THE
EMERALD
BEAR

By

Elizabeth Marsh

For my husband and son. Thank you for urging me on.

CONTENTS

PROLOGUE

Sergeant Bora, Razor to his friends, was progressing through the ranks fairly rapidly. He had always wanted to be a police officer, just as his father had been. He remembered his father well, who had died when he was just fifteen. He had grown up in a little village just outside Shrewsbury, called Allaburn. His father had been a Superintendent in the same station in Shrewsbury that he was in now. John was very handsome and never short of female company; he enjoyed female company and loved to eat out at expensive restaurants but only when he could afford it, which wasn't all the time.

He had met Susan, his first wife, at a concert; she was a musician and for John it had been love at first sight. However, Susan wasn't keen; she had just finished a four-year relationship with one of the doctors who worked in the hospital, arguing that she never saw him and when she did he was so tired that they never socialised anymore. So the orchestra that she played in became more and more important to her and started to take up more of her time. She always said, though, that if she met the right man she would cut down on her musical performances.

John persisted and eventually persuaded Susan to go out with him. After six months, having discussed that it was uneconomical to keep running two houses, when they were both at one house, they decided to sell one. They sold Susan's house on the Friday and she moved him with him on the Saturday. After six months they decided to get married. Susan was under no illusion what John's job entailed and he assured her that it wouldn't get in the way of their marriage; like a fool, Susan had believed him. After a while, however, the marriage started to break down as being a good police officer came at a price. At first Susan had accepted it but the last couple of years she had come to resent his job. Bora was a meticulous officer, who investigated every detail and left no stone unturned. He was six foot four inches tall with brown wavy hair and deep soulful brown eyes. That was what had first attracted Susan to him. They didn't have children as Susan always said that she didn't feel she would be a good mother, so instead they rescued a dog from the local animal shelter. Bora's dog was called Dinky and he and Dinky used to go on hikes around Shrewsbury, but all that stopped when Susan left him. They argued over who would keep the dog, but in the end Susan took Dinky.

John Bora was lean and athletic; he tried to go running at least three times a week, not only because he enjoyed it, but he felt it gave him an edge whilst doing his job. He prided himself on being very fit and able to give chase to criminals when they were on foot. Recently he had noticed that he was gaining a few pounds as he was having to adapt to life without his wife who he missed terribly. He missed the company of Dinky and didn't care to go on long walks now. He began frequenting a local café known affectionately as "The Greasy Spoon".

He remembered the day when he had been informed that he had passed his Detective Sergeant exam. He had been so proud, but unfortunately there was no special someone to share the news with. Bora had worked hard for this and felt as though he had sacrificed so much, so he reasoned that all his hard work had paid off and he deserved the promotion.

He was a quiet man who preferred to do everything in a methodical manner. When he interviewed suspects he never raised his voice, just presented them with the cold, hard facts. However, he was a person that you felt could intimidate you, with just a stare. Many criminals had been known to give up information just based on Bora's stare. The younger members of the police team found him a little abrupt and knew not to get on the wrong side of him.

Being a fearless officer, he had been called upon to

be a mediator in difficult situations more than once. He was specially trained to talk a person down from a difficult situation. Although these situations weren't a regular occurrence, they did happen and Bora would be shipped to the scene never knowing immediately what he would be dealing with. He would have to wear protective gear, a bullet-proof vest or a stab vest; he couldn't afford to take any chances. By the time he arrived on the scene the person causing it had already been approached by other officers. Bora was the last resort, but he was also the force's secret weapon, a position he took very seriously.

He had been Commended for Bravery twice, once when he had been able to avert a hostage situation and once when he had tackled a gunman without injury to either party. For his Commendations he attended the Divisional Headquarters to receive his awards. He would do his best dress uniform and stand there and listen to the speech given to him by his superiors, wishing the ceremony to be over. He preferred to dress in a casual fashion when he wasn't working, but he remembered his Superintendent's words when he was promoted. "Get yourself a good suit and look smart; no-one likes a scruffy detective." So John had always worn a good suit to the "office".

He had found it difficult when he had split from Susan, having to cook for himself and discovering microwave meals for one. Fortunately he had found a cleaners that could look after his laundry and he found that such a relief as when Susan was there she had always ironed his shirts and made sure his suits were clean and pressed.

Two years had passed and Bora had decided it was time to start socialising again; he felt he needed to relaunch himself into the dating scene.

Paula came into his life, quite by accident. She was an emergency call handler and John had cause to go to the call handlers' office. There had been instant chemistry between them and they were married shortly afterwards.

As John stood facing the gunman, he had been in this position a couple of times previously; he tried to reason with him, but he knew he was a dangerous criminal. John felt protected, though, as he had on his bullet-proof jacket.

As John faced the man he felt the adrenaline pumping through his veins and the hairs on the back of his neck stood on end. He had to be careful, this didn't seem like the other incidents that he had attended, and for the first time in his career he felt scared. No-one saw it coming, or predicted what might happen next. The gunman raised his arm and a shot rang out, hitting John in his forehead. He dropped to the ground, blood pumping from the wound. The attending officers were shocked and stunned and then another shot rang out and the gunman had been wounded; he fell to the ground where officers proceeded to handcuff him before bundling him into an ambulance. John had been rushed to St. Peter's Hospital for emergency surgery. His wife having been told rushed to the hospital and they didn't know if John would live or die. The emergency surgery managed to save his life, but unfortunately not his sight.

CHAPTER 1

She had arrived at the farmhouse a few minutes early; she never liked to be late. She looked at her watch impatiently wishing the agent would hurry as she was keen to get on. She quickly made a mental note of the layout of the farmhouse, planning where each activity could take place and mentally reckoning how much it would cost to convert. At the time it had seemed liked the ideal opportunity, but looking around the place now, she could see that it needed a lot of work doing to it and she wondered if she could afford it. She leant forward, stretching out a manicured hand and began to rub the crumbling window ledge. *Hmm, dry rot,* she thought. That would be expensive to fix. Maybe she would ask the agent to let her have the property at a reduced price as she was the one that was going to be renovating it. The farmhouse creaked and cracked as she moved around, but she was oblivious to the sound of someone entering the property; after all, she was expecting the agent. She glanced down and checked that her precious cargo was still in place.

He entered silently, it was important that she didn't detect him, he would approach her from behind and by the time she realised what was going on, he would have done the deed, or so he thought. He had thought long and hard how he would kill her. He could have used a gun with a silencer on; after all, he was used to using a gun. He dismissed the idea as he wanted to hear her speak one last time. He owed her that. So he had decided that it would have to be a knife.

His long bony fingers wrapped tightly around the knife. There was no room for error. This was for all the injustices he'd suffered. He knew exactly where the girl would be as he had been tracking her for many months. He despised her father and everything he stood for, especially the means he used to accrue more wealth. Well, this was all going to be over now.

The gleaming blade dripped with her blood. Drip, drip, drip. Her life oozing away, with every drip. Was it fair that she was dead? Yes, he was able to justify it and she would be silenced now forever. He hadn't wanted to kill her at first, but she had left him no choice. She had what he wanted and by silencing her she would no longer be able to tell of the secrets she knew. She had taken a gamble and lost, so her fate was death. He was quite surprised at the struggle she put up, but eventually he had overpowered her. There had been no traces of blood except hers. He had taken every precaution – gloves, hat, dark clothes.

He had spoken to her once, to ask where it was, but she was uncooperative. He gave her chances, but still she would not give up her secret. He felt compelled to murder her and as he leant over the lifeless body he ripped the item from her. He strode purposefully to his car, a job completed. He heaved his body into the driving seat, sweating profusely as the mobile he had taken from her flashed into life informing her that the agent was running late and would be at the property shortly. He didn't want to know what the mobile message said, he just wanted to get rid of it as soon as possible. He had killed before and now as he drove away from the scene he momentarily pondered on the act he had just carried out. It had to be done though and now he felt relieved if not a little sorry. After all, he had known the girl since she was very young, he remembered her growing up. It wasn't her fault that she had a bastard for a father. It had been easier than he thought, just two stab wounds to the heart, after the initial struggle; the sound of gurgling echoed in his ears as she gasped her last breath. He had replaced the knife in the sheath and felt relieved; he had picked the best night as the tyre tracks would be washed away by the torrential rain.

Driving furiously back down the dirt track he tossed the phone out of the window without reading the text and pressing the accelerator roared away at speed. He struggled making the car move as the rain was causing big puddles in the dirt. He began to panic. Would the rain wash away all the tyre prints? His task was becoming harder as the rain pelted down; his plan was to douse the car in petrol and set it alight, but the heavy rain would make it much harder to ignite. He eventually found the deserted spot on a dark road, where he had planned to ditch the car. The night was so bad that there weren't any cars along this particular stretch of road as it was known locally as a danger spot and the locals didn't dare to venture out on such a bad night. After several attempts he managed to ignite the petrol and the car began to burn eventually. He needed it to burn completely so there would be no trace, no DNA that the police could find. He found the car he had hidden earlier, opened the door and drove away. Her body, he presumed would be found by someone eventually, but he told himself he didn't care, it seemed to him a fitting end.

*

When John came around from the surgery he had been told the devastating news. The bullet had lodged in his head a millimetre up from his eye, but as a result he had lost the sight in both eyes.

It took many months for Bora to come to terms with the terrible accident. His wife struggled with her husband's life-changing injuries and to accept the new normal.

John Bora was blind. He had been an exceptional police officer, but now all that had gone. He was becoming very depressed as he could no longer do the job he had always loved. Even his love of music did nothing to brighten his mood. He remembered how he and Paula used to enjoy going to live concerts. The Philharmonic Orchestra, the Halle, the Prague Orchestra. They would go together after work. If it was a night when they were going to a concert, John would always try to finish work early. It didn't happen all the time, it very much depended on the case he was working on, but nonetheless he looked forward to their "Concert Evenings".

There was never anything else he had really wanted to do. Now he seemed doomed to filling his days with other things and he was finding it particularly hard.

One particular dark day John had picked up his white stick and ambled into the kitchen; the days seemed to merge into each other, he found, when there was nothing in particular to do.

"John, phone-call for you, stay there and I will bring the phone in."

"Hello, John. Ready to come back to work?"

He recognised the Area Commander's voice. He gulped a few times then replied, "How am I supposed to come back to work now I am blind?"

The voice on the other end still sounded cheery. "Oh it's not a problem, we have a arranged a driver for you and also a guide dog. The dog is called Louie. Well, Detective Inspector, what do you say?"

Wait a minute. The Area Commander had got it wrong; John wasn't a Detective Inspector, he was a Detective Sergeant.

"Congratulations on your promotion by the way, John, I'm sure you'll make an excellent Inspector."

John needed to discuss this new opportunity with Paula, who had misgivings. Having nearly lost her husband once, she wasn't overjoyed at the thought of him going back to work, however, she had to concede defeat if going back to work would make him happy again.

So John had returned to work. On the first day he felt very nervous; Paula had assured him that he looked fine.

"Good morning, sir. I'm Steve, your driver, and when we get to the station we will pick up your guide dog Louie."

It felt strange to John walking up the corridor, the one he had walked up so many times before, but now it was different, he couldn't see. He could remember the smell of the painted walls though. He was now firmly gripping onto the harness of his guide dog.

"Here, sir. This is your office." Steve directed him through a door and towards a table. He would have to get used to that. "Would you like a coffee, sir?" the young Constable asked. "You have your own kettle and coffee mug and little fridge."

Humph, thought John. *What use will that be if I can't see to make it?*

"Yes, a black, strong coffee would be great." John believed that having at least one cup of strong black coffee in a morning helped to focus the brain. Louie sat quietly under the table.

The Chief Inspector was briefing John on the latest murder. "A woman in her twenties, John, I want this cleared up as soon as possible."

"Yes, sir."

DI Bora gave a small tug on the dog's harness. "Come on, Louie. Let's go." The dog quickly arose and steered Detective Inspector Bora carefully through the open door. Bora let the dog lead him down the passage to his office.

*

"The car is at the front, sir."

Steve ushered John into the car and it sped away.

The Detective Constable cautiously opened the door of the farmhouse. Louie was already leading John to the body. The young DC began describing the scene to the older man. Although John couldn't see the body, his sense of smell and touch were heightened as a result of his accident.

He tried to imagine the young woman's body as

the Constable worked methodically, shouting things out to John as he saw them.

"How old, Steve?"

"She only looks to be in her twenties, sir."

Such a waste, a young woman in the prime of life.

James, the pathologist, was quickly on the scene. "Now John be careful where you are standing." The pathologist was pointing at something. "Look, Steve, a very unusual birthmark."

Steve described the birthmark slowly to John.

"Was there a struggle?"

"Yes, it looks like there was."

"So there should be two lots of blood that we can match with DNA samples then," Bora said hopefully. "When can you let me have the report?"

"First thing tomorrow morning, I will make it a priority."

DI Bora nodded. "See that it is, thank you."

Louie led John back to the car, Steve fastened the seatbelts around the Inspector and the dog and started the journey back to the station.

John had the forensic report stretched out in front of him, carefully feeling all the bumps on the page, as it had been converted into Braille.

The forensic report made for gruesome reading.

Just then, a knock came on the door.

"Come in."

A tall slim woman breezed into the Inspector's

office. She looked about thirty-five, with blonde hair and a ready smile. She was dressed in a smart grey suit with a white blouse, her blonde hair piled onto the top of her head in a bun.

"Good morning, sir, how are you today?"

"I'm well, thank you Sergeant. I would like you look at this, there seems to be no motive, no murder weapon and no suspect."

Christine Lockhead looked at the Inspector with her clear blue eyes; she really admired the Inspector. His lack of sight did not seem to affect his razor-sharp brain.

Christine Lockhead was known throughout the station, everyone was aware of the rumours about her, the fact that she was regarded as a bit of a vixen. The main rumour being that she had been seeing a senior officer, the senior officer's wife found out, and the officer in charge was promptly transferred to another station on the pretext of a promotion. It was not long after that, she managed a transfer to Shrewsbury. Christine had that effect on all the officers and as a result everyone was wary of her, however, despite her chaotic life she was an excellent officer. Her private life seemed to lurch from one crisis to another and it invariably involved a man. Moving to Shrewsbury meant that she had to relocate. At first it was a bit daunting, but she soon made friends as her easy-going nature endeared her to people. When concentrating on her job, however, she was ruthless and gained satisfaction out of seeing villains apprehended. She had been instrumental in getting a drugs ring smashed in Carsley, being Commended for Bravery. It had been a very daring arrest, one where she had been threatened, but she showed great courage by distracting the gang leader enough to let slip about the drugs. She had managed to infiltrate the gang and had been with them for a few weeks, the leader being flattered that such a beautiful woman wanted to date him. That unfortunately was where he had gone wrong. He had been discussing their latest consignment of drugs and where it was coming from when Christine had appeared by the door. Immediately the group had become silent.

"Oh Ollie," she said in her most provocative voice. "I'm so sorry, I didn't know you were having a meeting," she gushed.

"It's alright, my dear, we were just discussing the finer details of the pickup tonight."

So now she knew. She would stick to Ollie all night like glue and secretly alert the station. Unfortunately she didn't know the place or the time, but she figured if she stayed with Ollie, sooner or later, someone at some point would show up with the consignment. The night dragged on and then out of the shadows appeared a man dressed in dark clothing.

"Ollie, you never said about a woman," he fumed.

He whipped out a hand gun and pointed it straight at Christine.

"Speak. Tell us who you really are."

Christine tried to approach the man but as she attempted to move closer, he fired a warning shot.

"The next one's yours."

The GPS signal had managed to track the location and now there were three armed police cars in the disused warehouse, next door.

She knew she would have to let the exchange take place in order for the men to be arrested. She was scared, but the adrenaline was pumping and now she was beginning to feel fearless.

"I am Detective Sergeant Christine Lockhead, and now I'm afraid, gentlemen, you are all under arrest."

As the man with the bag took aim at her, he was tackled from behind by a Police Constable. The room had been dark and no-one had realised there was a back entrance to the lockup.

"Bitch!" the gang leader screamed. "You'll pay for this."

Christine was relieved that she hadn't been shot, still, that was what her job was all about, apprehending the villains.

It was after that, that she had started seeing DI Tommy Spencer. When the affair had been made public, it was thought best that Spencer was moved to another police station and her Area Commander had recommended to her that for her own safety she moved away from Carsley. So that is how she became a DS in John Bora's team. Bora, she knew was respected throughout the force, because of the meticulous way he apprehended criminals but without a thought for his own safety; that was why he was so decorated. When Christine Lockhead heard that her DI would be John Bora, she vowed to get her life in order and concentrate on being the best detective she could. After all, she hoped to make DI sometime soon. In the meantime, though, she would have to impress her new boss.

Bora had worked with her once before on the Rudheath Murder case, when he had been seconded to Carsley, so he knew that her methods were slightly unorthodox and she had shown this on numerous occasions, with scant regard for correct police procedures. It had to be said though that she did get results. However, he remained unimpressed. Before she joined the team Bora had her records sent over in Braille so that he could work out for himself, what type of officer she would be.

She read the transcript, which wasn't in Braille.

"It seems very unusual, sir, that there was no suspect and no motive. How do we not even know why she was murdered?"

"There is no name in the file, so I presume she is a misper for the time being."

Bora hated that phrase, but she was right. So far, they had drawn a blank as to who the woman was and why she had been murdered.

"The report says it was not an unusual birthmark, but on closer inspection it seemed to be some sort of tattoo."

"It says here that a passer-by thought that there was something strange about the house when her dog started barking loudly."

Bora scratched his head.

"I thought the agent that was selling the property or letting it or whatever he was doing, I thought he would have discovered the body."

"Apparently there was no sign of the agent and no appointment ever recorded for the old farmhouse," interjected DS Lockhead.

She continued reading. "The house is a farmhouse off the beaten track. Many years ago a family called Fallon owned the farmhouse and the surrounding land. Old man Fallon died. They had no children so the farm was just left derelict."

Sergeant Lockhead was confused.

"Sir, it says that Fallon died. Do we know if anybody else lived there after his death?"

"No, there are no records to show anyone lived there, so who was our victim and was she killed at the house, or was she killed somewhere else by someone who knew the old farmhouse was deserted? Get onto the local hospitals and homeless shelters and let's see if we can put a name to the face."

"Sir, I have a question."

"Well, Sergeant?" Bora was becoming slightly agitated now; he wished she would get out of his office and then he could carry on with his own work.

The Sergeant continued, "Do we know how the murderer got to the farmhouse or how they left? Only it doesn't say here."

"No, it doesn't say because Forensics were unable to find any tyre tracks due to the heavy rain last evening. The path to the farmhouse was just one big muddy puddle. Does that answer your question?"

"Yes, sir." Sergeant Lockhead pushed away her chair, got up and left the Inspector's office.

She began to ring around the local hospitals first to see if anyone remembered a brown-eyed woman, with brown hair and an unusual birthmark or tattoo.

*

John started to study the report again. Was there something he was missing?

The forensic report placed the murder between 4 p.m. and 6 p.m. but surely it must have been earlier as she was expecting an agent. So was she murdered in the afternoon and taken there or was she there already and the murderer slipped in unnoticed? John thought that it seemed strange. There was just a body, no identification on her, no personal effects, no phone, in fact nothing to give any kind of clue as to who she was.

"Her clothes looked expensive. They were not dishevelled so it doesn't point to a rape or a sex act gone wrong," continued DS Lockhead.

Sergeant Lockhead had begun trying to find out who the woman was. She had interviewed the dog walker, who was still in shock. She couldn't give any useful information except to say that she always walked her dog early in the morning. She always took the same route and she had never known anyone to be in the house since the previous occupier had passed away.

Christine wanted more information.

"Now, Mrs Cherry, did you know Mr Fallon?"

"Oh yes, but only to say good morning to. He went proper funny after his wife died."

"What do you mean, funny?"

"When Ada was alive they could often be seen working the farm together. They seemed to complement each other; she tended the dairy herd and he looked after the sheep. He had a grand dog called Timmy who went everywhere with him and was excellent at herding the sheep. Fallon had him very well trained. When his wife died, though, the farm became too much for him and he sold all the livestock. That was when he became a virtual recluse. He would have shopping delivered once a month, because he never ventured out of the farmhouse."

Christine was puzzled. The woman seemed full of contradictions, it was as though there was something to hide about what she was saying. When first asked, she had replied that she only knew Mr Fallon to say good morning to and then during the course of the conversation, she had proved to be quite knowledgeable about the Fallons.

"Well thank you, Mrs Cherry, you have been very helpful."

"Er, have you found out who the girl was? It is a sight I will never forget. Stabbed and the look on her face, it was one of sheer terror."

"You have had a shock, Mrs Cherry, and I will get one of my officers to stay with you, throughout the rest of the day and overnight. You should be quite safe."

"Thank you, Sergeant, that will be most agreeable."

Sergeant Lockhead revved the engine and her car roared into life. Now came one of the most boring parts she loathed about the job, writing up the conversation she had had with the dog walker. She needed to convey what she had learnt back to the Inspector. She liked to be out solving crimes, not listening to some old woman wittering on about a long-deceased neighbour. Curious though, when she started the conversation she gave the impression that they were only nodding acquaintances.

*

Steve dropped him at his house and watched Inspector Bora put the key in his front door; the key made a noise when Bora put it into the lock, to indicate that he had put it in the right place. Steve watched his boss and the dog safely in, then drove away.

It had been a long, unproductive day. He took off his work clothes and let Louie guide him to his favourite chair.

Paula had been home for almost an hour, during which time she had prepared their evening meal.

"Louie, sit." The dog sat patiently waiting for his master to give him a treat. John felt along the table and found a treat for the dog, before unclipping his harness and saying, "Go get your food, Louie. That smells good. What is it?"

"One of your favourites. Spaghetti Bolognaise," came the reply.

John began to take off his suit; he knew from experience of eating Spag Bol that if he didn't change out of his work clothes, they would end up a holy mess with stains on his tie and splashes on his shirt. Since being blind he had worked very hard to be able to eat almost anything, without subjecting his clothes to splashes and spills, however, Spaghetti Bolognaise was still proving a challenge for him.

Paula had left his clothes on the chair next to him, so he was able to feel for each item and dress himself.

Louie was a black Labrador, who was very

intelligent and obedient. The perfect guide dog. When John had first lost his sight he thought his world had come to an end, then came his job and Louie.

Paula had turned on the TV and the news was all over the story of the murdered girl. The Chief Super was trying to sound intelligent as he stumbled through an awkward interview with the press.

"We have no further comment to make at this time."

John sneered. *No further comment because we know bugger all about who she was, or why she was murdered.*

*

John had awoken with a banging headache. Was it that this latest case baffled him, or was it the whisky the previous night?

"Steve, yes, send the car round in about an hour."

"Yes, sir, will do."

"Well Steve, have there been any developments overnight that I should know about?"

Steve began, "Well, sir, the victim's name is Shirley Denacot."

The Inspector returned to the office and told the officer to see if there was a Shirley Denacot anywhere on their database. Armed with a picture the officer began trawling through the files. Suddenly he came across a newspaper clipping of a Francis Delacot at the British Embassy with his daughter Shirley; the picture on the newspaper clipping matched exactly the picture the officer had been given.

The newspaper headline read, "South African Diplomat Francis Delacot and his daughter were on an official fact-finding mission on behalf of the South African government, to further cement mutually lucrative relations with the two countries."

Steve had unearthed something. Was it relevant, was it important?

John felt the blood draining from his face, as though someone had pulled the plug.

"Oh God, no. I remember Delacot, he is a right pain in the arse. I met him one time at a Police Conference in London. He was complaining about protection and diplomatic immunity. He became quite verbal until the Area Commander managed to calm him down with reassurances that he and his family would be quite safe when travelling in England."

"Are you positive the deceased woman is Shirley Delacot?"

"Yes sir, positive. I looked closely at the picture, you can just make out a tattoo. Didn't you say our deceased woman had a tattoo on her arm?"

The phone rang. "John, I want you in my office now!"

John straightened his tie, pulled down his shirt cuffs and knocked on the Superintendent's door.

Superintendent Rodgers was not in the mood for niceties this morning; he had been given a stern telling-off from the Area Commander about the lack of progress on the murdered girl.

"Just how much progress have you made, John?"

"Not much, sir, all we know at this point is that she is the daughter of a South African diplomat and her name is Shirley Delacot."

"I already know all that," he boomed. "Now is there anything new you can tell me? You've had 48 hours, surely you must have found out something."

John shuffled uneasily in his seat; Louie lay beside his chair. He could feel beads of perspiration starting to form on his brow. "We're working on it, sir, I have Christine Lockhead investigating whether anyone in the surrounding area has seen or heard anything suspicious within the last few weeks."

"Ah, Lockhead, a good choice, John. If there is anything to unearth, I'm sure she will do it."

John nodded. "Now if there is nothing else, sir, I will take my leave and carry on with my investigations. Come on, Louie."

"Pompous twit," he muttered under his breath. *Delacot, Delacot.* He turned the name over and over in his brain, trying desperately to remember something about the diplomat. He walked into an office, guided by Louie, where there were several people working at computers. John had been told what the layout of the office was and he turned to his left and remembered the name Paul, he said,

"Ah, Paul, see if you can find me any more information on Francis Delacot."

"Yes sir, I'm on it. He was decorated in South Africa for bringing two warring factions together and offering them mediation and finally reconciliation."

John was unimpressed; he remembered Francis Delacot as an arrogant twit with a supercilious air about him. He asked Paul to read the sheet that he had just printed off; nothing life-changing there. Only daughter Shirley, currently attending a private overseas college on the outskirts of Shrewsbury.

John cleared his throat and said to the team, "A meeting at 3 p.m."

John walked up the corridor, back to his office, Louie walking in front. As he reached his office Christine Lockhead greeted him.

"Hello Christine, have you found anything?"

"No, sir."

"Well keep looking, knocking on doors, and keep your eyes peeled for a murder weapon. It's a bladed implement, either a knife or possibly a dagger. Has Delacot been informed of his daughter's death?"

"No, sir, not yet. He is in London having a meeting with the Foreign Secretary."

"Oh, bloody great, who is going to break the news to him?"

"I think someone from the Met is going to do that, sir."

"Thank God, I didn't relish the thought of telling him."

*

The Inspector asked Christine to read out the report again focussing on the angle of the blade as it pierced the woman's body. In his office John had his own kettle and Christine was on hand to make his coffee. John loved the aroma of hot coffee; he always found that it helped him to concentrate on the task in hand. As he sipped his coffee, he pondered on the fact that there were no fibres on the body, no tell-tale signs of what kind of knife it was; he presumed it was a knife.

The meeting was not going well.

"Have you found out which college she was at and what she was studying?"

"She was at Brewmans English Language College."

"Was she learning English, or was she teaching English? Spit it out, man, which was it?"

The young Constable opened his notebook and began to read it.

"The Principal's name is Ryan Evans, he told me that Miss Delacot had been about to start teaching English as a foreign language. The Principal thought it strange though, as she never turned up for her induction, she was supposed to meet the other teachers before she started."

"Well that didn't happen, did it! Have you an

address of where she was staying?"

"Yes sir, the school gave me an address."

"And, have you checked it out?" said the Inspector irritably.

"DS Lockhead is checking it out now, sir."

"Finally," roared the Inspector. "Someone is getting their bloody finger out at last. "I want to know why she was calling herself Shirley Denacot and who else knew her real identity."

"Sir, there is a Mr Jones in the front office. He's asking to speak to you."

"Hello Jonesy, don't tell me, you have some important information for me, but it comes at a cost."

The man stood in front of the Inspector, was slightly built with a gaunt face. He wore a grubby green shirt and a pair of brown corduroy trousers. He was unshaven and he had dirt under his fingernails.

John didn't particularly like the man, but sometimes he had his uses. Although he couldn't see him, he remembered what he looked like years ago.

"I saw a car the other night, you know, when that lass got killed. Well the fella that got into the car looked as though he tossed something out of the winder."

The man held out a hand to the Inspector and said, "Well, is that worth something?"

"No. That's not enough, didn't you see any more? For instance, the car's reg or the colour, or a description of the man inside?"

"No, didn't see anything else, just thought you'd want to know."

The man slunk out of the station muttering under his breath, wondering why he had gone to the police station in the first place. He had thought the Inspector would have given him a little something for his trouble, but no, the tight bastard wanted blood.

This investigation seemed to be going around in circles, with no-one having any relevant information. John knew he would have to step up his game as the Super would be on his back again.

"Team meeting at three o'clock, and I want some positive news, got that?"

"Yes, sir," the team said in unison.

*

John went into the conference room and began building up a picture of what they knew, which wasn't very much at this point.

Steve started pinning photos on a board and writing the name of the college and the deceased woman's address as John called out the timeline.

"So, what do we know?"

"The woman is the daughter of an influential South African diplomat. She had just taken a flat close to the college where she was going to start work. Have we found her phone yet? Has someone been to the house where she rented, spoken to the neighbours, has anyone seen anything suspicious?"

It was Christine Lockhart who spoke next.

"We have found a phone, sir, but all the numbers seemed to be wiped. There are several texts though, and at the end of each text she signs herself SD and adds kisses. I wondered whether it could be a jealous boyfriend."

"Where was the phone found?"

"On the dirt track. It was almost buried in the mud, as if someone didn't want us to find it."

"She has only been in the country two weeks, Sergeant. I checked that this morning," the Inspector interjected. "Has someone interviewed the teachers at the school?"

"I checked with the Principal, sir, none of the new teachers were there as they were all supposed to attend an induction on the Friday, when the girl was found."

"Get onto IT. I want to find out who the texts were to and see if there is any way we can retrieve any numbers she might have had in her phone. Have we found anyone who is likely to be a suspect?"

"No, sir."

"Right, people, I want interviews done, I want the area surrounding the farmhouse combed for any possible weapon, I want a list of the new teachers that were about to start at the college and their movements on that Friday morning. Now go, we all have work to do, we will meet up for an update tomorrow at three o'clock."

John turned on his heel and swept out of the room. This was unsatisfactory, most unsatisfactory, he thought.

"John, can you spare me a minute please?"

John thought, *No, not really,* but the Super had spoken and although it sounded like a request, John knew that it was a command.

"Where are we up to with the murdered girl case? Have we any suspects in the frame, have we found a murder weapon?"

"No, sir."

John looked down, wishing the Super would shut up. He had been railed again by the unpopular Super.

"If that's all, sir, I will get on."

"Yes, do that, I want some positive news within the next twenty-four hours."

It had been another trying day for John with not much accomplished.

As he got into bed that night he wondered if there was something he had missed. Paula had been in bed for an hour as she had been reading a particularly exciting novel.

"Goodnight, John. Try and get some sleep."

*

John had awoken early determined to get a breakthrough in the murdered girl case today.

As Steve drove the half hour to work, John

realised he hadn't had any breakfast and now his stomach was rumbling. He also needed a coffee; he always felt that a coffee in the morning awoke the senses for the day.

He parked outside the "Flowerpot" café, one of the DI's favourites.

The "Flowerpot" café, despite its attractive name was known locally as the "Greasy Spoon". It was run by a cheerful couple called Ronaldson.

"Hello, Inspector, the usual?"

"Yes thanks, Ray."

He gave John a wide toothy grin, displaying 3 gold teeth.

John could smell the bacon as it sizzled in the pan; he could smell the fat as the eggs and sausage were being cooked. He had ordered a "bin lid" today as usual; that meant 2 rashers of bacon, 2 sausages and a fried egg. He began to salivate at the thought. His wife had always said that it was a "heart attack on a plate".

John knew his waistline was expanding because just recently his trousers had become tighter.

As he waited for his breakfast, he listened to the gossip around him; they were all discussing the evenings news, and was the murdered woman on a secret mission?

Secret mission. John smirked. It wasn't a secret mission, to him it just appeared as a straight-forward homicide, possibly with robbery being the motive.

*

"John, this is Inspector Grieves, from the London Met. He will be assisting you as this is such a high-profile case apparently."

John got a sense of the man stood before him; cheap aftershave and probably a cheap suit. Was he not capable of solving a murder? After all, this wasn't his first murder case.

Inspector Grieves was a tall lean man in his early forties. He believed the local police force were unable to handle such a high-profile operation, and took no time letting John know his views.

John had taken an instant dislike to the man – crass and arrogant. He had probably solved more murders than Grieves had had "hot dinners", he thought.

This policeman had been fast-tracked up the promotions ladder, but John wondered how much experience he had in solving highly sensitive murder cases. It had become highly sensitive because this was a daughter of foreign diplomat, and John knew the press would be following and watching and analysing their every move, especially as the media had portrayed the murdered girl to be on some sort of secret mission. The public loved a good mystery, especially when it was inferred that someone might be a spy.

He began to bring the Inspector up to speed with the case, and was irritated as all the Inspector said was, "Mmm, yes."

He studied the photographs of the dead girl without much interest.

"Are there any known contacts, friends that she went partying with, did they take drugs?"

"No, not as far as I'm aware. She had only been in the country for two weeks, hardly enough time to become bosom buddies with anyone," said John.

Inspector Grieves was unconvinced that this was the woman's first trip to the country; he felt that the location and the school were just too convenient.

In the meantime Grieves would keep his theories to himself until it became more apparent what had actually happened.

The Operation seemed to be going slowly. Grieves was unwilling or incapable of offering much insight to the case. John noted he was about "as much use as a chocolate fireguard".

For the rest of the afternoon John witnessed the comings and goings of various people. People wanting to see the Super, people wanting to check out the IT department, people wanting to see Inspector Grieves. He felt side-lined, but this was his case and he was going to crack it with or without the help of "the chocolate fireguard".

He needed to go for a walk and get out of the office for a little while. He tugged Louie's harness and said, "Come on, boy, we are going for a walk."

He needed to clear his head and focus. Something

Inspector Grieves seemed unwilling to do.

As he walked he heard some activity down by the river. Louie was well accustomed to this walk and was very careful with his master.

"Hey sir, we've found something," the police diver shouted, and told John to hang on and he would bring the item over.

John held his breath in anticipation that it could be the murder weapon that had killed the young woman.

As the diver fished the implement out of the water, John held out his hand and his heart sank; it was probably a murder weapon, but not the one he had hoped it would be. It was a long heavy crowbar, misshapen at the top if he wasn't mistaken.

"Good work, lads, keep looking and get this bagged up for Forensics."

John didn't want another unsolved mystery on his hands; this one was quite enough, thank you.

*

Release from the office over, he started to trudge back to the station, his footsteps heavy. He knew his shoes would be covered in mud as it had been raining. No doubt the Super would say something if he spotted that. He could just hear the Super. "Shouldn't you be trying to catch a murderer, not going out for walks?"

Back in the office, Steve made John a strong coffee and he settled down once again to his reading. He felt sure there was something he was missing about this case, but he just couldn't fathom what. A dead diplomat's daughter, residing near Shrewsbury, why this location? Who knew her identity? He started to mull the names over. Ryan Evans, was the Principal of the college; obviously he had met her but the other teachers had not yet met her, as she hadn't turned up for the induction.

"Come in," shouted John.

It was Christine Lockhead. He was relieved to know it wasn't the useless Inspector Grieves. He must be out trying to catch the perpetrator, some hope of that!

In the harsh lights of the office Christine looked older, her usually sparkling eyes looked dull and her forehead wore a frown.

"I've done some digging on Ryan Evans. It seems he had a conviction in the US ten years ago, for a felony, fraud to be exact. As it was his first felony, he only served three years in prison. He travelled back to England, but knowing he had a criminal record, he decided to start his own school and then there would not have to be any background checks on him for a job."

"Hmm, what was the fraud about?"

"Teddy bears, sir."

John nearly fell off his chair laughing. "Come on, Christine, be serious."

"I am, sir. Apparently being an arctophile, a person

who collects teddy bears, is very big business and very lucrative in the US."

"So, what was his crime, kidnapping teddy bears?"

"No sir, defrauding unsuspecting buyers out of thousands of pounds, by falsely stating that he had various bears for sale. His website was very professional looking, and he also offered a service for sourcing rare and unusual bears. He would get in touch through the website with potential buyers, promise them the bears and charge exorbitant amounts for them, after buying normal teddy bears and putting fake tags on them."

John consulted his desk calendar which was also in Braille. No, it wasn't April the 1st.

"Are you being serious, or is this a wind-up?"

"No sir, no wind-up, here is the evidence to prove it."

With that, Christine pulled out a sheaf of papers and read them to the Inspector.

John chewed the end of his pen while listening.

"Well I never, a teddy bear fraudster. Who'd have thought it? I must say that Ryan Evans didn't come across to me as being that bright."

"That's what I thought, sir, when I interviewed him, but obviously he has hidden talents."

"I should say so, but come on, Christine, how does a teddy bear fraudster make the leap from fraudster to killer? No, I don't think this is our killer at all."

CHAPTER 2

He put the bear up on the shelf to join the rest of his collection. This bear had been made at the turn of the century, one of the first string-jointed bears ever to have been made. He had had the letter to inform him where and when to collect the teddy bear.

"Daddy, is that the newest addition to our bear family?"

The little girl danced around the room clapping her hands in glee.

"Yes, darling. Our very newest, but you can't touch him because he is very, very old."

The little girl looked crestfallen; although she wasn't allowed to play with the teddy bears, her father always allowed her one touch of them. He told her they had to be in pristine condition without any sign of wear or marks on them. Although the little girl didn't know what pristine meant, she knew that she could only look at the bears in the glass cabinet and for the time being that seemed to satisfy her, as she had lots of other toys to play with.

Paul Plumpton was a respected pillar of the community. He owned his own business; an electrician by trade, he was now in Property Development. He was given a helping hand by a mutual friend who introduced him to Billy Haskins, known to his mates as "Big Billy". Billy had liked his work and saw it as an opportunity to expand his own business, while playing the benefactor and displaying a respectable front. He had offered Paul the position of manager for his Property Developing business. Paul had worked hard and learnt about Property Development while all the time being aware that Billy Haskins was watching his every move. Every so often Billy would turn up with a large amount of money and ask Paul to put the money into his business account so Billy could access it at any time. Billy had offered to help Paul set up his own Property Development business and Paul had been delighted, but Billy added, "There are conditions."

Billy Haskins was of average height with blue eyes and a crooked nose. He had a scar just above his right eye. It was rumoured that he was into extortion and blackmail, to name but a couple of his illegal activities. Although he regularly executed illegal activities he was always under the radar, and if anyone ever got caught, he would ensure that it was never him. He liked fast cars and going to watch horse-racing where he gambled and invariably lost. He had always been in the lower league, a grubby little petty criminal although he liked to think he was Shrewsbury's answer to the mafia. He was also a known loan shark but he had influential friends. Friends the police were unaware of. He was never seen to intimidate people, but he had an army of low-life associates willing to do his dirty work, as he inevitably held something over each and every one of them. Mainly it was unpaid debt or a scam that had gone wrong. His other passion, though, was rare teddy bears; there was one in particular that he wanted to get his hands on, and he would stop at nothing to secure the bear.

Billy had begun pestering Paul to do more of his bidding. When Paul refused, Billy said acidically, "You didn't think I wasn't serious when I said there would be conditions. I have a collection of teddy bears, that I want you to keep for me until such time as I ask you for them. I will pay you to mind them for me and then maybe that will go some way to assuaging the debt you owe me."

That was how he got into teddy bears.

Slightly scared of Billy and not wanting to arouse his wrath, he agreed to having the teddy bears. Besides, it would help fund his wife's extravagant lifestyle.

He had left his first wife, because she didn't want children, although Paul thought he could persuade her otherwise when they were married, but it wasn't to be. His wife had been very domineering and dug her heels in every time Paul mentioned children. He was still a young man so he decided to divorce her in the hope of finding a partner that he could love and wanted children.

Now in his forties he had met Julie; after six months they had moved in together and within a year they had married. Julie was ambitious and greedy, she always wanted more and being ten years his junior expected to be given everything she wanted. They hadn't had to try very hard when Julie fell pregnant. Paul was delighted, especially when it was revealed that it was a little girl. Now his little girl was five, she went to an expensive private school and had the best of everything.

Julie was becoming more and more demanding; first it was a sports car, which Paul thought highly impractical considering they had a child, then it was expensive holidays with her friends and now she was complaining that they didn't live in the right neighbourhood and that they should move.

Emily, his daughter, had beautiful blonde hair, she was slightly built and not very tall with clear blue eyes and a mischievous smile.

Frightened of losing his beautiful daughter, he had agreed to be part of this, he needed the extra money.

They hadn't been looking long when a house came onto the market. It was a four-bedroomed detached house, with enough land for a couple of horses. This was Julie's next thing, she wanted to keep horses, "To teach our daughter how to ride."

So that is how they came to own the biggest house in the village. Although it was called a village it was in fact a town. Julie thought that somehow village sounded more genteel than town. The house had a sweeping drive with security gates at the entrance and enough space for five cars. Now they had moved into a more affluent neighbourhood, she wanted to have dinner parties and entertain the local gentry, believing this would raise her standing in the community.

Paul felt that they had overstretched themselves financially and was worried about the bills that were piling up. There seemed to be no end to Julie's capacity for spending, usually on herself, until Paul would remind her that they had a daughter.

Paul was six feet tall, and before he met Julie he had been a healthy weight for his height. He had a full head of black hair and sported a little goatee beard. Now as the years had passed, he was greying at the temples and had put on a few pounds. He recalled their wedding day, Julie had wanted a grand affair; bridesmaids, pages, flowergirls, the whole ensemble. It had cost Paul an absolute fortune.

"Paul, darling, you can't possibly have that beard on the wedding photos, I think you need to be clean shaven." So, Paul had shaved off his beard.

When Paul first met Julie, his Property Development business was thriving but over the years she had worn him down physically and mentally; his clothes weren't right, he needed to lose weight, she needed more money from him, she drained his money like a tap being constantly left on.

The marriage was breaking down more every day and Paul knew that he needed to get himself and his daughter away from there. He knew it would take time and some careful planning. He could leave the house, but he needed money to support himself and his daughter. The money that accompanied the teddy bears could end at any time.

He had met Ryan Evans at an arctophile convention, where they had discussed among other things the real value of rare bears. Paul seemed the consummate collector, interested and knowledgeable about his subject.

"So, have you got a favourite bear then?"

Paul took time before answering; he didn't like to give too much away.

"Yes, the last bear I acquired. It was made at the turn of the century."

Paul didn't want to offer any more explanation and turned on his heel to go when the other man called him back.

"Paul, what's the rush? Let's talk more about your bears."

Paul was getting more irritated; the less people knew the better.

As he entered the driveway he heard the squeals of delight of his daughter who no doubt was playing with something she shouldn't.

"Hello, darling."

The little girl swung round and ran towards him.

"Have you brought us another teddy?"

"No, Emily. I was just looking today."

"Oh well, never mind. I have been playing shop with my toys."

He knew he had to get himself and his daughter away from here as soon as he possibly could, the mood in the house was becoming more toxic by the minute. Julie was more controlling and forever asking him for more money, money he didn't have.

His mobile rang.

"Paul, it's Ryan Evans, I'd like to meet up with you."

"How did you find my number?" Paul snapped.

"A mutual friend," he continued. "I have an interesting proposition for you. I think it will make us both a lot of money."

"Who was it?" demanded Paul.

"Ah, you don't need to know that."

Paul was annoyed that a virtual stranger had phoned him out of the blue, but he was intrigued, was this the way out of his problems that he was looking for?

"Next Tuesday, yes. That's fine."

Paul entered the date in his diary.

"Julie, you will have to look after Emily on Tuesday as I have an important planning meeting to attend," he lied.

Julie pulled a face; she had agreed to go out for lunch with her friends, now it wouldn't be happening.

"Oh, very well, if I must."

"Yes, you must. If you want to continue the lifestyle you have with me funding it."

Julie knew that Paul had to attend these meetings as that was how he obtained most of his business, that and his arctophile conventions. She often wondered what "teddy bear" collectors talked about.

Paul had been studying the world's stock markets for a couple of years now; he knew the best stocks to buy and whether the gold and precious stones markets were making profit or losing money.

His Property Development business had blossomed and after a few years had begun to make a profit. That was pre-Julie.

He had been given the teddy bears and told to "guard them with his life and remember they were not his, he was just the protector for them." For this Paul was paid handsomely every month regular as clockwork. If that money kept arriving in his bank account, he was able to keep his avaricious wife happy until such time as he would leave.

For a while Billy Haskins left him alone, just occasionally sending him notes on when and where to pick up another bear and he would hurriedly have to make space in the cabinet for the new arrival. He often wondered what was so special about the bears; some were cute, some were ugly-looking. These were Haskins' conditions. The cabinet was nearly full and when he had cautiously approached Billy about this, he had been told not to worry as the bears would be collected very soon. That meant the end of his payments from Billy. He was sorry that he had ever got mixed up with Billy Haskins, but now he was in too deep and was becoming desperate, to make more money; he needed another source of revenue. That was what had been a deciding factor in meeting Ryan Evans. He had been unimpressed with the other man on first meeting, assessing him to be somewhat of a dimwit.

Paul had never suffered fools gladly and wasn't about to start now. However, he was intrigued about a new business venture.

Ryan Evans was a creature of habit. Every morning he would go downstairs, light his cigarette, check whether he had any emails, grab a quick coffee and then prepare to start his day as Principal of his Language School. It didn't pay as much as his previous career, but it afforded him some sort of respectability.

He was short in stature with a bald head and a body that looked as though it belonged to a person of increased height. In effect his body looked out of proportion; his hands were big like shovels and yet his feet were quite small. The most exercise he took was walking from the school dining room to his office and back again.

He drove an old car that had been his pride and joy, but now it was time to upgrade, as his school was doing well and giving him a healthy revenue.

"Ah, Paul." He greeted Paul as though he was a long-lost brother. "So glad you could make it."

Paul nodded his acknowledgement and indicated that they sit down away from the other people in the bistro, so as not to draw attention to themselves. He began loosening his tie before slipping it off, then opening the top button of his shirt, which made him feel more comfortable. Ryan watched in amusement.

"What's with the suit and shirt and tie?"

"My wife thinks I have gone to a planning meeting and this is how I always dress for it."

"Oh."

Ryan looked at his own attire; usually he was dressed in a smart suit with a shirt and tie, but today as he was not working, he was dressed casually with an open-necked shirt, corduroy trousers and sneakers.

"Well what have you brought me here for? You said to make us both some money. Then get on with it, man, I haven't got all day."

Paul had strict instructions from his wife to be home by two so she could still meet up with her friends. Emily was on half-term break so therefore she was at home. He didn't want to leave his little girl with her for a moment longer than he had to.

He began, "Have you ever heard of Francis Delacot?"

"No, why, who is he?"

"He is a South African diplomat and rumour has it that he is very rich."

Paul stroked his chin. "So what has it got to do with us?"

Ryan was in his element. "He collects teddy bears."

He waited for Paul's reaction. When Paul showed no reaction, Ryan became frustrated.

"Do I have to spell it out, man? Rich diplomat with diplomatic immunity, and a love of teddy bears that he lets no-one touch. Occasionally one of his bears comes up for auction in an auction house – they are sold for hundreds of thousands of pounds. The auctions are never advertised and take place behind locked, closed doors. There is obviously something in the teddy bears." Here Ryan stopped.

Realisation began to dawn on Paul. Had there been something very special inside the teddy bears he was looking after? So far, apart from mentioning Francis Delacot no other name had come up in conversation and Paul wondered just why this man had brought him here and whether there really was a plan to "get rich quick".

"Delacot contacted me and asked if there was a vacancy at my school for a language teacher. I was flattered and not just a little curious why a South African diplomat had approached me, when he could have had his pick of schools in London. When I asked him about this, he shrugged and said that he had been researching myself and the school and thought it was the perfect place for his daughter, as it was away from London, where she may be in danger. I agreed to take her on as a teacher, as he was paying me a lot of money, but he said I must keep her identity a secret. She never showed up for Induction and as you know she was found murdered in an old farmhouse on the outskirts of Shrewsbury."

Paul was curious. "But what can it possibly do for us? The girl is dead."

"Yes, she is dead, very dead, murdered, as it was all over the papers. What wasn't splashed all over the papers, was that she was carrying something very special, that she was supposed to deliver to an anonymous person."

"How do you know that?"

"She always travelled with a battered teddy bear and my client will pay us both £50,000 if we manage to locate the teddy bear and hand it over to him."

"Who is your client?"

Ryan gave a wry smile.

"You don't need to know that. Suffice to say it was you he told me to seek out. He knew that you could probably do with the extra money."

Paul gave a whistle. Fifty thousand pounds would ensure a good start for him and his daughter.

That was when he decided to be in.

"My client wants that teddy bear. We need to look for it."

"How do we know what it even looks like?"

"When Shirley came to the school, I needed to find her somewhere to stay that was inexpensive and inconspicuous. That was when your name came up and your property portfolio seemed a perfect match for Ms Delacot. So, you see, Paul, you did meet her when you showed her around the flat."

Paul hadn't realised that Ryan Evans had facilitated in her renting the flat. He hadn't personally met the young woman, as he had been busy the day of the viewing and had sent another of his colleagues to deal with her.

Paul shrugged. "I didn't meet her."

"Oh. At that time, I hadn't heard of Francis Delacot, but he was paying me very well and said that I needed to keep his daughter's identity a secret as it was a matter of national security. I didn't ask any more questions and he never volunteered any more information. A couple of days before she was due to come for the Induction I decided to go and see her as some paperwork needed signing. She invited me into her flat where she had an open suitcase, with a teddy bear in it. She quickly shut the suitcase and signed the papers and I promptly left. The next day a man showed up at the school. He asked about Shirley and I pretended not to know who he was talking about. That was when he made the offer of the money if I could locate the teddy bear. As you know, the girl was murdered shortly after and the teddy bear along with the other possessions from the flat had all gone missing."

"Why are you asking for my help?"

"Because you know about teddy bears."

With that, Paul was in.

*

Evans had been sworn to secrecy about who his client was that wanted the bear so desperately.

"Have you any idea what we are looking for? How much of a look did you get of the bear when you were in her room?"

"Paul, slow down with the questions, we have to take this carefully and slowly."

Paul didn't want to wait, he wanted to locate the bear and then they could collect the money from his client. After all, time was of the essence for Paul. He needed more money as soon as possible.

"The bear was brown and was wearing a green jumper."

"Humph. That's not much to go on. Was there anything else you remember about it? For instance, was it an old bear or one of the more modern makes? Have you any idea where we can start looking?"

Ryan began, "I think it must have been stolen just before the girl died."

"Well think, man, did you see anyone else apart from yourself either entering or leaving her flat? Did anyone apart from you know her identity? You didn't let it slip to another teacher or colleague?"

"No, I did not." Ryan felt very affronted. "I gave my word to Delacot, so why would I, especially when he was paying me so well?"

Paul looked at his watch; ten minutes to two. If he wasn't home soon Julie would be very annoyed.

"I'll ring you in a couple of days and we can discuss where we go from there."

Ryan was not happy; he felt Paul should be looking with him straight away, but as Paul had pointed out he still had responsibilities.

Paul dusted down his suit but hadn't bothered to put his tie back on.

"Hello, Julie."

It was ten past two and Julie was fuming. She looked him up and down disapprovingly.

"That warm, was it, that you needed to remove

your tie? It makes you look scruffy."

With that, she flounced out of the house.

Even without his tie, Paul thought he looked quite dapper in his Dior suit, although he had been uncomfortable in it all day. After all, Julie had been the one who had advised him to buy it, along with the shirt, the tie, the shoes.

He remembered her words when he purchased the outfit. "Darling, you simply must have the whole ensemble; you look so smart and sophisticated."

And it was so bloody expensive, he thought.

That had been the last time she had ever remarked about the way he looked, except to criticise some aspect of his attire.

She never said anything nice to him these days, unlike when they were first married, and she always said how handsome he looked in his suits. Then, her favourite saying had been, "I adore men in smart suits, it makes them look so handsome."

Paul went upstairs and started to take off his suit. As he removed his trousers, a business card fell out. It was the first time Paul had really seen this; he turned it over in his hands for a few moments. He had remembered Evans giving it to him, but he hadn't really taken any notice of it. Now he began to scrutinise it. It read:

Ryan Evans
Principal and Owner of the Brewmans Language Academy.

It gave a phone number and an address to call.

At least Paul would have one phone number to call should the need arise.

His daughter came running in.

"Daddy, Daddy, all the bears have gone."

Paul looked down at his daughter.

"Yes, I know, darling. They have gone to someone else to be looked after now."

"Ooh, I liked them, especially the one that rattled when you let me touch it."

Paul gave his daughter a quizzical look. "What do you mean, Emily, when you touched one it rattled?"

"Yes, don't you remember? It was the small one with a little bow and a bell round its neck."

Paul sighed; he had missed an opportunity to find out why the bears were classed as being so expensive.

"Can we play football, Daddy?"

Paul looked out of the window at the perfectly manicured lawn and not wanting to incur Julie's wrath when she came home by churning up the lawn and not wanting to disappoint his daughter, he said, "Come on then, let's go to the park."

*

Billy Haskins was stood by a tree smoking a cigarette. Paul pretended not to notice him.

"Ah, Paul, I have the bears. Thank you. Your last payment will go into your bank account tomorrow."

Paul nodded. "Thanks for that."

Billy Haskins finished his cigarette and made his way to an expensive Rolls Royce with a personalised number plate.

Paul looked after him. What was so special about those teddy bears and what did Haskins not want Paul to find out?

They had been on the park for about half an hour, when Paul made someone out in the distance. He screwed his eyes up against the strong sun in order to get a better look at the person. It was just as he thought. Ryan Evans, and he was talking to someone who had his back to him.

Was that the client?

Paul was really straining to see, but just at that moment his daughter shouted with joy, "Daddy, it's a goal. I have just scored a goal."

Paul turned to face his daughter with a big smile on his face, but when he turned back to get a better look at the two people he had seen, they had both disappeared.

It had been an eventful day in more ways than one, now he would have to go home and brave the wrath of his wife again, when she launched into an attack on him about how dirty their daughter looked.

"Can't you ever look after our daughter without

her getting her clothes dirty?"

Paul shrugged. *Just once she should let her be a child,* he thought.

"Mummy, we played football on the park and I scored a goal."

"Yes dear, but now we have to give you a bath and change your dirty clothes."

"Mummy, all the bears have gone now, to someone else to look after."

"Finally, I get my cabinet back!"

She took the little girl's hand and led her to the bathroom, muttering all the time under her breath about how irresponsible Paul was for letting her play football.

Her daughter was a tomboy and it was all Paul's fault!

All Julie was interested in was what expensive items she could now fill the cabinet with and then when any of the neighbours visited, she would be able to show off her displays.

*

The phone rang.

"Ryan Evans here."

"Have you located that bear for me yet?"

"No, I need more time, it has only been four days."

"Sort it."

Ryan replaced the receiver, but his hands were shaking. There was something menacing in his caller's tone. Although he didn't like to admit it, he was a little scared of his client and wondered if he would turn nasty, if he didn't find what he was looking for.

He needed to get in touch with Paul right away. His hands were still shaking as he dialled Paul's number.

*

Billy Haskins stood in the locked auction room, where there were only a handful of people. These people were the highest bidders; the other bidders had been eliminated in previous rounds. The bidding commenced and finally ended up with the winning bid. Haskins was pleased with the outcome; he had sold one of the teddy bears and for a tidy sum. His bears were his insurance, but also his pension and he would add that to the fortune he had already amassed.

He reflected, "Was it about the bear, or the money?" He couldn't decide which. All he did know was that the bear he desired had not been given to him yet and this made him angry and growing more impatient by the day.

He would ring that Ryan Evans again and find out what his £50,000, no wait, £100,000 as there were now two people on the job, were doing for their money.

*

The Inspector was late into work, and as he strode briskly up the corridor, he was met with an excited Constable who had been on surveillance duty all night telling him about the night's proceedings.

"All right, Constable, let me get in. I'll have a coffee and then listen to what you have to say. Was DS Lockhead with you?"

"Yes, sir. She's a wild cat, isn't she?"

"Constable Johnson, kindly do not refer to your superior in that way," he reprimanded.

John listened attentively to what the Constable was saying; he was reading from his notebook. And then at 10:35 p.m. two men arrived, they let themselves in and after about half an hour at 11:10 p.m. they left.

"Hmm, is DS Lockhead in yet?"

"No sir, she said that she needed to go home and freshen up and take a few hours off, then she would be back in this afternoon."

"Right, Constable, get yourself off home and I will see you this evening before your shift."

*

"Christine, I hear you had some activity last night at the surveillance house. Opportunists, do you think?"

Christine sat down and crossed her long legs. It was clear to see why everyone in the office liked her; she was a very likeable person.

"No sir, I don't think so, they seemed to have a purpose."

"Did you not think to arrest them for breaking and entering, especially when it is a crime scene?"

"Well no, sir, because they had a key, there was no breaking and entering."

"How do you know they had a key?"

"I saw one of them take a key out of his pocket and watched as he tried the door and the key obviously fitted, as they went straight in."

"Have you descriptions of these men?"

"Well, sort of."

"What do you mean 'sort of'? More like you and that Constable were eating your bloody pie and took your eye off the ball."

She looked at him with piercing blue eyes. "I don't eat pies. It was pitch-black at the house, there are no streetlights immediately outside," she continued in an acidic tone. "One man was shorter than the other: they were both wearing dark clothes, they were there for about half an hour and then they left. I have the registration of the car though, it was a black Insignia. I instructed Johnson to check the number plate this morning, before he left. It turns out the Insignia belongs to our friend Mr Ryan Evans."

"What, the dodgy teddy-bear collector?"

"Yes," she nodded, "the very same."

"I hope he is not trying to start his fraud business up again."

"Well, bring him in for a chat, let's see what he has to say about his nocturnal habits."

Inspector Bora didn't usually attend these chats, he

left it to the DS, but this was a murder case they were trying to solve, so he needed to be at the interview. Besides, he wasn't going to let Inspector Grieves anywhere near any suspects, if that was what Evans was. He resented Grieves and thought his presence unnecessary. He was quite capable of dealing with a murder, it wasn't the first time in his career that he had solved murders. He wanted to go out in a blaze of glory that would look good; a high-profile murder case solved.

In the meantime, though, he would busy himself with the report again and then he could prepare for the interview with Evans.

"I hear you have someone coming in for a chat later, Bora."

"Yes sir, a fraudster teddy-bear collector."

The Super looked at Bora. "Is it April 1st, Bora, is this a game?"

"No sir, no game. This man is a felon, he defrauded customers out of thousands, on the pretext of having valuable teddy bears for sale. Being an arctophile is huge business in the US."

The Super clicked his tongue. "Well if you say so, Bora. Keep the 'chat' friendly and let Inspector Grieves sit in."

John left the office. *Hell*, he thought. *I didn't want that useless lump muscling in on my enquiry.* So far Inspector Grieves had not really contributed anything useful to the enquiry.

John straightened his tie, put on his jacket and walked down the corridor to the interview room.

"Well, Mr Evans, this is a friendly chat, would you like some tea or a coffee?"

"Tea would be nice. Milk with two sugars, please."

Ryan Evans was neatly dressed in a blue suit, the kind a Principal of a school would wear.

"Now can you tell me what you were doing last night at a murdered girl's flat?"

Evans answered without hesitation.

"Yes; I was looking for some important paperwork that Miss Delacot should have completed. It was important for our records. You see, being a prestigious language school we are constantly monitored and audited."

Bora wasn't impressed. He continued, "How was it that you were able to let yourself in with a key?"

Evans thought before answering. "The other person who was with me was the landlord and he had the key to the property. We have known each other for a while, because he regularly rents out properties to my students," he lied.

"Why did you go in the dark though, surely it would have been better in the daylight?"

"Yes, you are probably right, but I was in meetings all day and Plumpton was in planning meetings all day."

Inspector Grieves sat scribbling notes, or at least that was what Bora hoped he was doing. He looked up, cleared his throat and began, "Was that Paul Plumpton you were referring to? The Property Developer?"

Evans nodded. "Yes, the very same."

"I hear he has just won some award for building, hasn't he?"

Evans stumbled. "Er, yes." He didn't really know that much about Paul Plumpton.

"What award was it?"

"I'm not too sure, he is always winning something."

Inspector Grieves looked down at his pad and continued scribbling.

"Well, thank you Mr Evans for coming in and chatting with us. It is much appreciated."

Bora was not much further with his investigation; it was perfectly plausible what Mr Evans was saying and at this point he hadn't committed any offence, so the Inspector showed him out of the office.

CHAPTER 3

"Don't you think it was a little suspicious?"

"What?"

"That Evans didn't seem to know too much about Plumpton. If that was my friend, I would be proud to know someone who had just won a prestigious building award and I would let others know too."

Bora shrugged. Inspector Grieves had a point; Evans didn't seem to know too much about his "supposed" friend.

"John, I think I'll do some digging and find out more about our Mr Evans and Mr Plumpton."

"Look in the file, you will find out all about Evans." He muttered under his breath, "If you had been prepared to look." Paul Plumpton, though, hadn't really appeared on any radar, so as far as everyone knew he wasn't doing anything wrong.

"Ah, Billy, fancy seeing you here." It was a figure of speech as Bora had recognised Haskins voice.

Bora was seated at a table in his local pub called

the Goose C Gander. John always thought this was a curious name for a pub. He once asked the landlord why it was called the Goose C Gander and not just the Goosey Gander. The landlord explained to him, that when the brewery was taken over by Battleton Breweries, one of the main owners was called Charles and he insisted on adding it to the pub's name when it was refurbished.

Billy Haskins looked around nervously.

"Inspector."

"Out for a quiet drink, are you Billy, or are you waiting for someone?"

"What business is it of yours?" he grunted.

"Nothing, Billy, just being friendly, unless you have something to hide, that is."

Billy finished his pint, looked at the expensive timepiece on his wrist and shuffled out.

That idiot Evans was late again. He really hoped that he had some good news for him. The longer it went on, the less chance he would have of finally getting his hands on the bear.

Ryan Evans had recently bought a new car; it was a black Insignia. He came charging up to the pub, giving the car full throttle. He jumped out of the car and looked around him. There was no sign of Billy Haskins. *Damn it,* he thought. *I must have just missed him.* If it hadn't been for that crash on the motorway, he would have made it in time. He was about to get back into his car when he felt an icy grip on his shoulder.

"Evans, have you got me my bear?"

"No, we are still looking."

"Well, look harder, otherwise there will be consequences."

Billy turned on his heel and left a scared Ryan.

Ryan didn't know where to start looking and now he was aware that if they didn't find the bear soon, the murdered woman might not be the only dead body.

He knew he would have to come up with a better plan because Billy was losing his patience.

*

Francis Delacot was beside himself with grief. His beautiful, clever daughter had been murdered. Someone was looking for it, that was the only explanation he could think of, why else would she have been murdered? She had known it was a risk coming to England, but she had volunteered to do it. Not only to please her father, but receive her handsome remuneration. It would be enough to set her up and keep her in the style she was accustomed to. She had been primed vigorously before she had come and told what her role was to be. As she was a fluent speaker of five languages, she had found it easy to get a job, but this job had been specifically picked out for her, in a place that no-one would think of looking. She would have been able to blend in sufficiently, so as not to attract attention. That is why her father after much deliberation had decided on Ryan Evans' Language Academy. He had known that Evans hadn't always adhered to the law and that he was a felon, but in his world it didn't really matter. Yes, he was a diplomat, but he had also amassed a large fortune, under the noses of the South African government. He enjoyed his "Diplomat" status as it gave him diplomatic immunity to travel freely as and when he wanted to.

Francis Delacot was a willowy weasel of a man with sharp features and an angular jawline. He was used to getting his own way, he was arrogant and frequently rude to people. His wife had died when his daughter was very young. She had been brought up by a succession of nannies. She had developed into a lovely, clever young woman, shrewd like her father and ambitious.

She had studied International Studies at the University of Stellenbosch and graduated with a first-class honours degree. When she arrived in England, she had met a contact who had taken her to Shrewsbury, where she was to take up a post as a language teacher. Although she thought she would find this quite boring, her real ambition was to set up an International Centre for the furtherment of business and skills, where she would invite some of the foremost and most distinguished leaders in their fields and have people pay "mega-bucks" to listen to them. She planned to run Seminars and Workshops, in the hope of attracting the very rich. She knew, however, this couldn't happen at the Language School, so she would just have to bide her time.

. This was where Paul Plumpton's business had been called in. Plumpton hoped to receive a high rent from the property. He had also found her a place that he thought would be "ideal for her to set up her Centre". As this was also on the information she had filled in.

They had explained to her that it was a farmhouse down a dirt track, but that it had quite a few rooms; ideal for visiting guests, once it was renovated. Shirley was excited at the idea and arranged to meet Paul at the farmhouse, the following day. Unfortunately, Paul never showed and now she was dead. Paul had been dismayed not only about her death, but thinking about the lost revenue for the farmhouse. This was just another blow to his finances and one he could not afford.

*

"So, people; what leads have we got on the dead woman? She was going to start at Brewmans, and rented a flat from Paul Plumpton. Has anyone checked into his background? Any dodgy dealings, not paying his taxes etc?"

"No sir, everything he has done and all the properties he owns are totally legitimate."

Inspector Bora groaned. "Nothing, nothing at all?"

"No sir, not even a parking ticket."

Bugger, he thought. Now Billy Haskins was a "different kettle of fish". Slippery and slimy with lots of fingers in lots of pies, they just could never find something to convict him for.

"I want you to bring Billy Haskins in for 'a chat'. I want to know who he was waiting for at the pub the other night."

Christine Lockhead nodded. "Onto it, sir."

Bora looked at the file again. Who knew about the woman apart from Ryan Evans and Paul Plumpton? There was something not quite right with Ryan Evans, but Paul Plumpton seemed an upstanding member of the community; he was a family man and by all accounts doing alright for himself. Now the only suspects in this case were Ryan Evans and Paul Plumpton. He would have them both in for questioning and see if they had convincing alibis, alibis that checked out.

*

"Well, Inspector, I was at home all night when that girl was murdered, my landlady can vouch for that as we ate our evening meal and as I was tired, I went up to my room and stayed there all night."

"You are the Principal of the Academy, surely you must have a house somewhere near to the school."

"Yes, quite, but it suits me to have a landlady, and to live just outside the village; that way I am not constantly pestered by people whom I have no time for."

"Hmm. We will have to check out your alibi with your landlady."

"Yes, do, I have nothing to hide. Now if we are finished here, I would like to leave now, as I have a governors' meeting tonight."

Bora took a long breath in. "Before you go, what was Delacot's reaction when he found out about his daughter? Especially as she should have been starting at your school."

Evan's face flushed; he wasn't expecting that question. He had to think quickly.

"He was furious and threatened to take me to court to retrieve the money he had paid me, so I returned his money in full. I don't want a scandal like that hanging over the school, it's not good for the reputation."

Bora allowed himself a little smile. "Rightly so, Mr Evans."

He was not taken in by this smooth-talking Principal. Did the man think he was an idiot? Or was he so arrogant that he thought himself above the law? Either way he felt sure this fraudster had something to do with the girl's death.

*

Christine Lockhead sat at the desk, her long legs stretched out in front of her. Shuffling the papers on the desk, she looked up at Paul Plumpton and began.

"So you were pleased about the sales you managed that week, were you? The farmhouse you hoped would now be a going concern. That must have been a relief for you after so many years of it being empty. Was it three or four years?"

Paul looked her in the eyes and noticed what an attractive woman she was, far more attractive than his wife.

He gave a cough to clear his throat. "Yes, it was three years, I was going to sell it at a knock-down price to Miss Delacot, because she, like me, wanted to start somewhere and own her own business. It took me back to when I first started my business and I wanted to help her as much as I could."

"Does the name Billy Haskins mean anything to you?" she continued.

"Yes, I know Billy Haskins, he was the first person to give me my real break."

"What is your opinion of Mr Haskins?"

Paul was beginning to get nervous; how should he answer that question?

"Well, erm, no comment," he said.

He didn't want to elaborate on the point, because he thought he was a slimy bastard. Although he had helped Paul, there were strings attached and he never did anything for nothing, but he had helped keep that very expensive roof over his family's heads and afford his wife the lifestyle she had. Now though, all that would end. He had received his last payment from Billy. When his wife realised that the money wasn't as forthcoming as previously, she would probably go into "meltdown". He could hear her now. "Why, Paul, where has all the money gone? Have you been having an affair? Have you got another woman tucked away in a house somewhere? Really, Paul, it's too much."

Christine Lockhead was surveying the man sat in front of her.

"Have you ever owned a weapon?" She was blunt and to the point.

"Excuse me?"

"You know, a weapon, a gun, or a hunting knife maybe."

"No! I have a young daughter in the house, what would I be wanting with any kind of weapon? I am a responsible father, Sergeant, and I do not believe in violence of any kind."

"Thank you, Mr Plumpton; you are free to go."

*

Paul was sweating profusely when he entered the house. How was he going to explain to Julie where he had been?

"About bloody time. Don't tell me, a planning meeting."

Paul frowned; he hated Julie swearing in front of their daughter. He didn't want her picking up Julie's bad habits.

Julie gave him a defiant look. "Don't tell me about swearing in front of our daughter, when you can't even keep her clean for an afternoon, allowing her to play football in her pretty dress, what were you thinking? Oh wait, no, you weren't thinking, were you?"

Yes, he thought, that had been a bit stupid. He should have told her to put on her old trousers and a tee-shirt. Then, maybe Julie wouldn't have been so mad.

Things were getting more intolerable for them both; they seemed to be constantly rowing and Julie took great delight in belittling him whenever she could.

He needed that bear. It was his passport out of his miserable life, where he felt trapped.

*

"Sir, we've found a knife. It was buried deep in the undergrowth in Knotts Wood."

"Well done, now get it bagged up for Forensics to examine. Finally we may have some sort of breakthrough."

Forensics confirmed it was the knife that killed Shirley. That was good news, but they were no nearer to finding the killer or even a motive.

Evan's alibi checked out and as for Paul Plumpton, he had taken his daughter to visit his parents in Bridgenorth on the night of the murders. It had been a last-minute decision as he had a phone call from his father saying that his mother had been taken ill. Not wanting to leave Emily with Julie, he decided to take her with him. He had phoned Shirley to let her know, but had got no answer, so he left a voicemail, explaining that one of his colleagues would be along shortly.

"Is that Plumpton?"

"Yes. Who is this?"

"My name is Francis Delacot, I believe it was you who rented the flat out to my daughter."

"Yes. That's right."

"I would like you to show me exactly where the flat is."

"Mr Delacot, please take a seat, I will personally drive you to the flat and then we can see the farmhouse."

Delacot nodded.

At the flat it was obvious that Francis Delacot was looking for something.

"When the police searched the flat was there anything missing?"

Paul coughed, then answered, "No, I don't think so. The police had an itinerary of exactly what was in the flat."

"Has anyone else been in the flat?"

Again Paul was getting nervous. "No," he lied.

"Very well. Drive me to the farmhouse then. I want to see where my beautiful daughter was found."

"Well, if you're sure."

"Damn it, man, I have just said so, haven't I? This is by no means the end of this, Plumpton, the police investigation is ongoing and I expect you to keep me informed of your business activities. I am travelling back to South Africa tomorrow after the funeral, but I will be in touch, mark my words."

Paul was visibly rattled by the other man.

He pressed the accelerator and roared up the road, towards the dirt path that led to the farmhouse. He didn't like Francis Delacot; there was something menacing about him. He hoped the pair would find the missing bear soon, present it to their client and then he would be free from all this.

*

"Paul, I must see you." It was Ryan Evans; he sounded quite breathless.

"I think I have located the bear, but I need you to help me retrieve it. I have been doing some digging around and I managed to find someone in the pub that had seen a young woman with a teddy bear just before she died. He thought it was an odd thing for a grown woman to be carrying in her bag; the arm was just visible and my friend thought it might be a teddy bear. I had been drunk a couple of nights ago and let slip that we were looking for a teddy bear. I'm sorry, Paul. He decided to follow her, curious about the bear. She had a rucksack on her back and a purse was in the rucksack.

"As my friend is a pickpocket, he brushed past her and was able to seize her purse. It was too risky for him to try and get the bear, so he settled for the purse instead, as it had an address written on a piece of paper tucked deep inside. That was when he called me.

"My friend shared that information with me for a cut of the prize money."

Paul was not happy, someone else was now involved in retrieving the bear.

"So where is the flat then?"

"Out towards Bridgenorth and surprise, surprise, it's one of your properties, so I presume you have the key."

Paul looked up the address on his office database. Yes, it was indeed one of his properties, he had acquired it several years ago as an investment.

"No-one has lived there for at least eighteen months, the flat has been empty."

"So, what are we waiting for?" Evans' voice was raised, and it had an impatient tone.

Paul jotted down the address, picked up the keys for the property and soon they were speeding towards Bridgenorth.

The house smelt musty and very damp. Evans was not surprised no-one lived there.

"We need to take this house apart to try and find that bear."

"So who is the anonymous person, I wonder? Have you a name for the person you have let this property out to?"

"No, because as I told you it has been empty for at

least eighteen months, but obviously someone has been here."

"Whoever it was left in a hurry, or was forcibly removed – look at the walls." The rooms had been ransacked and the walls were splattered with blood.

They had both been searching for a couple of hours when suddenly Paul found something sticking out the side of an old battered sofa. He pulled it and suddenly the bear was free.

"I've found it!" he shouted triumphantly.

Evans rushed over and checked the bear. Yes, it was the one he had seen in the girl's flat when she had arrived.

"We need to get in touch with my client and arrange to hand it over as soon as possible."

Paul presumed that this bear had something hidden inside, but he wasn't bothered just as long as he got his £50,000. He had already began planning how to spend it in his head. As soon as he was able he would take himself and Emily on a holiday to begin with and with some of the money that he had put aside, money that Julie didn't know about, then he would look for a property in France where they could live undisturbed. He had to make sure he knew where Emily's passport was and check that it was up to date. Although Julie went on at least four foreign holidays a year, she always went with friends, never him or their daughter. It was always left up to him to care for his daughter and ensure she had holidays and fun things.

They carefully dropped the bear into a plain brown bag and headed off.

"Hello, we have found the bear."

"Excellent, excellent. I will arrange for the money to go into your accounts once I have verified the authenticity of the bear."

"No, that won't do. I want the money in our accounts before we hand over the bear. No money, no bear."

"Alright, alright." The voice on the other end of the phone was shouting. Paul thought the voice sounded familiar. Wait a minute, it was Billy Haskins, he was sure of that. So that was who the mystery client was. He would enjoy taking the money from him.

"Tomorrow night outside the Goose C Gander, at seven thirty and this time don't be late. You got that?"

"See you then."

The phone clicked off.

*

Billy Haskins could hardly contain his excitement. At last he was going to be the richest man in the world. The bear would make that possible, he felt sure.

The men arrived at the allotted time and place. The handover went smoothly, and Haskins jumped into his car and sped off.

As he handled the bear with shaking hands, he

noticed something unusual. It didn't seem as heavy as it should be, but no matter. It was now his, all his. He took out his penknife and started to slit the fur of the bear, anticipating with bated breath, the "jewel" that was about to be revealed. He reached into the stuffing and nothing. Where was the thing? He began to frantically pull the stuffing out of the bear, when suddenly something dropped onto the floor. Billy looked down at the floor and then could hardly contain his rage and disappointment. This was not what he was looking for. He had just lost £100,000 to a useless pair of idiots. He cursed and vowed to get even.

*

"Mr Haskins, what a pleasure it is to see you again."

"Sod off, copper, go and 'arrass someone else."

"Oh, Billy, now that isn't a nice greeting. Has someone upset you?"

"Like I said, copper, shove off and leave me alone."

Inspector Bora thought that Haskins was acting suspiciously, and he was determined to find out why.

"Copper, I've told you if you don't leave me alone, I'll do for you."

"Come, come, Billy. That's no way to talk to someone who is just being friendly. We could continue our little chat down the station, if you'd prefer."

Haskins glared at the Inspector, eyes wide and his nostrils were flaring.

"What, what is it you want to know?"

"Well for starters, why you seem in such a bad mood."

"It's none of your business, but if you must know I've been scammed and lost £100,000 into the bargain."

Bora gave a little smile to himself. It looked as though this thug that always managed to avoid prosecution, had finally got his come-uppance and been scammed out of money he had probably scammed in the first place.

"Do you want to make an official complaint, Billy?"

"No, I bloody well don't. I don't need nosey coppers sniffing around and looking into my business."

"Have you something to hide, Billy?"

"No! Now get lost, will you?"

*

The Inspector was driven home and as Paul poured himself a stiff drink of his favourite whisky they sat down and he reflected on the conversation he'd had with Billy Haskins.

Haskins knew more than he was saying. Did he have something to do with the murder of the young woman? John would never put anything past Billy; he could be slippery and dangerous. John would get him in for an interview in the morning to try and ascertain some more information. As yet they didn't have a motive for the murderer, or really any concrete evidence about anyone.

"A murder, Billy, a diplomat's daughter, what do you know about it?"

"I don't know nuffink about it. Why should I?"

The Inspector continued, "We all know you do some dodgy things to get your own way, but murder, Billy, I didn't have you down for that, and not just one murder but a diplomat's daughter no less. You could be looking at life imprisonment if you were found guilty of this."

Billy's hands were sweating profusely and there were beads of sweat on his brow.

"What was it you needed so badly, Billy, that you were prepared to murder for to get it? I hope whatever it was, was worth it."

"No, I went to see the murdered woman about a purchase, but she told me she didn't know what I was talking about. We had a row, but then I left. I swear I din't lay a finger on her."

He was scrabbling about desperately for an alibi.

"Anyone see you in her flat?"

"No, oh yeah, an old woman."

"Where was she?"

"Two doors down from the girl's flat, I think."

"How do you know that, Billy?"

"Because I watched her turn into a house and then I got in my car and left. Now, Clueless, if there's nothing else can I go. You have no evidence against me that I have done anythink wrong, so you can't keep me 'ere."

"That's fine for now, Billy, but stay in the town as I might want to speak to you again."

Billy stuck his finger up at the Inspector and left.

Inspector Bora needed to find out what it was that Billy had wanted to purchase from the young woman. He did not ask Billy outright, for fear of him being given false information and then that would hamper the investigation further.

He would play it softly with Billy and eventually find out what the purchase he had hoped to make was. Sooner or later Billy would fall into his trap; his arrogant way and the way that he felt he was above the law would be his downfall.

He would let Christine Lockhead interview him next time. There would be a next time, he felt sure about that.

"Christine, can you check out the old woman and see if she remembers anything about Miss Delacot, or someone visiting her before she was murdered?"

*

Josie Tanner was a grey-haired lady in her sixties. Yes, she had seen people visiting the young woman before she died.

"One was in a Rolls Royce, I think it was. Then there was another man who visited her. He looked all official, he was carrying a black briefcase. He was there about twenty minutes and then he left.

"Thank you, Mrs Tanner, that has been very helpful. Just one more question before I go. Do you remember what kind of car the man with the briefcase was driving?"

The old lady thought for a minute.

"It was a big fancy black one. I remarked to Benji that there were strange comings and goings at that flat."

"Benji?" DS Lockhead said enquiringly.

"Yes, that's my little dog. He's quite old now you know so usually I just take him for a walk round the block. That was how I was able to tell you about the goings on. I always walk around the same time every day."

"Can you remember the time you saw the man with the briefcase?"

"Oh yes, it was about six o'clock."

"And the man you said you saw getting into a Rolls Royce, what time was that? Can you remember?"

The woman thought for a few moments then answered, "Two o'clock, yes it was two o'clock."

"Are you sure about that?"

"Yes, yes, I had just come back from my luncheon club."

At this point as if on cue a small dog came nuzzling up to his owner. "He is telling me he wants to go for his walk now." She bent down and patted the dog gently and produced a treat for him. "Alright, Benji, we will go in a minute. Now if that is all will you excuse me? It's time to take Benji out."

Christine bent to stroke the little dog, but he began growling so she decided not to.

"Well thank you again, Mrs Tanner, and this time I really am going."

"Goodbye, dearie."

*

So, two people could now be potentially in the frame. "Do we know yet who the other visitor was?"

"We could bring that Ryan Evans in again and ask him, see if it was him at Ms Delacot's flat. The old lady said the second man was in a fancy car. He was there at about six o'clock. That would have been after school had closed, I suspect."

The Inspector stroked his chin. "There is something not quite right about that Evans."

"I know, sir. That's what I thought."

"Are we getting nearer to either a killer or a motive, do you think Christine?"

"Well currently we have our friend Billy Haskins and Ryan Evans, but no evidence on either linking them to the murder."

*

Paul had booked the flights and the hotel; he was going to take his daughter to Spain for a holiday and then look at either buying or renting a villa in France. He felt relieved and a little apprehensive, about taking his daughter away from her mother, but he convinced himself he was doing the right thing.

The phone rang.

"Mr Plumpton, we would like you to come down to the police station and answer a few questions for us."

Paul's heart sank; he would have to ask Julie to look after Emily while he went to the police station. He thought it best not to arouse Julie's suspicions, so he lied and said he had been called to an emergency development meeting. Julie didn't believe him and again accused him of having an affair. Paul shrugged and said nothing. Now was not the time to pick a fight with his wife.

*

"Mr Plumpton I understand it was you that let that flat to the murdered woman. Is that true?"

Paul took out his handkerchief and mopped his brow.

"Yes. That's right."

I presume you were charging a high rent knowing that the woman was the daughter of a wealthy diplomat."

Paul looked down at his feet, then said in a small voice, "I didn't know who she was. I just saw the opportunity of charging a high rent, as she stated on her form that she would be starting at Brewmans Language School as a teacher. I figured she would be able to afford the rent and when in discussion with a colleague she remarked that she had the money to pay for the old farmhouse, well, I jumped at the chance. It meant someone else would be able to fix the place up and it wouldn't cost me or my company."

"So all this about wanting to help a young woman fulfil her dream, has all been a load of lies?"

"Yes, pretty much," Paul confessed. "I really only thought about the money."

"We have been looking into your affairs and we noticed there was a substantial payment of £50,000 received into your bank account two days ago. Would you like to tell us about that?"

Paul coughed nervously and began, "I, er, I sold an investment property."

"Would you like to tell us who you sold it to?"

"Another developer."

"Not Billy Haskins by any chance?"

Paul could feel his cheeks burning. He hadn't killed that woman and he didn't know who had. After all, he had just gone along with finding the teddy bear. He wasn't involved in any other way.

"Only Billy suggested he had been scammed out of £100,000 and it just seems strange that £50,000 just popped into your account a few days ago. Were you working with someone else for Billy?"

Paul felt the Sergeant's blue eyes piercing into his soul. He shuffled in his chair.

"I never murdered anyone, I didn't stab anyone."

"You must admit that it looks suspicious, you owning both the properties where the dead girl was renting and wanting to buy from you? You said previously that you didn't own a knife. I will ask you again and this time I urge you to tell the truth. Do you own a knife, or not?"

"Most definitely not," was the reply.

"In that case, you may go, but don't plan to leave the country anytime soon. We may want to ask you more questions to assist us with our enquiries."

Paul felt more miserable than he had ever felt. He wouldn't be able to take his daughter on holiday or start his new life anytime soon.

Damn Billy Haskins and damn Ryan Evans. It was his greed that had led him to work with Evans. He convinced himself that they would become very rich very soon, with no repercussions. But that was not meant to be!

CHAPTER 4

Francis Delacot was a weasel of a man; thin, willowy and shrewd. He was disliked by his colleagues and had no-one he could call a friend. He was not unduly troubled by this, as he argued, who needs friends when you have power? And he did have power – lots of it. He was able to travel through countries unchallenged as he had diplomatic immunity. He had amassed a great deal of wealth, including diamonds, paintings, etc., sometimes from not exactly legal channels. He was known to be a bully and people who crossed him invariably suffered the consequences, although his outward persona remained squeaky clean. However, the thing he had desired most in the world had been ripped from his grasp and now it was, well, he knew not where.

The death of his daughter had hit him very hard; he kept reminiscing of when his beautiful daughter was young. She had the same brown eyes and brown hair that his wife had had. She had also had ambition and a shrewd business brain, where she hoped to make lots of money before she was thirty. She knew of her father's precious cargo and had agreed to transport it to England.

As he mourned the death of his daughter, he also mourned the fact that the "thing" had gone missing and he didn't really know where to start looking.

That was why he had been so insistent on looking round his daughter's flat and the old farmhouse. Nothing had yielded any results, however.

*

"Mr Delacot, so pleased you could spare us the time. I am very sorry for your loss."

"Yes, yes, man, that may be all well and good, but have you found my daughter's killer?"

John despised this weasel, but keeping his tone civil, he answered, "No, not yet, but we feel we are very near to making an arrest."

"Well that's just not good enough. Do you have a murder weapon, or a motive?"

"We have a murder weapon."

Delacot's brown furrowed, he was in deep thought.

"I expect this case to be cleared up imminently before I go back to South Africa. If you require anything else from me I will be staying at the South African Embassy, and I suggest you get your men working harder to solve this case."

John pushed his chair back and raising himself to his full height, gave Francis Delacot a forced grin and wished him good afternoon.

John was puzzled. There was something decidedly odd about Delacot. There was definitely something he was hiding.

*

Billy Haskins was still fuming. How could he have been so stupid to let two complete imbeciles, in his eyes, try and locate a very valuable bear? He began to wonder if he had been double-crossed by either or both of them. Were they in it together? Either way, he had just lost one hundred thousand pounds. That would have been a paltry sum if the bear was the one he thought it was, but instead it had just been a copy. So where was the real bear and who had it? A lesser villain would have wondered if the real bear existed, but not Billy; he felt sure it did and HE was going to find it and it would make him very rich and very powerful. He would have progressed from being a small-time villain to one of great standing within the criminal fraternity.

*

Delacot had been relentless in pestering the police and the Home Office about his daughter's murder. He had demanded they arrest someone immediately.

"Sir, it might happen like that in your country, but in ours we have to follow strict guidelines and have enough evidence to back up our claims before we can make any arrests."

The Commander was getting slightly annoyed at being told what to do in a murder case.

The diplomat was becoming more and more anxious. Where was it and who else knew about it?

"John, have you made any progress in the woman's murder?"

"We have two suspects, sir, but nothing that can tie them to the murder completely."

The Superintendent puffed out his cheeks. "What is Inspector Grieves doing? Has he any theories on who might have killed this young woman and why, and what about Lockhead, has she managed to uncover anything?"

"Only the fact that Shirley Delacot was visited twice in the same afternoon, once by Billy Haskins and once by Ryan Evans."

"Ah, our old friend Billy. Have you checked out his alibi?"

"Yes sir, it is rock solid."

"Pity. I would love to see that bugger go down for something; we have been after him for years, but we can never get anything to stick. So frustrating."

"Yes sir, I know."

Haskins had been brought to the police station again on the pretext of "helping the police with their enquiries".

"Now, Mr Haskins, Billy, do you mind if I call you Billy?"

Looking at this attractive woman in front of him, she could have called him anything she liked and he would not have minded.

DS Lockhead was dressed in a smart black suit and as she crossed her legs under the desk she shot Billy a smile. Billy smiled back; this copper was going to be a pushover, an attractive one, but still a pushover, he thought.

"I believe you are an arctophile. Would you like to tell me about it?"

Billy gave a loud cough as if getting ready to clear his throat; he was going to have some fun with this copper.

"Well I just like collecting teddy bears, you know some of them can be very expensive."

"Can you tell me about the last one you purchased? The one that you spent £100,000 on."

Billy's face turned crimson. How the hell did she know that was what the hundred thousand pounds was for?

"It must have been a very valuable bear, Billy, to spend that kind of money on."

"Like I told Inspector Clueless out there, I was scammed out of my money. No-one said it was over a bear."

"Yes, Billy," she continued in her sweetest voice, "but it was a bear, wasn't it?"

"So bloody what? I'm not asking you to investigate

it so what's the problem?"

"The problem is, Billy, you paid a lot of money for a bear and a young woman is dead, the one you visited just before she was murdered. You said that you went to make a purchase but you came away without it. Is that why you killed her, Billy?"

"No, no, no!" he roared. "I 'aven't killed nobody."

"Did you get someone to kill her for you because you couldn't have the bear?"

"I got the bear, Miss Clever Clogs, but it was after she was murdered."

"And was it the bear you expected it to be?"

Billy glared at the Sergeant. "No comment."

"Why was it so expensive, Billy?" she persisted with her line of questioning.

"No comment."

*

"I don't think we are going to get anything more useful out of him, sir."

"Do you think he did it?"

"No, I don't think so. I don't think he has the brains to do it, even if he has the motive."

Billy Haskins was not a suspect, or was he?

The police hadn't said whether they were going to charge him with any offence. He knew he would have to keep his head down for a while, in case the "coppers come snooping again."

*

Billy sat in his lounge fuming. He had been scammed out of one hundred thousand pounds and that Paul Plumpton and Ryan Evans were going to pay him every penny back as there would be consequences.

First, he was accused of murder and to be made a fool of by not having the right bear, was too much for him to take. He had seen the bear at her flat and then when she had been murdered the bear had disappeared. He was convinced it was the right bear, that was why he wanted it so badly.

*

BANG, BANG, BANG, came the knock on her door. Julie looked up to see two burly men stood outside on her front porch. She put the chain on the door and was able to open it a little.

"Mrs Plumpton? We're debt collectors."

Julie looked at the pair quizzically. They were both dressed in black. One was unshaven and the other was clean shaven, they both wore black hoodies, with the hoods up, partially concealing their faces.

"What do you mean, debt collectors? We are not in any debt. I think you have the wrong house."

"No," said the tallest of the men. "This is where Paul Plumpton lives, isn't it?"

"Yes," said Julie in a small voice. "He's not in though."

"Tell him his friend Billy wants to have a meeting

with him tomorrow night at seven o'clock. At the Goose C." And with that, the two men left.

Paul returned home and Julie began shouting at the top of her voice. What had he done now, he thought?

"You, you!" she screamed. "What have you got yourself into?"

Paul thought she was charging around like a demented banshee, shouting and pointing one of her long elegantly manicured fingers at him.

"What are you on about?"

"You know very well what I'm on about. The two debt collectors that came around here earlier and demanded you talk with them. I told them you were out and they left a message. The message was to meet Billy Haskins tomorrow at seven o'clock at the Goose C."

The colour drained from Paul's face. He presumed she knew what it was about.

It hadn't been a request, it had been a demand and the men, Julie had screamed, looked very menacing.

*

"Ah, Paul. So glad you could make it."

As Paul looked around him he saw he was circled by three men, one being Haskins.

"You tricked me; and I want my soddin' money back. Every last penny."

Paul froze, then suddenly he felt a sharp searing

pain to his jaw.

"Do as the boss says or else."

Another blow was aimed at his head and suddenly he was falling to the ground.

Haskins' face was an inch away from his. He could smell his putrid breath on his face. Haskins produced a knife.

"Maybe I should slit you up the back like I did with the bear. What would happen, Paul, if I did? Would your stuffing come out?"

Paul felt the blood oozing from his mouth where he had been punched. He didn't want to die like this.

Haskins waved the knife in front of his face.

"How's that pretty little daughter of yours? You shouldn't be depriving her of a dad, now should you?"

"Leave my family alone. I'll get your money, just don't involve my wife or my daughter."

"Two days, Paul, and if you don't deliver, the debt collectors will come to collect your debt. Transfer it to this account and make sure it is not traced."

Haskins pulled Paul up roughly and flashed a toothy grin.

"I look forward to it. Boys, our business is concluded for the time being. Come, let us celebrate."

The three men set off in the direction of the pub and Paul was left to stumble to his car. His jaw was beginning to swell and his left eye was black and bruised where one of the thugs had punched him.

"God in heaven," Julie shrieked when he reached the front door. "What has happened to you?"

Paul looked at his bloodstained clothes, but could hardly speak as his jaw was so swollen.

Through swollen lips he managed to tell Julie that he had some business to sort out, but it got a little out of hand.

"A little out of hand, a little out of hand?" she repeated. "I'd say it got a lot out of hand. Are you going to the police?"

"No. I am going to bed though. Goodnight."

Julie and Paul had slept in separate bedrooms for the last two years.

"Don't bleed on the pillows."

Christ, is that all she was concerned about? She had never once asked him how it was or if she could do anything to help his pain. Spoilt brat, but some of it was his own fault as in the beginning he had never wanted to say "no" to his new wife. Then over the years, she had become much more demanding and self-centred.

His head ached as it touched the pillow; his mind was racing. He hadn't got the whole £50,000; as usual Julie had demanded money from him and not wanting to arouse suspicion, he had given her £5,000.

"I sold a property to an investor," he lied. What was one more lie to her? She couldn't care less where the money came from as long as she was able to spend it.

Paul checked his bank account again. He was still £5,000 short to pay to Billy. Maybe he wouldn't query it or wouldn't notice it, or maybe he would and he would send his Haskins thugs round to give him another beating.

*

"Ryan Evans has been found hanged. They reckon it was suicide."

Christine Lockhead was imparting this information to the Inspector.

"Well, well, I guess that is one murder suspect out of the picture. Did he leave a suicide note?"

"No, one hasn't been found."

"Well, Mr Ryan Evans, what was so bad that you had to commit suicide? Or was it that you had been threatened by someone? It's a mystery. I want to see the pathologist's report as soon as it is ready."

"Yes sir, I'll arrange that."

At that moment his phone rang.

"What is it, Constable?"

"A Mr Jones says he wants to see you urgently."

"Tell him to bugger off. I haven't got time for his jokes today."

"But sir, he is very insistent."

"Oh very well, show him in."

The man stood in front of Bora looked dirtier than ever.

"You been sleeping rough, Jonesy?"

"No I bloody aint, yer cheeky bugger."

"You smell like you have."

"Ah, that's 'cos I bin doin' some digging."

"Where, for God's sake? Down a coal mine?"

Jones smiled. A row of crooked black teeth that looked like uneven crazy paving greeted the Inspector.

"Well get on with it, man, I haven't got all day."

"'Ow much? 'Ow much is me information worth? And then I'll decide if I want ter give it to yer."

Inspector Bora was running out of patience.

"Here's twenty, now give me the information."

Jones produced from his pocket a crumpled picture of a teddy bear. The writing underneath it read "The Emerald Bear".

Bora took the dirty crumpled picture from the man and showed it to DS Lockhead.

"Is that it?"

"Yeah."

"What do think, DS Lockhead? Is it worth twenty quid?"

"No sir, definitely not."

"Get out, you just robbed me of twenty quid."

Jones held on tightly to the cash, in case Bora demanded the money back.

"Dickens!" he shouted and a young Constable came in. "Photocopy that picture for me."

"Yes, sir." The Constable took the picture from Lockhead and held it by a corner. He didn't want to catch anything from the dirty paper.

"Right, people, listen up. I think we might have the motive for our murderer of the young woman."

He held up the picture of the teddy bear, captioned "The Emerald Bear".

Bora could hear the sniggering and sarcastic comments, about teddy bears and being found in woods.

"Concealed inside the Emerald Bear is reputed to be the most expensive emerald in the world with a price tag of four million pounds."

The room was hushed; you could hear a pin drop.

"Questions? Don't all speak at once."

There remained a stunned silence. Then a Sergeant broke the silence.

"So, is it a teddy bear we're looking for?"

"Looks that way, Sergeant. Look at the picture and familiarise yourself with it. That bear must be out there somewhere."

"How do we know this was the target or the motive and do we know who has it?"

"We don't yet, that is what we need to find out and why. Inspector Grieves will talk you through the rest of it."

Grieves looked stunned. How the hell was he supposed to talk anyone through it? He hadn't familiarised himself with it yet.

Inspector Bora chuckled to himself as he left the room.

"Let's see how you handle that, Mr Smarty!"

Inspector Grieves was thumbing through magazines and looking at websites on precious gems.

Apparently the darker the emerald the more it was worth. This particular emerald was not used to be bought and sold; no, it was used as currency. The person who possessed the emerald would have an enormous wealth and power.

Grieves looked at the picture of the gem and thought to himself wistfully, *If only that was mine.*

"Yes sir, right away."

As John walked down the corridor to the Super's office, he wondered what kind of mood the Super would be in today. Was he in for another ticking off?

"Have a seat, John. So, what was the motive? Robbery? Greed? And why was that girl murdered?"

John didn't have the answers, well, not yet anyway.

*

Paul Plumpton knew he had to get away. Short-changing Billy Haskins was not a good thing to do and he knew that sooner or later the Haskins thugs would return because Billy would want his pound of flesh, literally. It was too dangerous to take his daughter, but as soon as he could, he would come back for her.

He picked up his passport and his hold-all; he didn't take a suitcase as he wanted a quick getaway at the other end, not waiting for his luggage on a carousel.

Emily was at school and Julie was on one of her lunches with her cronies, so Paul ordered the taxi to the airport and slipped away. He left Julie a quickly scrawled note and ended by saying, *Look after Emily and I will be back as soon as I can.* He conveniently forgot to say that he would be back for Emily. The less Julie knew, the better.

As the aeroplane took off Paul heaved a sigh of relief; 40,000 feet up in the air, it didn't seem too bad. He ordered a whisky, drank that and then settled down to try and sleep. It seemed like ages since he had had a proper sleep. The swelling on his face had gone down and the bruising on his eye didn't look quite as bad. He had panicked about going through customs as his eye was still black and it didn't quite match his passport photo, but he needn't have worried. He was waved through with everyone else.

He had been to America several times before, but this time was different. As the plane touched down at JFK airport, he knew he was on a mission.

Francis Delacot had rung him from America.

"I want that bear, and I will stop at nothing to get it, do you understand? Your flight is booked. I want you and that bear on American soil by 2:30 p.m. tomorrow. I will send you the tickets through by email and then you can print them off, is that understood?"

Maybe this was a way out for Paul. He had been told not to leave the town, but there was no-one watching him and he hadn't had to surrender his passport, so he could slip out of the country relatively unnoticed because at the moment, he wasn't a suspect for anything, just "a person of interest".

Delacot had discovered by some means that Billy Haskins had the bear. He had told Paul that he must steal the bear from Haskins and present it to him. Large amounts of money were discussed and again, Paul thought about the money and agreed to help Francis Delacot. He knew the bear must be very important, but he didn't really care just as long as he was getting a very fat paycheque.

He touched down at John Kennedy Airport armed with the teddy bear stolen from Billy Haskins. It had been quite a clever plan and brilliantly executed.

He had enlisted the help of his friend Don to help him get the bear. He was sure Haskins still had the bear. It was just a matter of getting it out. Paul had described the bear to Don and had assured him that when he had the bear, he would pay Don for his trouble.

Don was to be disguised as a TV Director, wanting to make a film about successful people and convince Billy to take part in a TV documentary. This had appealed to Billy's vanity as then at last the world would see him as a respectable businessman, no longer a joke in the community, but a force to be reckoned with.

"Of course, we'll have to do some filming in your house, the viewers just love to see where people live and the bears of course. There are lots of people that will be so interested in your bears."

So, Billy had agreed.

"I couldn't believe it was so easy," said a delighted Don to Paul. "The man is a total idiot and so vain."

"But will you have access to the bears?"

"I think so. I told Billy that the viewers would love to see his collection of bears. I have arranged to meet him for the film next Tuesday."

*

"Have you got the bear?" Paul was breathless with anticipation.

"Yes, yes, I have it. Billy had to slip out of the room to make a phone call and I popped it into my camera case. With a bit of luck, he won't notice it is missing until we are long gone."

"I don't think he knows what he is looking for, really."

Paul had been contacted by Delacot a week ago, so now he was eager to leave the country with the bear and under Billy Haskins' nose, as he didn't relish another beating.

"I do want my cut, Paul. I have not risked

everything for you for nothing."

Paul had plans of keeping the money Delacot was going to pay him for himself, but now there was an added complication. His friend Don was now asking for some money.

Paul could be ruthless and was thinking of a way not to pay Don his cut. He had become devious over the years, with his Property Development dealings. He hadn't set out to be like that, but family pressures, namely Julie, had forced him to earn as much money as he could so that she could live a jet-setter lifestyle. Although not quite, that was how Paul viewed it.

He used to find out where the most gullible or rich clients might be and then work on them to either rent or invest in his properties. Now he just had to quietly skip the country and disappear to America, where he could conclude his business.

It would be several days before anyone knew that Paul was missing. His wife would have got the letter by now, and she didn't care anyway.

Don would want to meet up with Paul for his share, but Paul had left his phone behind so the only thing that anyone would hear on his phone was the voicemail.

CHAPTER 5

Paul paced up and down the hotel room, waiting for the phone call.

"Is that Paul Plumpton? Have you brought the bear?"

Paul hesitated. He had to be sure that he was speaking to Delacot. They had devised a code word and Paul listened intently for this before answering.

When the voice on the other end said the code word, Paul then answered.

"Yes, I have the bear."

"Right, stay in your hotel room and I will pick it up tomorrow at 2:30 p.m. I'll have the money for you only if it is the right bear."

Paul had secretly opened a bank account in America, one that wouldn't be traced in England. He thought about the cheque he would receive, and sank down into the plush armchair. He then went to bed. He needed a good night's sleep as he still felt jetlagged.

He could wait until tomorrow to hand over the bear.

*

He looked at his watch. 2:30 p.m. Delacot was late. Suddenly there was aloud banging on the door.

"Plumpton. Are you in there?"

Paul blinked. He was still jetlagged from the journey. *That didn't sound like Delacot's voice,* he thought.

"We need to speak with you urgently."

Who is we? thought Paul. What had happened?

The voices outside the door were becoming louder and more agitated.

"Open the door, Mr Plumpton, now!"

Cautiously Paul began to move towards the door. What or who would be on the other side? At the moment the door seemed the only thing dividing them and maybe not opening the door would afford Paul some degree of safety.

"Where's Delacot?"

Paul was beginning to panic.

The voice on the other side of the door replied, "He's no longer with us."

Oh, shit, thought Paul, *they have murdered him and now my life could be in danger.*

They began furiously banging on the door.

"Open this door or we will have to break in. You wouldn't like that, Paul. Could be very messy."

Paul was quaking with fear. The whole thing had turned very nasty. What he had thought would be a straightforward delivery was now turning into a nightmare. He quickly stuffed the teddy bear behind the back of a wardrobe and went to open the door.

"Where is it?" demanded a man with a gun pointing straight at Paul.

"Where is what?"

"The bear, the one Delacot was to take delivery of."

Paul was trying and not succeeding to act calmly.

"Oh, that bear, didn't you know it was picked it up earlier? So, I'm sorry, gentlemen, but you seem to have had a wasted journey."

The man with the gun raised his hand and pointed the gun at Paul's head.

"If you are lying, we will find out."

The men left and Paul heaved a sigh of relief, but would he be the next one to be killed because of that teddy bear?

He must try and arrange a flight immediately back to England. He deliberated for an hour, whether it was worth the risk taking the teddy bear back. Maybe he should have just let those men take it, but would they have spared his life? Possibly not when they had the bear. They didn't look like reasonable men.

Paul pulled the bear from its hiding place at the back of the wardrobe, and as he was pulling it he felt something else. He carried on pulling and discovered it to be a stack of old newspapers. Out of curiosity he began flicking through the copies.

On one the headlines read, "Francis Delacot South African Diplomat narrowly escaped prosecution today, as he pleaded diplomatic immunity." Paul carried on reading; it told how Delacot moved from continent to continent and amassed huge sums of wealth on his travels. No-one quite knew how he did it, but the authorities were seeking to remove his diplomatic immunity, so he could answer questions about his wealth. Paul put the newspaper down and picked up another one. It had a picture of Francis Delacot, with the caption, "Is this the world's biggest teddy bear lover?" He was holding aloft a bear and smiling.

What was it about this man and teddy bears? How many did he have and why did they seem to play a big part in his life?

He put the papers down, and just as he was placing the last one on the coffee table, there came a knock at the door. It was a woman's voice.

"Mr Plumpton are you alright in there? Only we haven't seen you since you checked in and I was just wondering if you needed anything."

Was this another trap to get him to open the door again? He felt the blood freeze in his veins; he wasn't cut out to be a criminal mastermind.

"No, I'm fine thank you, will be out shortly."

"Oh, that's alright then, have a nice day."

A nice day, she must be joking. This had turned

into the worst day of his life, now he needed a plan to get away from there.

*

Paul awakened to a very sore head. He was still in his hotel room. He looked for the bear but it was gone.

Shit, he thought. No Delacot, no bear and now no bloody money. He needed to get out of this place, he frantically searched for his wallet and although there was no money, he discovered his credit card that he always kept in a secret compartment in his wallet. Whoever had stolen the bear and knocked him unconscious wanted that bear. Desperately. *Desperately enough to kill*, thought Paul.

He would go back to Shrewsbury and try to continue his life pretending none of this had happened.

He had frantically made phone calls and manged to get a flight out on the Wednesday. Until then, though, he would have to concentrate on keeping himself safe, as he was sure the visitors from the previous day would come and visit him again.

*

As he scanned his passport at the airport he was waved through and he breathed a sigh of relief. He was going home and nothing bad had happened to him. He thought he would never be so pleased to see his daughter and even his wife again.

He put the chair into the reclining position and

closed his eyes.

"Sir, sir, it's time to put your seat in the upright position as we will shortly be landing at Heathrow, and if you could also fasten your seatbelt. Thank you."

He opened his eyes and blinked a couple of times trying to get his bearings; he felt so sleepy. Ah yes, now he remembered. He was safely on the plane and touchdown at Heathrow was a matter of minutes away. His next thought was how he was going to get back to Shrewsbury. He looked in his wallet, took out his credit card and paid for his ticket.

He collected his luggage and proceeded to customs. A sniffer dog momentarily took an interest in Paul's case, then moved to the next person in the line. He really needed to get out of this airport.

Paul's train was late, and as a result it was the early hours of the morning when he finally put his key into the lock. *Home at last,* he thought.

"Paul, is that you?"

It was Julie, she didn't seem particularly bothered.

"Yes, it's me."

"Oh, glad you're home," she said in a sleepy voice. "Those men have been here again, you know, the debt collectors."

Before Paul could ask her any questions he heard her snoring loudly from her bedroom. He figured she had been drinking again, she always snored when she had been drinking.

*

Billy Haskins was fuming. He had been double-crossed by Paul Plumpton again. He felt sure that it was Plumpton who had stolen the bear. Apparently the threats and the violence had meant nothing to him, so now it was time for Billy to wreak his revenge.

Since he had discovered the theft of the bear, he had vowed to get revenge on Paul Plumpton. He would start by intimidating Plumpton's family, the little girl and that useless wife of his. Then he would move on to Paul. He owed him at least £5,000 and a bear.

As Billy dressed he carefully slipped a loaded revolver into his trousers; he wouldn't use it on Plumpton's family, but he knew it would be a good bargaining chip, if he didn't get his own way.

"Hello again, Billy, out on the rob are we?" Inspector Bora's dog was now sniffing round Billy. "I would know that cheap aftershave anywhere so it has to be you, Billy."

Billy swallowed hard. It was that nosy Inspector again.

"No, just been to a funeral if you must know. That's why I am in black. Not that you can see, Clueless."

"Yes, a likely story," said the Inspector. "Who is it this time, Billy, a long lost cousin, or your grannie perhaps? That poor woman has been buried more times than a vampire."

"Huh, very funny, copper. If you must know it is a friend of mine."

The Inspector mocked, "You've got friends then, have you Billy? Care to give me their names?"

"No, I don't have to."

"That's very true, Billy. But if I find you have withheld information about anything, especially that young woman's murder, then I will arrest you for perverting the course of justice. If I don't arrest you for her murder in the meantime."

Billy strode briskly to his car, trying to keep out of the way of the Inspector. If he had been caught with a gun, then he would be a prime suspect in a murder case, the Inspector would see to that.

He drove around the block a couple of times, circling like a vulture ready to snatch his unsuspecting prey, making sure each time that he was noticed by Paul's family. In the garden, Paul's daughter was playing. His wife came out shortly and shouted her daughter in.

"Darling, I'm going out now, Daddy will look after you. Try not to let her get into mischief and dirty her clothes, or it'll be you that is washing them," and with this throwaway comment she swept past Paul and into her sports car. Before she had backed the car out of the drive though she had noticed a man driving around, perhaps he was lost. Julie took out her mobile and rang Paul.

"There's a man outside, he looks as though he is lost, are you going to ask him if he needs some help?"

Paul went to the window; his face paled as he saw the man in the black shiny Rolls Royce. It was Billy Haskins. Surely, he wouldn't try anything with his daughter being there, but who knew how Billy's mind worked? He had seen first-hand that Billy had a temper and a violent streak. Now Paul feared for his daughter knowing what Billy was capable of.

"Daddy, can we go to the park please?"

"No, darling, today we are going to stay in and play hide and seek, then Mummy won't be cross when she comes in; she'll be happy when she sees how clean you look in your pretty dress."

Emily pulled her tongue out at her father. "But I can change out of my pretty dress and into my trousers and tee-shirt, you know, the one with the pink rabbit on it."

Paul looked down at his daughter. "Okay, change into your trousers and tee-shirt, but we are NOT going to the park. We can play football in the back garden."

"Oooh Mummy won't like that," the little girl said excitedly. "She said it spoils the garden playing on it."

Paul repeated himself.

"We are not going to the park, now, either we play football in the garden or hide and seek in the house. Which is it to be?"

"Football, football, in the garden."

He led her upstairs and helped her to change her clothes. Hanging her dress carefully on a hanger, he undid the buckles on her shoes and found her pumps to play in.

Billy drove up to the house and unbeknown to Paul stopped his car and walked up the driveway. He was able to peer over the back gate and see Paul playing with his daughter.

Hmm, he thought. Such an idyllic scene of family bliss. Armed with the knowledge he could shatter that whenever he felt like. Perhaps today wasn't the day. He didn't really want the little girl to get caught up in the feud with her father. He thought, stoically, he would keep. Then when he did get Plumpton alone he would give him the thrashing he deserved and force him to tell him all about the bear and where it was.

*

"Anything else on that mobile phone? Names, phone numbers, anything." Bora was not happy. It had been days now and they had turned up nothing to do with the woman's murder and now they couldn't even get in touch with Francis Delacot to ask him some questions. It was as if he had disappeared off the face of the earth. They had been ringing the Foreign Office, they had rung the South African Embassy, nothing. Nobody seemed to know where he was, or they were purposely withholding information if it was of a sensitive nature.

John Bora felt weary; this case had really got to him. Every road they turned up seemed to lead to a dead end. He felt sure Billy Haskins had something to do with it, but without proof he couldn't arrest anyone.

Christine Lockhead knocked briskly on the Inspector's door.

"Come in, you don't need to break the door in. "Well, Miss Lockhead." He never called her Miss Lockhead, it was always Christine or Sergeant. "Take a seat, would you like a coffee?"

"No thanks, sir. I have an update on the murdered woman."

She felt him looking at her quizzically.

"I'm off to a police conference, don't you remember? It was you who gave me permission to go."

"Ah yes, I remember now. About the murdered woman, you said you had an update."

"Yes, Inspector Grieves said he would investigate it, but I thought I would keep you updated as well."

"Oh. That's very good of you, Sergeant," he added sarcastically.

His tone had changed. So she had told Grieves about it first.

"Well, Inspector Grieves told me he was at a loose end and wanted to be of more assistance in this enquiry, so I told him about the tattoo."

"Please do go on," the Inspector said acidically.

"Well the tattoo, it wasn't a birthmark after all," she continued, unperturbed by the Inspector's sudden change of tone. "It was one of a teddy bear. It was such an unusual design that I rang around the local tattoo parlours and then arranged to go into them and show them a photo of the tattoo. They all said they had never seen a design like it and it hadn't been done locally."

"So, where does Grieves come into this?"

"He said he had friends in London who could ask around in local tattoo parlours, to see if anyone had inked that tattoo within the last twelve months or so."

"Well, thank you for that." His tone towards her was cool. "Now bugger off, you don't want to be late for your conference."

She had turned to Grieves of all people, before letting him know. Was this investigation slipping away from him?

He poured himself a nightcap and then went to bed. He tossed and turned all night, thoughts of Susan kept awakening him, then dreams of him losing his job and his pension for incompetence.

With Ryan Evans no longer a suspect, his thoughts turned to Paul Plumpton.

He was a cool customer, all sweetness and light, a true family man. *True family man my arse, he was a money-grabbing nobody, but he did have some money. After all, he*

117

couldn't live in the house he lived in without money. That wife of his seemed at least ten years younger than him; she could always be seen out and about in her sports car.

Paul Plumpton knew something, but what was it and how was he going to find out?

"Come in, Christine." He had calmed down since yesterday.

She thought he sounded tired.

"Was it a good conference?"

She shrugged her shoulders.

"Yes, I suppose so as conferences go. I find them rather boring though, to be honest. I would rather be out catching criminals."

He smiled.

"Good answer."

"I think we need to bring Paul Plumpton in again and ask him to bring his passport with him."

"Sir?"

"I think he has been out of the country without anyone knowing. I want to check his passport."

*

"Mr Plumpton, may I call you Paul? I have asked you to bring in your passport in as I wish to check it."

Paul coughed nervously.

"Check it for what? It is definitely my passport, I have had it for seven years."

"I don't doubt that, Paul."

Paul was looking for any distraction he could so

the DS wouldn't look at the pages where he had the American customs stamps on.

"Ah, I see you have been to America."

Paul looked straight at the DS. "Yes, I have been a few times. That's why there is American stamps in it."

"And what about the last time you went there, Paul. What happened?"

"I, er, don't know what you are trying to infer, Sergeant, if you look at the passport the date tells you it was four years ago."

DS Lockhead examined the passport more closely.

"This entry looks as though it has been changed. Do you realise it is a criminal offence to alter a passport? Now Paul, let's start at the beginning, otherwise I am going to charge you with the murder of Shirley Delacot. Did you see the murdered woman before she died?"

"No."

"How well did you know Ryan Evans?"

"He was more of an acquaintance, than a friend."

"Have you remembered the name of the investor that you sold a property to, that gave you a cool £50,000? It seems very strange, that one day the money was in your account and then shortly after it was transferred out again, all except for £5,000. What did you do with the five thousand, Paul?"

"My wife, I gave it to my wife, she has a certain lifestyle that she likes to maintain, and I enjoy funding it," he lied. He hated Julie for the wasteful way she spent his hard-earned money, but he wasn't going to tell the Inspector that.

"Hmm," the Inspector said thoughtfully. "If I'm not very much mistaken this passport says you were in America very recently."

Paul looked at his feet and then mumbled, "No comment."

"Paul, Paul, old son, you need to start talking or I will arrest you for tampering with a legal document."

CHAPTER 6

Francis Delacot slowly began to awaken. He blinked several times and tried to work out where he was. He was about to move his hands to get his phone out, when he realised, he was bound with nylon twine. Where was he? What was this place? He looked around to try and work out what time it was, there was not a single clock in the room, then he remembered his watch would tell him. He glanced at his wrist expecting to see the expensive Rolex, but it was gone. With no indication of where he was and no clue about what time it was, reality began to dawn on Delacot; he must have been kidnapped. But how? How had he been transported to this place without his knowledge?

He looked at his clothes to try and give him some clue as to what he was doing, prior to being kidnapped. He still had on his dinner suit, although it looked grimy now; his bowtie was in a crumpled heap next to him. He suddenly remembered, it was a special Embassy Ball, black tie. The Embassy Balls were always a grand occasion. He had phoned Paul Plumpton that night about the bear and had arranged to meet him later the following afternoon. Whoever had kidnapped him, hadn't thought it was necessary to strip him, so he had been left in his suit.

Had he been drugged? How had he got to this place, had he walked?

His shoes held a clue; the black patent leather was covered in mud. He was in his stockinged feet. So he must have been able to walk at least some of the way. Kidnapping a diplomat would not have been easy. So how had it been achieved?

At that moment a man burst into the room.

"Delacot, where is the bear?"

The man gave him a swift kick to the ribs. It hurt like hell.

"What bear? I don't know what you are on about."

"Well maybe this will help you to remember." The man rained down a blow that caught Delacot squarely on the jaw, knocking out one of his teeth. He began to bleed profusely.

The man was violent and losing patience with Francis Delacot.

"I won't ask you again, where is the bear?" he thundered.

Delacot tried to answer through his bleeding lips. He realised that if he didn't give the man some information he was seeking he could end up dead. "It is with a man called Paul Plumpton, in the Sherise Hotel, room 58."

Someone was lying. Was it Delacot or Plumpton?

Had Delacot already given them this information? Everything seemed to be a complete blur. He remembered the phone call with Paul Plumpton, but then nothing. Had Plumpton run off with the bear? Was he going to be massively out of pocket? He was supposed to be paying Plumpton. Again his memory did not come. He then found himself at the mercy of his captors.

"You're lying, Francis, we went to the hotel and the room number you gave us, and the guy called Plumpton insisted that you had already collected it. We searched the room thoroughly but didn't find anything. So where is it?"

Three more men had now entered the room.

One of the men had a gun. "Now Francis, start talking." He was waving the gun at Francis' face.

Francis' face was stinging from the last blow, but he was determined to find out how these thugs had managed to smuggle him out of the Ball without causing suspicion.

"Tell me, tell me, how did you manage to kidnap me in front of all those people?"

"It was easy. I posed as a policeman and I was in a dinner suit. I slipped something in your drink, that made you slightly dopey. I announced to the others that you were feeling unwell and I felt it was my duty to see you home safely."

He grinned.

"The van was parked a little way up the muddy road and you were still able to walk and the rest you know."

Now it was the turn of the man with the gun to speak.

"So, you see Francis, no-one will be looking for you as they just thought you were unwell."

Francis did feel unwell, very unwell. His ribs hurt and his face was swollen.

"We will be back in two hours; I suggest you have the correct information ready for us or else."

With that, the men left.

They had left Francis tied up; he couldn't reach into his pocket for his mobile, but it was probably dead now anyway. Just as he would be if he didn't come up with a plausible story about the whereabouts of the bear.

For many years Francis Delacot had lived a good life as a South African Diplomat. He owned expensive cars and houses, he owned a few paintings by the Masters and various other things he had acquired on his travels. Sometimes the things he had acquired were not always acquired legitimately, but nevertheless he was quite wealthy.

He reflected on his position. His wealth would not

help him now; it was the bear they wanted, not his offer of money. He still couldn't work out where he was and no idea of an escape plan was in sight.

*

Billy Haskins was going to exact his revenge on Paul Plumpton. He presumed that Plumpton had stolen the bear from him. There was never going to be any TV documentary, he had been scammed again!

Plumpton's wife was attractive, he thought. He would try and have an affair with her under Paul's nose, that would surely piss him off when he found out. This would hurt Plumpton more than anything else he might do.

She was a classy lady though, so he had to smarten himself up if he was going to seduce her. He looked at his clothes – worn, grubby and his filthy nails and unkempt hair completed the picture. He knew her husband always looked neat in his suits, that was probably what she went for. Smart businessmen.

He would visit the barbers in the morning and then buy a whole new wardrobe and scrub his fingernails. The last item was to lease a sports car, that would be sure to impress her. He had been following Julie for the last few days and knew what her routine seemed to be. She would meet friends for lunch, then go out in the evening to one of the swanky wine bars in the town.

*

Bora had left Paula at home. He fancied walking to the pub tonight and he wanted a drink, so he and Louie had set out. The thought of his whisky on the bar made him quicken his step. It was a warm summer's night when he and his trusted animal companion embarked on the pleasant walk to the pub. He had discarded his suit in favour of lightweight shirt and trousers. As he passed someone he heard a voice he thought he recognised. Expensive aftershave, no-one he knew, then he dismissed it.

Billy Haskins was walking towards him, dressed in a navy suit with a crisp, clean white shirt and a silk tie. His hair had been well cut and he was clean shaven.

John heard the voice again and this time he did recognise it.

"Billy, Billy, is that you? Expensive aftershave, bet you look quite dapper as well. New suit, is it?"

"How do you know, Clueless? You can't see what I looks like. As a matter of fact though it is a new suit, I am going to meet a lady, not that it is any business of yours."

"I hope she appreciates the effort you've made."

Billy walked on. His clothes felt uncomfortable; he wasn't used to wearing a suit and shirt and tie, and his shoes were pinching his toes.

He hadn't quite yet managed to snare his victim, but he hoped tonight might be the night that he did. He slipped into the wine bar and found a quiet corner; he only ordered a glass of wine, he didn't want to eat anything for fear of spilling it on his suit.

Julie swept in, she was with two other friends.

God, she is gorgeous, he thought.

Her figure-hugging blue dress accentuated her curves perfectly. He would enjoy this.

Billy got up and walked over to where the three women were seated.

"Ladies, may I join you until my colleague arrives?"

The women stopped their conversation in mid-flow and each one in turn scrutinised him. He felt like a bug under a microscope.

Finally, it was Julie that spoke.

"Yes, please do. I'm sure your colleague will be along shortly." She flashed him a smile with her even pearly white teeth.

"In the meantime, ladies, what are you drinking?"

He had bought the round of drinks and the ladies where chatting merrily.

He looked at his watch; time to put step two into action. He picked his mobile out of his inside suit pocket. He kept it there because someone had once told him that if too many things were in trouser pockets it would cause the pockets to bulge and it would ruin the cut of the trousers. He had spent so much on the expensive suit and the rest of his ensemble, even down to the gold cufflinks on his silk shirt sleeves, that he was going to make sure that didn't happen.

He flicked open the phone and pretended to have a conversation with someone.

"Yes, that's such a shame, but I understand, until tomorrow then. Goodbye."

He clicked off his phone and placed it back inside his pocket.

He returned to the women and looked crestfallen.

"I'm sorry, ladies, I must be going. My colleague can't make it tonight."

He got up to leave.

"You don't have to leave, you can join us for the rest of the night if you would like to."

"That's very gracious of you, ladies, but maybe it is best if I do leave."

Julie had spotted her opportunity when the man came in; he had introduced himself as Tom.

Relations with Paul had almost broken down completely, especially when he was unable to give her the money as and when she demanded it. This man was polite, presentable and by the look of his wallet, loaded. Was this man going to be her next sugar daddy?

Yes, he was about fifteen years older than her, but no matter. She liked him, or was it the thought of his money she liked?

The friends dispersed, but Julie hung back. "I'll catch you up later."

"Er, would you like to have dinner with me?

Unless you have already eaten," said Tom.

Julie thought, *Yes, this is my opportunity. If my husband can have an affair, then so can I.*

"That would be very nice. Thank you."

"My pleasure."

He led her to a red sports car and held the door open while she sidled in.

Billy started to drive, a huge smile on his face. That was step two completed.

After driving for a while they arrived at a small but exclusive country pub. Haskins thought this was better as it was more intimate and he intended to get to know Julie better. He stopped the car and whipped round to the passenger side to hold the door open for Julie. Julie was impressed. What a perfect gentleman, she thought; impeccable manners and a very smart dresser, yes, she was going to enjoy getting to know him.

The waitress took their meal order. Billy was dying to get out of his suit, his new shirt scratched against his skin and he longed to take off his jacket and tie and slip his feet out of the confounded shoes that were hurting him so much, but he knew he couldn't, for fear of tarnishing his image in front of her. Julie looked at the menu and ordered the most expensive meal on it, as if testing her dinner date to see if he would pay.

Billy gave her a smile and said, "Would you like a glass of wine or maybe champagne?"

Julie stared into the man's eyes. "Champagne would be lovely."

"Waiter, a bottle of champagne please." This was going to be a very expensive night for Billy. First his new clothes, then the lease of the car and now this, but he concluded it was worth it.

Julie ate her meal and drank her champagne. Billy picked at his food. After all, he didn't want to show himself up by splashing food on his new suit. He usually devoured his food without any heed as to whether he spilt any or not, but tonight was different; he had to act the perfect gentleman. It was about 2 a.m. when he dropped Julie off and she had left him with the promise of meeting him again the next Tuesday. This way her husband would not suspect anything, as she told him Tuesday was her night out with the girls.

Once in the safety of his own home, throwing caution to the wind where his suit was concerned he quickly kicked off his shoes, pulled off his jacket, loosened his tie and undid his shirt before throwing them all carelessly in an untidy heap on the floor. Ah, that was better. He sat in his pants and lit a cigarette. Step three was complete, he thought.

*

Paul could hardly bring himself to talk to Julie these days, so when she had made an extra effort when she was going out on Tuesday he didn't question her, or even notice. She had agreed to meet "Tom" in a different wine bar to her usual one so as not to arouse suspicion. She had been in touch with her friends and told them that she would not be going out tonight as she was feeling unwell.

*

After throwing his clothes into a heap the previous Tuesday, and not bothering to hang them on hangers he realised they had become quite crumpled and a bit grubby and on closer examination his white shirt had acquired a dirty black mark on it where he had trodden on it on the floor, and one of the shirt sleeves had a tiny rip where he had yanked the cufflinks off in his hurry to be rid of the trappings of respectability. He picked the clothes up, dismayed at the state of them. That would never do, so he had put the clothes into a bag and taken them to the dry cleaners. The cleaners had remarked on what a shame it was for such a lovely new suit, to be in such a state and especially the tiny rip on the silk shirt cuff. They had mended it invisibly and cleaned and pressed his suit and shirt.

Now Billy was going through the same ritual as the week previously, taking care to attach the gold cufflinks properly to his shirt cuffs so as not to rip the shirt any further, then taking a different tie out of his drawer, and fastening it round his neck before straightening it, he proceeded to put on his trousers and jacket before slipping on his shoes that pinched his feet. He stood in his stockinged feet and noticed a hole in his sock and gave a wry smile. That was the Billy he knew, the one with holes in his socks. Besides, no-one would see his holey socks.

Julie was enchanted by this man; he was so generous and witty and funny, she found it easy to like him. They ate, drank and talked, Haskins being careful not to reveal too much about himself.

Julie remarked that she was surprised he had ordered pasta, as it usually splashed everywhere mainly on their clothes and it was an absolute nightmare to try and get the sauce out of the clothes.

Instantly he had regretted ordering it and prayed that his napkin would catch the splashes and not his tie.

*

"I've met someone, not that I suppose you care."

Paul looked up from his paper momentarily and simply replied, "Oh."

"His name is Tom and he is a real gentleman, dresses immaculately and is generous to a fault. I'm thinking of moving in with him. Of course you would have to keep Emily with you, because I don't think there is much room for the three of us."

*

"But darling, we haven't really discussed this." Billy was getting jittery, it was all moving too fast and he didn't really want to be saddled with a money-grabbing gold digger. This, making Paul Plumpton jealous, had seemed to backfire on him. He thought he would have found out by now and have been consumed with jealousy, but that hadn't happened and now this woman was proposing they move in together.

*

Paul had a glimpse of someone picking up his wife in a sports car; for a moment he thought it was Billy Haskins and then convinced himself that it wasn't because this man looked too smart and was driving a sports car. Haskins had deliberately driven up to the house again, on the pretext of wanting to see the beautiful garden. Julie had agreed.

This time Paul got a good look at the man and yes, it was Billy Haskins. He felt the colour drain from his cheeks as the powerful sports car roared away.

Although he hated Julie, he feared Billy Haskins even more and was determined to try and talk her out of her dangerous liaison.

"If you are going to cheat on me, you really should find someone more suitable," he snapped acidically.

"What do you care? He is everything you're not."

"That is just it, don't you see? He is not the person you think he is."

"I don't care what you think, I am moving in with him."

*

"Well what do you think of Billy Haskins, then, Sergeant?"

He motioned to the Sergeant to sit down.

"I saw him a while ago, suited and booted, even his greasy black hair had been washed and cut," she replied.

"I don't like it, Christine, he is up to something. When I asked him about his changed appearance, because I could smell the aftershave, he informed me that he was wearing a new suit he told me to mind my own and he was meeting a lady."

Christine stretched out her long legs; she looked uncomfortable.

"I agree, sir, he could be up to something. The question is what though?"

Inspector Bora grimaced. His back had recently started to hurt him; he shuffled around on his chair.

"How far are we along with this murder enquiry, and has Inspector Grieves come up with anything astounding?"

Christine Lockhead gave a small cough as if clearing her throat.

"Billy Haskins. He is seeing Paul Plumpton's wife."

DI Bora gave a small laugh. "Come on, Christine, is that the best you can come up with?"

"It's true, sir."

"From all accounts she is a stunner. How has that

scruffy toerag managed to bag a classy lady like that? Mind you, she can't be that classy if she is seeing Haskins."

"Well that is the point, sir. He is passing himself off as a rich businessman."

"That would explain the clothes, I suppose."

"He calls himself Tom."

"But why? How is he mixed up with Paul Plumpton?"

"Roy Johnson was having a quiet drink in the pub and Haskins came in. He recognised him from being at the station. He was talking about the Plumpton woman with his cronies and saying it had all got out of hand, and how she was on about moving in with him."

Bora gave a long snort.

"Does she know who he really is and how he lives?"

"Apparently not, she thinks he is her next sugar daddy."

"Does Plumpton know?"

"There are rumours that he does know, but Haskins and Plumpton are sworn enemies of each other."

"That's odd. Wasn't it Haskins that helped him to set up his own business years ago?"

"Yes, that's what it says in the file, but Haskins has always been a loan shark and yet he gave Plumpton money to set up a business. Haskins has many dealings, as we know, but I wonder what Plumpton did to totally piss him off."

Christine stretched out her long legs. "Then of course there was that investment that Plumpton was very vague about. Do you think that had something to do with Haskins?"

"I wonder how long Haskins will keep up the pretence with Mrs Plumpton now he knows that she wants to move in with him."

"I'd say it seems like revenge, taking Plumpton's wife, but he obviously got more than he bargained for and now he wants out."

"Have we got anything on Haskins that we can bring him in for and rattle a few cages?"

"No, sir, he seems completely under the radar at the moment."

Bora stroked his chin. "Hmm, he will make a move over something sooner or later and then we will have him banged to rights."

*

"Sir, we have managed to trace where the knife may have been bought."

Bora said, "About time, make some more investigations, then bring me what you know." He really wanted to know how Grieves had got on. "How are we doing with the tattoos? Has Poirot unearthed anything interesting?"

"If you mean Nathan," she continued, "no, he hasn't had any luck yet, but he still has a few contacts to try."

"Nathan, now is it?" Bora said in a derisory tone.

"Aw, he's not that bad when you get to know him."

"I suppose I'll take your word for it."

*

"It's about time I had the bear. God knows I've waited long enough for it. Spent thousands and crossed continents, but now I have it."

He proceeded to slit the bear up the back, his eager hand ready to catch the emerald, but all that came out was stuffing. Now he was furious. His large six-foot frame shook with anger, his dark eyes held a murderous quality. "Wait till I catch the bastard. I'll kill him!"

He had been tricked but who was it by?

Delacot? The Treveries? They were a nasty lot, violent thugs and thieves.

He could trace Delacot, he thought, but the Treveries, were a different matter. They were elusive, violent and slippery. Just when you thought you had them in your sights, they would disappear as though they had never been there.

*

The pretence with Julie had to stop. It had become way too serious. How was he going to be able to drop her though? She was already making plans for moving in with him. As he donned his suit, he hoped it would be for the last time; he had grown to hate the new clothes and now it was time to put an end to his double life and just go back to being Billy Haskins.

He had picked her up from round the corner from where she lived. Although he knew the house well, they had driven to an intimate country pub and Julie had expected him to present her with the key to his mansion. She felt sure it would be a mansion as he seemed so wealthy. She had made such an effort tonight ready to accept his offer.

He cleared his throat as Julie sipped a glass of champagne.

"Well you see, my dear, I'm so sorry but my business overseas requires quite a lot of my time at the moment," he lied. "I really have no idea when or if I will be back in this country, so I'm afraid this must be the end. I don't expect you to wait for me to come back, not knowing when that may be."

He held his breath and tried to study her face; she looked crushed and confused, then angry.

"Take me home NOW," she demanded. She felt deflated. No man had ever treated her like that.

He dropped her off around the corner from where she lived and was able to breathe a sigh of relief. He was free of her at last, but he was not going to let Plumpton get away with robbing him blind, so he would just have to come up with another plan to make Plumpton pay.

*

"John, I have come up with something regarding

the tattoos."

"Okay then, let's hear it."

"Well I have this mate that lives just outside Canary Wharf and he owns a tattoo parlour. When I showed him the picture of the tattoo, he said he remembered doing one about four months ago."

"And," the DI said impatiently, "so what did he tell you?"

"Nothing really, that was it."

Bora was getting more angry. Not only was this Inspector annoying, he was also a useless idiot.

"Oh, there was one thing he said. He said it had to do with some sort of guild."

Bora was in disbelief at what the Inspector had said.

"Are you for real, Inspector? What, are you telling me that it is some sort of clandestine teddy bear guild?"

"That's about it, John."

John Bora had reached the end of his patience with this incompetent fool.

"Well then, I suppose you better go back to London and try and find out more about this guild."

John thought with Inspector Grieves out of the way, that he might be able to do some real policing and find the killer. At least if he was in London he wouldn't be bothering the local nick for a few days.

"I'll go first thing tomorrow then," Grieves said. He was secretly relieved as it meant he could spend time with his girlfriend, whom he had been missing since coming up to Shrewsbury. He much preferred the Met and the lively atmosphere of London; he wished he didn't have to be up here investigating a murder about a teddy bear. *How ridiculous and a waste of my time,* he thought.

The train pulled into the station and Inspector Grieves alighted it; his girlfriend was waiting on the platform. She threw her arms round him and declared, "Darling, it has been simply ages since I last saw you. How has Shrewsbury been treating you?"

Grieves gave a slight smirk. Was he really going to tell his girlfriend that he was on the trail of a teddy bear?

"Let's go for something to eat, I'm starving," he said, trying to steer away from the topic of the teddy bear tattoo. Cheryl, his girlfriend, would think he was barmy. So he preferred not to tell her that he was here to try and find out who the owner of the teddy bear tattoo was and what the "Guild" was.

He went to his friend's tattoo parlour. Aspey was just completing a very intricate-looking tattoo on a very macho-looking male. "Be with you in a few minutes, Nat, make yourself a cuppa."

Mug in hand, Nathan sat down and was surveying his surroundings. Everywhere he looked there were pictures of tattoos and people proudly displaying their latest one. Aspey was always busy and he made a good living out of creating tattoos. Grieves had often thought of having one, but he was too much of a coward and a skinflint to pay for one.

Aspey came into the room and lit a cigarette. "Whew, that was a long session," he said as he took a long puff. "That's the second part of the tattoo done, when it is finished the daft sod will have paid me over £1,000."

"Nice work if you can get it," said Grieves.

It was the second time he had visited Aspey that week; the first time he had asked about any unusual tattoos, especially of teddy bears.

Aspey had told him about a teddy bear tattoo that he had done for a young girl about four years ago, and then he told him about an unusual one that was the initials of some kind of guild. When Aspey had asked the man said, "Oh, it's just one of those, you know, to do with toymakers."

Grieves put down the cup he was drinking out of. He cleared his throat and then began, "Tell me more about this Guild and the teddy bear tattoo again."

Aspey gave a tired yawn.

"Not that again, I told you the last time you were here that it was some sort of Guild. Something to do with toymakers, or toysellers or something, I'm not sure which."

Grieves had seemed to come to a dead end and he wasn't sure where to go from here.

CHAPTER 7

Francis Delacot was in considerable pain. He'd received a terrible beating at the hand of his captors. He truly didn't know where the bear in question was, but somehow, they didn't believe him.

Bloodied, bruised and battered, they had bundled him into a van and left him for dead on the roadside. Finally a passing motorist spotted him and offered him a lift.

"Jeez, mate, looks like you've had a good hiding. I think I should drive you to the hospital and then you can get seen to."

After all, this man didn't want a stranger dying in his truck. He hated the police and never liked to give them any opportunity to look closely at what he did.

"Here you go, mate, I ain't coming in with you. Good luck."

With that, the driver turned his truck around and exited the scene.

In the hospital Delacot felt safe; hopefully his ordeal was over, his captors realising he hadn't got the booty they were so looking for.

Now in a comfortable bed and with a hospital gown on to protect his modesty, Delacot needed to make some phone calls.

"Yes, I'm in Queensbury Hospital, four broken ribs, a fractured skull and a broken arm."

A car with blacked out windows came to pick up Francis Delacot, after a week.

Delacot struggled to the car and lay back in the seat relieved to be alive. He needed to call in some favours, he thought. He needed to know more about his captors and more to the point how much they knew about him.

He picked up a paper; the headline read, "South African Diplomat beaten and left for dead."

Francis groaned. He didn't need this kind of publicity as it could affect his future deals.

He returned to work a few days later. It was clear to him now that his captors had been an organised crime group, who knew exactly what Francis had been up to and had been determined to get their hands on the bear at all costs. However, this had not happened. Greed was always a strong motive for killing someone, he thought.

He needed to ring Scotland Yard to find out if they were any further along with finding the killer of his daughter. He needed to know this as a matter of urgency, as the killer could come for him at any moment.

"Ah, Mr Delacot, our enquiries are ongoing. We have one of our Special Officers dealing with the matter and the police force in York are assisting."

"Assisting, ASSISTING. Good God, man, what kind of tin pot service are you running down there?"

"Mr Delacot, please be assured we are doing everything we can to catch your daughter's killer. We just need a little more time."

Commander Ericson loathed this arrogant man, and it took him all his patience to try and keep calm and defuse the situation.

Francis Delacot was becoming more and more desperate; the bear was missing and his daughter was dead. Life could become a lot more uncomfortable for him. His unscrupulous dealings and questions about how he had acquired his wealth could all be about to revealed. This, he knew would cause a political outcry and brand him a thief and a cheat. It could even threaten diplomacy with other countries as more and more questions would be asked. Francis knew that it was now a political time-bomb – he had to find the bear at all costs.

*

He was now growing tired of Julie Plumpton; she had been more trouble than she was worth. He had already spent a mint on her and now this, she wanted to move in with him. He was annoyed with himself that his plan to wreak revenge on Paul Plumpton was spectacularly backfiring on him. He had only meant to make Plumpton suffer and become jealous, not take his wife off his hands permanently. He looked at his bank account which was quickly diminishing. First the hundred thousand that he had been scammed out of and then the drain on his finances by this woman, who demanded the dearest things whether it was jewellery, or clothes. She wanted to be taken to fine dining establishments where she would order the dearest item on the menu and the champagne and expect "Tom" to pay for it. Billy pondered on his double life; it was affecting his real businesses, the ones that were extortion and intimidation. This was how he made his money, not mincing around the countryside dressed to the nines with an although beautiful, very demanding woman. No, as far as he was concerned Paul Plumpton could have her back. Billy hated defeat, so he would have to think up another way of punishing Plumpton, but the mystery remained. Who had the bear? If it was Plumpton did he know what it was? Billy wanted that bear. Delacot's daughter had been killed, yes, he knew all about that but where was the bear? He would have to devise a cunning plan to sound Plumpton out and find out whether he still had the bear. He knew about Plumpton's meeting in America with Delacot. He also knew that Delacot hadn't got the bear. The obvious person then must be Paul Plumpton.

Billy needed to come up with a plan. He assembled his cronies in the Goose C.

"What have we got on Paul Plumpton, apart from the obvious?"

"We could rough him up a bit and then threaten him with shooters," a greasy-looking man sat to the right of Haskins said.

"No, we have already done that, it didn't work very well, it just made him fly off to the States."

"We have to be cleverer than that."

A lanky individual who sat facing Haskins suddenly said, "Kidnap, bundle him into a van, take him somewhere out of the way and then torture him until he talks."

Haskins was liking this plan; he had a lock-up down on Meadow Lane, and it was down a dirt track which was usually deserted. It had to be thought out properly, though, a daring kidnapping like that would take some planning.

Two days later the plan was put into action.

Lanky Lennie would drive the van, and Midge would kidnap Plumpton. They would lure him to a property that he had for sale and arrange to meet him, then they would bundle him into the waiting van.

At the arranged time Paul Plumpton put the key in the lock and he was immediately pushed to the ground. Before he got his breath back he could feel something sharp being pushed into his back.

"Get up, get up." Lennie quickly tied his hands behind his back. They brought the van round to the back of the property and bundled Paul inside. The van roared off in the direction of Meadow Lane.

Paul was terrified; he had never seen these men before and now he was holed up in a van with his hands tied and no visible means of escape.

The van finally pulled up outside an empty lock-up.

"Get out, and no funny business or I will shoot you."

Paul had no option, but to obey. They bundled him roughly into the dark, smelling lock-up. Lennie found a light and clicked it on. In the middle of the room was a chair. Paul was pushed into this and now Midge was tying him to the chair as well as tying his feet.

"What is all this about?" Paul was trembling.

"You know, Plumpton." It was Midge who was speaking. "Where is the bear?"

Plumpton replied, "What bear? Don't know what you are on about."

"Aha, want to play games, do you?"

Lennie fired a warning shot over Plumpton's head.

"The bear, Plumpton, where is the bear?"

"You'd better tell us, otherwise something might just happen to that happy little family of yours."

Paul was panicking. He needed to convince these thugs that he didn't have the bear. This bear was turning out to be a lot more trouble than it was worth. He wished he had never got involved with the bear.

"I, I err, haven't got the bear, I don't know where the bear is."

Another warning shot was fired; this time it whistled past Paul's head.

"Please believe me." He was becoming more and more desperate.

"Why should we believe you?" rasped Lennie. "We know you took the bear to America, you were supposed to deliver it to Francis Delacot. We know he hasn't got it so where is it?"

Paul could not answer. All he could remember was that he had been knocked unconscious but he didn't know who by.

Lennie fired another shot; this time it grazed Paul's shoulder. Paul shouted out as a searing pain gripped him.

"I don't know where it is, I don't know where it is!"

He was beginning to lose consciousness. Lennie turned to Midge.

"Suppose we better get him out of here. Before we kill him. We was only supposed to frighten him. Not kill him."

Midge's face was grave. He clicked his tongue and said, "Yep, you're right, don't want a smelly old carcass on our 'ands."

Paul was bundled back into the van and then pushed out at the main road. Shoulder bleeding profusely through his jacket, he stumbled against a wall and phoned for an ambulance.

"Well sir, we need to stem the blood and then take you to the hospital for a check-up. I think it is only a superficial wound, but better be safe than sorry."

Paul was feeling exhausted. He explained the injury as having fallen onto a sharp object. He was fooling no-one, but it wasn't the paramedic's place to question him. Arm in a sling, Paul went home.

When he arrived Julie looked worried. "Where the hell have you been and what have you done to your arm?"

"I had an accident."

"So I see."

*

Billy Haskins was beside himself with rage.

"You blundering buffoons. I knew I should 'ave done the job meself."

"Sorry, boss, but we don't think 'e 'as the bear."

*

Paul Plumpton was trying to keep a low profile.

"I don't trust that Paul Plumpton, Christine, I think he knows more than he is telling us."

"I agree, sir, do you want me to bring him back in?"

"Bring him back on the pretence of wanting to

check something on his passport."

DS Lockhead was seated at the table. "That looks painful, Mr Plumpton. What have you done?"

"I er, fell."

"Oh really? Now would you care to tell us what really happened?"

"Am I being charged with something?"

At this point DI Bora interjected, "I don't know, Paul, have you done anything that we need to charge you for?"

Paul squirmed uneasily in his chair.

"No comment."

"Come, come, Paul, we haven't charged you with anything yet, so why are you saying no comment?"

Paul was scared. He had worked it out that Billy Haskins was behind the kidnap plot; he was scared how much further Haskins would go in order to get information about the bear.

"Sergeant, check Mr Plumpton's passport again. Is there anything remotely odd about it?"

Christine scrutinised the passport again, it seemed in order.

"I think it is alright, sir."

"Very well, Paul, you are free to go for the time being."

As Paul exited the station, he looked around him cautiously in case anyone was lying in wait for him.

The murder trial had gone cold. No-one could

contact Francis Delacot and even the South African Embassy in London didn't know how to locate him. Delacot, meanwhile, was recovering from his ordeal in his secret hideaway. The one that no-one apart from him knew about. Here it was easy to convalesce as no-one bothered him. It was a house in a sheltered little bay. The locals in the village went about their own business, not giving any heed to the diplomat. In fact it was doubtful if anyone recognised him, and that is how Delacot liked it. He was growing stronger by the day and soon he felt ready to resume work. After all, work meant more wealth.

"Hello, Delacot. We thought you had disappeared off the face of the earth. Have you heard anything more about your daughter?"

"No, nothing. Seems like those lazy buggers in England aren't doing anything to try and find my daughter's killer."

*

Louie was sniffing around the man in Reception.

"What do you want, Jonesy?"

"I got information, but I ain't telling unless you make it worth my while," he sniffed.

Bora was in no mood for playing games. "Tell me what you know or I'll have you arrested for wasting police time."

"Okay, okay, Inspector, keep your fur on."

Louie started growling at the man, this was never a

good sign.

"Keep that dog away from me or I'll do for it."

"May I remind you that this dog is police property."

Jonesy seemed to admit defeat. It looked as though he wouldn't get any cash out of the Inspector today.

CHAPTER 8

"You're late. I expected you to be on time for our meeting that was scheduled for 9 a.m., wasn't it?"

Bora knew what time it was because the clock in his office relayed the time when asked. Bora marvelled at the technology.

Christine Lockhead needed to get her breath back before she addressed the Inspector.

"Yes, sir. Sorry, sir."

"Well I hope you have some news for me."

DS Lockhead took another deep breath and made herself and the Inspector a coffee. She felt she need to compose herself.

Sat on a chair opposite the Inspector, she took a sip of her coffee and began.

"Nate has tracked down a tattooist in London who remembers doing a teddy bear tattoo on a young girl several years ago."

"Who the bloody hell is Nate?"

"Inspector Grieves, sir."

Bora suspected that Christine was up to her old

tricks again, dating an officer above her rank. Although he didn't want to come out and actually say that.

"Well, Miss Lockhead, what else have you and Inspector Grieves learnt? And in my team I expect you to call him Inspector Grieves, not Nate."

Christine felt ticked off as she had been seeing him for a couple of weeks. He had ended it with his girlfriend in London, citing that a long-distance relationship wasn't working out. However, no sooner had he finished with his girlfriend, he had jumped into bed with DS Lockhead. They had both tried to keep the secret, but Christine had been particularly tired that morning and had let it slip by referring to her senior officer in a very familiar way. Bora was no fool, she thought; now he would have worked out what was going on with his DS. She was aware of her reputation but since coming to Shrewsbury she had made a concerted effort not to get involved with a senior officer, although there were a few who she knew would like to go out with her.

"Now," began Bora, "is there anything else you or Grieves have found out about the tattooist or the person he tattooed or when?"

"Nate," she began and corrected herself, "I mean Inspector Grieves, was given a book by the tattooist with the exact picture in of the tattoo. There was no address of the girl, but there was a photo of her holding up her arm displaying the tattoo. Aspey the tattooist said he was quite proud of the tattoo and that is why he took a photo of the girl."

"Have you been able to match the photo with the one of our victim?"

"Yes, but that is the mystery."

"What do you mean?"

"Well after seeing the photo of the girl in the tattoo parlour, Inspector Grieves began asking around the locals if anyone remembered her. It transpired that the girl was twenty and she was called Shirley Denacot."

Bora rubbed his chin. "Are we sure it is the same person?"

"Yes, but we don't know why she was calling herself Denacot."

"Thank you, Christine, can you ask Inspector Grieves to step in?"

Relieved that DI Bora hadn't railed her for seeing Inspector Grieves, she left the office with a sigh of relief and directed one of the Constables to find Grieves and tell him that the DI wished to see him.

Bora just did not like the man, but he still needed to work with him.

"Come in, sit down, Grieves, help yourself to a coffee."

"No thanks, John, I've just had one. I'll make you one though if you like."

John nodded his approval. Louie had raised his

head when Grieves had walked in, but had now settled down again by the DI's desk.

"Tattooist and dead girl. What, if anything, have they got in common?"

"Well at this point, John, I'm not sure."

"What do you mean you're not sure? Haven't you been in London for the last few days?"

John was beginning to lose patience with what he saw as an incompetent officer.

"Yes, but Aspey is really hard to pin down, he doesn't like the police much."

"That's irrelevant. Was he able to tell you more about the tattoo or the girl?"

"He told me about something called the 'Guild', though he didn't really know what it was except that it had initials and was to do with toys or toymakers."

"Right, you need to get on the internet and research teddy bear tattoos and toymakers' guilds."

John had completely forgotten about the photocopy of the teddy bear known as the Emerald Bear. He had dismissed it shortly after when he mentioned it to the rest of the team.

John jerked the harness and Louie was up on his feet, ready to lead his master out of the office. Steve was waiting ready to drive the DI home.

"God, I feel knackered, Steve. This murder investigation is going so slowly. Have you heard anything useful?"

"No sir," the young officer replied.

John wanted a quiet night in, but when he got home, Paula said, "Come on, John, or we'll be late for the concert."

"What concert?"

"You know, the one we booked last month, I especially phoned to see if they would allow Louie in and they had agreed to it. So come on, get ready."

John let out a large groan. So much for his quiet night in.

*

John was tired when arrived at work the next day. The concert had gone on until quite late and he hadn't had much sleep, thinking about the case and how the pieces fitted together. At the moment there was nothing concrete that linked anything to anyone, except Paul Plumpton.

"Christine, I want you to bring Paul Plumpton in for a friendly chat. Make sure he knows he is not being charged with anything and he doesn't need a solicitor."

Paul Plumpton sat in front of the Inspector; he looked dishevelled and his suit was creased as though he had been wearing it for several days, a very notable difference from the last time they had seen him, thought DS Lockhead, although his injuries had healed.

"What do you know about a teddy bear tattoo?"

Plumpton shot a quizzical glance at the DS.

"I don't know anything about a teddy bear tattoo, why should I?"

"Well we know you went to America with a rather special parcel, it was a teddy bear, wasn't it, as I recall?"

"Yes but," he blustered, "I was supposed to deliver it to a Francis Delacot."

"So Delacot has the bear then?"

"No, I was supposed to deliver it to him, but before I could someone else came into my room and knocked me unconscious. I tried to put up a fight but the man was a lot stronger than me and when I woke up the bear had gone."

"A likely story, Mr Plumpton. What was so important about that bear and how much money were you going to get paid for delivering it? What were you planning to do with the money, Paul?"

The DI was firing questions at Plumpton and he became uncomfortable.

He wriggled and squirmed in his chair, his body odour lingering on the air. He ran his hand through his greasy hair and shouted, "Stop."

"Stop what, Paul, asking you questions about a teddy bear? You know Shirley Delacot has been murdered, did you also know that Francis Delacot was her father?"

Paul had become red in the face. Suddenly he felt faint as though he was going to pass out.

"Get Paul a glass of water, will you Sergeant?"

The Sergeant returned with a glass of water.

"Well, I am so glad we had this little chat, Paul. Don't do anything silly and don't try to leave the country or we will have to confiscate your passport.!

*

Paul Plumpton felt wretched. Things were not going well for him. His wife had left him and taken his beloved daughter to her mother's. The bills were piling up and he had no way of paying them. Since his trip to America suddenly all his businesses had dried up. People cancelling appointments to view his houses. People not renewing their rent contracts. It was as though he was a pariah and no-one wanted to do business with him.

Billy Haskins rubbed his hands in glee. Trying to have an affair with his wife hadn't particularly hurt Plumpton, but ruining his business, well, that was different. He was finally paying for crossing Billy. He grinned a toothy grin to himself and said, "Let the fun begin."

Paul Plumpton was driving home still quite shaken after his chat at the police station, when a car with blacked-out windows pulled across the road effectively blocking his way. He slammed on the brakes and the car was millimetres in front of him.

The headlights of the other car flashed brightly and Paul recognised the figure of Billy Haskins. Quick as a flash Haskins was out of his car and pointing a knife at Paul.

"Now then, Plumpton, got rid of that greedy cow 'ave you?"

"Yes, you know she has gone."

"Yeah, that's right. I know. Me and you need a little chat though, don't we?"

Paul could feel his chest tightening as he looked at Billy who was brandishing a knife perilously close to him. He looked around for other motorists, but it was a lonely stretch of road and there were no cars passing. Haskins had chosen his spot well, knowing it would probably be deserted.

"You have something I want."

Paul felt his chest tighten even more.

"What is it, what do you want?"

"Come on, Paulie." Now Haskins was taunting him. "I want the bear, it is rightfully mine, now hand it over."

"I, I haven't got it."

"Wrong answer, Plumpton." He began waving the knife around near Paul's face. "I could slit you from ear to ear, you know that."

"Yes," squeaked Paul and with that he collapsed onto the floor writhing in agony.

"Oh shit." Haskins didn't want the lying, cheating, lily-livered man to die, noting that if he did, he would never get his hands on the emerald. It seemed like he was having a heart attack; he was clutching at his chest.

Billy got into his car and before he drove away he phoned 999 and asked for an ambulance, giving the directions to where Paul was lying, but not leaving his name.

"Phew. That was a close one." How was he supposed to know Plumpton was going to have a heart attack? That still didn't solve the mystery of where the bear was. The bear that he felt was rightfully his. After all, he deserved it for all the services rendered he had given to Francis Delacot over the years.

*

DI Bora was working late; he had sent Steve home, saying he would get his wife to pick him up later. Steve was relieved not to be working overtime as he wanted to get home to see his wife and play with his baby son, before the child went to bed. It was not very often that Steve went home early, as being Bora's driver he would wait for him. For this role of driver he got paid more money and the extra money came in handy for his family.

"Sir." It was Christine Lockhead.

"Christine, I thought you were on a day off, so why are you ringing me?"

"Well sir, I was visiting my friend in hospital, when suddenly there was a commotion outside. Two paramedics were rushing through a patient to Resus;

when I explained who I was they told me they had been called to a remote spot on the Peveril Road and they had found a man writhing on the floor in agony. They suspected a heart attack and brought him here as this was the nearest hospital."

"I see." The Inspector clicked his tongue. "And do we have a name for this man?"

"It's Paul Plumpton, sir."

Christine detected the note of irritation in his voice. "Thank you, Christine, now go home and get some rest. We can discuss this more in the morning. Goodnight."

Paula was waiting for John as Louie guided him out of the building.

"Long day, was it?"

"Yes and it's not over yet."

Paula looked at her husband; he looked completely drained. "John, you must slow down a little, your stress levels are through the roof and if you are not careful you are going to end up having a heart attack or worse."

John thought to himself, how ironic, the person that was causing all the stress was lay in a hospital bed suffering from a heart attack!

*

"What was Plumpton doing on the Peveril Road anyway?"

"Apparently he thought he saw someone following

him and he had turned up Peveril Road to try and give them the slip."

"Do we have any idea who was following him, or why they were following him?"

"No sir, I have sent a DC to the hospital to try and find out more, but he has just called me and said Plumpton is not being very co-operative and claiming he doesn't know who was following him."

"Do we know who called the ambulance?"

"No sir, it was from a payphone."

"I didn't know there was a payphone on that road."

"Neither did I."

"Well, someone must have known."

"Has anybody checked the road for clues as to who it might have been?"

"Yes sir, uniform are checking it now."

"I want to know as soon as they find something, anything."

"Yes sir."

DI Bora's day passed uneventfully; there was nothing to report from any of the uniformed team.

John needed to clear his head and try to think about the scenario that was presenting itself.

"Come on, Louie, walkies."

The dog instantly arose, glad to be going for a walk.

Where was the wretched bear, and why was it so important to people? Was it really true that it contained one of the most expensive emeralds in the world?

Plumpton either didn't have it or he was a bloody good liar, John thought. He didn't seem cunning enough, though, to be such a good liar. He wasn't assaulted on the Peveril Road, there were no marks on his body consistent with an assault, so who was it that had terrorised him enough to bring on a heart attack?

Paul Plumpton had decided to check himself out of hospital against the doctors' advice, but he felt safer being out of hospital than in. Haskins was devious and bold enough to try something while he was in hospital. So on the Thursday Plumpton had signed himself out. Thing was now, where was he going to go? Was he going to go home, or back to his mother's? If he admitted it to himself he was scared no matter where he was, as it would only be a matter of time before Haskins and his mob caught up with him.

John's mind was in a whirl; on the one hand there was Paul Plumpton and on the other hand there was Francis Delacot, Francis Delacot's name kept cropping up, but how was that even possible as he was the dead girl's father? Perhaps the teddy bear had been given to his daughter as a parting gift or a more sinister motive. Perhaps she was to deliver it somewhere and the killer found her and the bear before she could, knowing that she was leaving for England.

Plumpton, though, had said that he was supposed to meet Delacot and deliver the bear to him, so what had happened that Delacot hadn't received the bear?

They had attained from Plumpton that he had had a call out of the blue from Francis Delacot. Delacot had bought his airline ticket and offered him a considerable amount of money to deliver the bear. Now though, Plumpton was in hospital and he definitely didn't have any money to speak of. John had even heard that all Plumpton's business interests were floundering, and he was desperate for money as his wife had left him with all the debts.

He needed to see Plumpton, but he knew it wouldn't be that easy, as whoever had terrorised him may come back and finish the job. Maybe Plumpton would tell him what was going on, but he didn't think for one minute, that he would.

"So, people, who is in the frame for the murder of Shirley Delacot? Anyone any ideas?"

"I think it could be that Paul Plumpton, sir. I think he is lying. He has the motive and he saw the dead woman a few hours before she went to the farmhouse. The farmhouse was one of Plumpton's properties, although no-one had lived there for many years. He saw a quick sale and that is why Ms Delacot was viewing it that day. I bet he rung up pound signs, knowing that the old dilapidated place was coming back into use and that Ms Delacot was prepared to spend money on it to get it into order."

"Hmm," said Bora, "but now this is all speculation,

we need hard evidence before we can accuse someone."

"Sir," it was Johnson who was speaking, "what do we know about Francis Delacot except that he is a South African Diplomat."

DI Grieves pinned a picture of Delacot on a board next to Paul Plumpton. "We know that these two men made contact with each other, but where does the bear come into it?"

"Plumpton had the bear, Delacot wanted it, was it the Emerald Bear or was it just a memento of his daughter? Whichever way, he seemed pretty desperate for it and was prepared to pay a huge sum of money so he must have known something about it."

"Seems dodgy to me, sir." It was Johnson again.

"I quite agree."

John was no nearer to finding the perpetrator. Had he taken on too much?

Should he be handing the case over to DI Grieves?

In the past he had always had a clear plan of action, but now with his disability he was not sure whether he could deliver the outcome. DS Lockhead had missed a chance to question Haskins about the tattoo when they had him there, now it was all a mess.

CHAPTER 9

"Francis Delacot, widowed with one daughter, Shirley, a member of the South African Diplomatic Core. Decorated twice by the South African president for services to the country. Personal wealth undisclosed."

"Hmmm. I bet it is undisclosed, probably got an offshore account somewhere."

"Nothing to indicate how he gained all his personal wealth."

"I want every possible detail checked out about him, from the car he drives, to where he goes, right down to his pants."

Christine pulled a face; it was not the image she wanted in her mind.

Christine continued to look at the file while reading it aloud to Bora. "Says here that he was suspected of fraud, but it never went to trial because the South African government feared it would cause too much of a backlash him being a diplomat."

"Right, Sergeant, I want you to go and find out all you can about our friend Mr Delacot."

Christine alighted gracefully from her chair, smoothing her skirt as she went. She would proceed to the ladies' toilets, where she would be able to apply fresh lipstick should it be needed and also add a squirt of her favourite mega-expensive perfume. Just on the off chance that she would bump into Nathan Grieves in the corridor. They practically collided in the corridor, both trying to be professional so as not to arouse suspicion that they were an item. Nate, she observed, looked rather tired and the frayed cuffs on his shirt subtracted somewhat from his appearance. It was a good job Bora was blind as she knew from bitter experience from other police stations, as a detective you always needed to look smart and tidy and at the moment Grieves was looking neither.

"The DI wants a meeting in fifteen minutes with you."

Oh bugger, thought Grieves. He wasn't feeling at his best this morning, after having a late night last night, where he and Christine Lockhead had danced the night away.

"Well, have you found out any more about teddy bear tattoos and secret guilds?" Bora said with a distinctive attitude to his tone.

"Well actually, John, I have found some things out." He paused to make his words more dramatic.

"Well come on then, spit it out. What have you found out?"

"I've found out there is no such thing as a toymakers' guild."

"Well I never," said Bora sarcastically.

Unperturbed by Bora's comments, Grieves proceeded to tell the Inspector about the letters.

"You see, John, it is a secret code for something, but I don't know what."

Yet again, Grieves had come up really with precisely nothing.

"Have you spoken to Forensics or any of your colleagues about what the letters might stand for?"

"No, not yet."

"Well don't waste time, man, go and check out those initials and if you don't know, ask one of the older men if they have ever heard of a secret organisation with those initials."

DS Lockhead was looking at some old paper clippings. She stumbled on a picture with Francis Delacot on it. He seemed to be with other people, holding a banner up, saying, "Save our bears."

There was something strange about Francis Delacot.

DC Lockhead wanted to probe further into the life of Francis Delacot, so she could try to understand more about the murdered woman.

"Sir, I have been looking at all these clippings regarding Francis Delacot. I'm sure I can see Billy Haskins in the background."

"No, Christine, you must be mistaken, why would Delacot be involved with a lowlife like Haskins?"

Christine took a magnifying glass from a shelf and began to study the picture in more detail. There was a group of people all in evening dress, but in the background was a man in dark jacket and trousers. She scrutinised the picture even more, yes, she was sure it was Billy Haskins.

"Sir, I am sure it is Billy Haskins in the background."

"Well what the hell is Haskins doing there? Where was the picture taken?"

Christine looked at the picture and read the information underneath the picture.

"It says, 'South African Convention Centre Opening 2015'."

"So five years ago then."

"I think we need to have another chat with our friend Billy."

"Twice Paul Plumpton has ended up in hospital in unexplained circumstances. Do you think Haskins is terrorising him?"

"Hmm, could be."

"We need to arrange a search warrant, then Haskins will have to comply with our wishes."

*

"Listen up, folks, we are going to search Billy Haskins' house, this afternoon. You all know your roles. Don't take any unnecessary risks with anything, is that clear? I will be with you and I will be guided by Louie. If you see anything suspicious use gloves and pop it into an evidence bag. Is that clear? Any questions?"

"Sir, are we hoping to find something or are we just having a general search?"

"Constable, use your brain, course we will be looking for something specific, it could be guns, or knives or even crowbars," was Inspector Grieves' sharp retort.

Oh, Grieves has finally woken up, thought Bora. *Now let's see what he can do.* Bora was not going to hold his breath though as Inspector Grieves hadn't been much use and his contribution to the investigation had been practically nil. *If that was how he worked at the Met, I bet they couldn't wait to second him to us.*

The Inspector knocked on Billy Haskins' door. Billy's face was puce with rage when he saw the policemen.

"What do you want, Clueless? You ain't coming in 'ere with that animal."

"Oh Billy, we can come in, we have a search warrant. DS Lockhead, showed the warrant to Haskins."

The officers searched the house but found nothing.

"Well Billy, I think you've got off lightly this time, but I am still watching you."

"Get lost, Clueless, you ain't got nuffink on me."

Inspector Bora was very irritated; they had found nothing at Haskin's house even though he thought Haskins was instrumental in bullying and intimidating Paul Plumpton. Twice in hospital in a short time seemed very unusual, especially when he never offered any real reasons as to what had happened. Bora had hoped to find a gun, or a knife, something that would tie Haskins to Plumpton and he was bitterly disappointed they hadn't found anything.

"I'm not satisfied. I want Billy Haskins brought in again. Even if he won't admit to intimidating Plumpton, I want to know why he was on that picture with Francis Delacot."

*

The phone rang. "Haskins, it's Delacot, I need a favour."

"'How much?"

"Does forty thousand pounds sound good?"

"What do yer want?"

"I don't have the bear, you don't have the bear, so I want you to find out who does have it and where it is being kept."

Haskins groaned. He had attempted twice to try and get some information out of Plumpton, but he had been unsuccessful. Twice he had threatened to kill him, but Plumpton had not been forthcoming. Did he really know nothing about the whereabouts of the bear or was he just playing dumb? Haskins was not going to be made a fool of again.

"Okay, I suppose I will see what I can do."

"Not good enough, Haskins. I want reassurance that you WILL find the bear and return it to me."

The phone line went dead.

Billy needed to assemble his cronies to try and work out a plan.

"Meet me in the Goose C at 7:30 and don't be late."

Haskins proceeded to tell the group about the visit from the police and the search of his house. "Clueless didn't find anything, though. Lennie, do you still 'ave the gun?"

Lennie looked up from his pint and said in a small voice, "Yes, still got it."

"Well make sure it's well 'idden."

"I will, boss."

"Midge, 'ave you still got the knife I gave you?"

"Yes, boss."

"Well make sure no-one can trace it back to me or there will be trouble, lots of trouble."

"Okay, boss, I get the picture."

All the men assembled around the table with Billy knew just how ruthless he could be and they were all scared of the consequences, as each one owed Billy some kind of debt.

Lennie had a drug habit that Haskins fed, but only

on his terms. Midge had a massive debt problem and Billy had let him off many times, allowing him to still live in his mother's house. Gorsy had a gambling problem and had lost thousands at the roulette table, to an unscrupulous money-laundering ring. Billy had managed to smooth the debt by threatening to expose the ring, a move that did not sit well with the gamblers.

"The point is, we 'ave to find that blasted bear. It's too risky pulling Plumpton again, the police, especially Clueless, would be all over us like a rash."

*

Delacot sat in his apartment. He was getting desperate and had called in all the favours that he could. Prominent South Africans were on his list to talk to. He looked at the Rembrandt on his wall – that had been one of his most recent acquisitions; he had bid for it behind closed doors and was lucky enough to win the bid, but it had left him with severely depleted assets. He needed money and fast, not least to maintain his opulent lifestyle to the detriment of others less fortunate. He had bank accounts in various countries, including a Swiss bank account where no-one knew his name. His account was just a number; this was where most of his money passed through. He thought about his daughter. The English police didn't seem to be getting very far with their investigations. It was a sad fact, though, that his daughter had been used as a smokescreen to hide what Delacot had been up to. He congratulated himself on being the doting father to the outside world, but in reality this was not the case. They had argued bitterly before Shirley came to England, the second time. The first time being when she was only twenty and had grown tired of her father's manipulative ways. She had settled in a suburb of London, hoping that he wouldn't find her; it was then that she changed her name to Denacot. That was when she had got the teddy bear tattoo. At that time she just thought it was cute, not realising that it was something that her father had influenced her to get in previous years. She had worked in an office for three years quite anonymously. She had just come home from work one evening and fed her cat, Mr Suki, when a knock came at her door. It was a special agent belonging to her father.

"You need to come back with us, your father will be so pleased."

With that, she had been bundled into a car with her passport and before she could raise the alarm she had been packed off back to South Africa and her father.

"So glad to see you, my dear, safe and sound."

"What do you want?"

"Well, I have this problem. Some undesirables are after me and I need you to go back to England and take a teddy bear with you. I have it all arranged, and you shouldn't be in any danger as long as you keep hold of the teddy bear."

"No, I won't do it."

"Oh but you will, my dear, you will be perfectly safe as long as no-one knows your true identity and when everything has calmed down you can come back, I will have the bear and the vast fortune and kudos that goes with owning the bear. We will be able to live in opulence for the rest of our lives. You see, the bear will be my insurance policy, no, I mean our insurance policy," he corrected himself.

Once again, he had won his daughter round and so she had set out for England. He had flown over for the funeral and then made hurried excuses stating that he had to go straight back to South Africa because of pressing engagements that he could not cancel. He had told the British Embassy, though, to keep him updated about the progress of his daughter's murder.

Delacot was beside himself with worry. There were so many questions but no answers.

Who knew about his daughter's identity?

Who was desperate enough to kill his daughter?

Who knew about the bear?

Where was the bear now?

Now Haskins was involved again, maybe he could find the answers. After all, he did owe him. Meantime, Delacot would have to carry on as before so as not to arouse any kind of suspicion.

*

Billy Haskins found himself once again at the police station. They had brought him in on the pretext of wanting to just have a chat, but Billy wasn't buying that.

"I want my solicitor if you's going to question me. I ain't saying nuffink without my solicitor."

DI Bora and DS Lockhead were both sat across from Billy.

Bora took the lead.

"Tell me about your relationship with Francis Delacot."

"Don't know what yer on about, Clueless, and who is this Francis Delacot? Never 'eard of 'im."

Bora was beginning to lose patience with the slimy weasel sat before him.

He continued, "I think you do know Francis Delacot, or why would you be on a picture with him otherwise?"

Haskins began to squirm nervously in his chair, his body language betraying him.

DI Lockhead showed him the picture of Francis Delacot with him in the background.

"Oh, that was 'is name then, yeah, I did some personal security for some guy, but I don't remember who it was."

"I think you do know, Billy, so you'd better start giving me the information that I want, or I'll arrest you."

Billy laughed, "On what grounds, Clueless?"

DI Bora continued in a calm voice, "On possessing a firearm with intent to inflict harm, intimidation, do I need to go on? I'll ask you again, Billy, what is your connection to Francis Delacot?"

This time Haskins knew the Inspector wasn't playing games.

"No comment."

"Was that the first time that you had met Delacot?"

"No comment."

"I'll take that as a no then, hey Billy?"

"Drop dead, Clueless. I ain't sayin' another word till my brief gets 'ere."

DI Bora clicked his tongue and said, "Come on, Louie, time for a walk I think."

As the dog passed Haskins he gave a low growl.

"An' I don't want that mangy dog anywhere near me."

Bora smiled to himself; so he was afraid of dogs. *That bit of intel might come in useful in the future,* he thought.

After two hours of getting nowhere, DI Bora conceded that they would have to let him go. The only thing he was saying was "no comment".

"I'm sure we'll be seeing you again very soon, Billy, so don't try and leave the country, will you?"

"Huh. Fat chance, Clueless."

"Inspector Bora to you."

John hated being called Clueless, but he knew that

it was the best derogatory name that Haskins could come up with. He wasn't the sharpest tool in the box, although he thought he was. Bora knew that the people he associated with were far cleverer than him, but because he had something on every one of them, they accepted him and even helped him, for fear of the consequences.

Paula was asleep when John arrived home. It was happening again; the job was becoming the foremost thing on his mind. He needed to check himself That was why his first wife had left him, because she had felt neglected because of all the unsociable hours her husband kept. He knew he had to try and leave the job behind even if only for a few hours. He justified to himself that Paula understood and knew how important his job was. Paula, however, was beginning to tire of John's late nights. Although she did understand, she felt neglected.

Louie settled down at John's feet. Paula opened her eyes and began manoeuvring her way towards him.

They argued and then Paula ended it after eventually putting her point over, calmly made herself a hot milky drink and left John to his own devices. She didn't care if he slept in the lounge all night with the dog, or whether he came to bed.

John reached for the whisky bottle that was on his table, felt for the glass that had been left there for him and poured himself a generous shot. It wasn't important if he had a drink late at night, because he couldn't drive. And he knew Steve his driver would be there in the morning to pick him up and take him into work.

*

After the previous evening, John was distracted; he didn't like arguing with his wife and began to question whether it was the right thing coming back to work. He was having misgivings. In the past he had been able to clear up cases relatively quickly, even murder cases. Was he losing his edge, or his confidence or both? He sat in his office waiting for the arrival of Christine Lockhead.

"Good morning, sir."

"Is it?" replied Bora.

Christine made herself a coffee and sat across from the DI.

"Sir, I've been thinking. You know when we interviewed Haskins yesterday, didn't it strike you as funny that he said he didn't know Delacot?"

"Course it did."

"Well, sir, I noticed on his arm, it was very faint, a tattoo, but thinking about it now the tattoo could have been of a teddy bear."

"Why didn't you point this out to me earlier, Christine? We could have questioned him about it then, but now we will have to wait for another opportunity to question him about it. I'm sorry,

Christine, but this is just not good enough. You are a Detective Sergeant and you didn't think to tell me about this."

John was really in a very bad mood; an opportunity with Haskins had been missed. If he could see he certainly wouldn't have missed the tattoo on Haskins' arm. He would have been on him like a ton of bricks.

Christine was perturbed. "Well I've told you about it now. I'm sorry, sir."

She left his room muttering to herself.

Damn Haskins and damn his lack of sight. What else had the DS missed?

"DI Borra here. Margaret, would you like to come to my office please?"

Margaret Loughey signed out of her computer and proceeded to the Inspector's office. Margaret was a diligent and competent officer; she was quite shy, which Bora thought was unusual given the office she worked in, but he trusted her implicitly as she had always provided the information that he needed, a very good information officer, in fact.

"Come in, Margaret, take a seat. You are aware of the murder of Shirley Delacot," he began, "but did you know that Francis Delacot, the South African Diplomat was her father?"

"Yes, I knew that."

"Well it seems that every man and his wife are after this wretched teddy bear. Apparently, everyone involved with it has a tattoo of a teddy bear on their arm. I want you to find out everything you can about the teddy bear tattoo and anything else you can find out. I am very interested to see what this is all about and how it all ties in with our murder."

"Yes sir, I'll get straight onto it."

Margaret loved a juicy mystery; she often thought about writing her own book, but that was just a pipe dream, as were many of her other dreams. She was an attractive woman in her thirties, but the right man had never come along to sweep her off her feet, so for the present she was still single. She lived in a modern apartment in town with her cat, Mr Pukistix. Her week was carefully planned out although the routine never really varied. She wasn't unhappy with her life, she just hoped that one day Mr Right would come and sweep her off her feet and they would live happily ever after, with at least three children. Margaret loved children and spoiled her nieces and nephews all the time.

She walked the short distance from the Inspector's office and went back to her desk to log on and start finding out about the teddy bear tattoos. She began to type in "teddy bear" and all manner of things came up – Stieff bears, teddy bears picnic, children's cartoon teddy bears. Then she saw it and was quite taken aback; it showed a picture of a teddy bear and next to it the biggest emerald she had ever seen. The caption read "The Emerald Bear". The emerald had been sewn into a bear for safe keeping, but at this point in time no-one knew where this bear was. It was rumoured to be in Asia, or South America or South Africa but no-one seemed to know for sure. And those that had any dealings with it were reluctant to give up their secrets. So not only was this bear hugely expensive it was also shrouded in secrecy. She tried again, typing in "teddy bear tattoos", but nothing came up in any searches. This was a mystery that would take some time to crack. By the end of the day Margaret was nursing a headache and no nearer to finding anything out about the teddy bear tattoos. Well, at least now she understood what all the fuss was about surrounding the Emerald Bear.

Sat in her apartment later that night, she couldn't get out of her mind the massive size of the emerald. Surely it must have been sewn into quite a big bear to be able to conceal its identity. Had it been sewn into an existing bear or had there been a bear specially made to house the emerald? These were the thoughts going round and around in Margaret's head, as she tried to sleep.

*

Paula greeted John with a cheery, "Hello." The argument of the previous night forgotten. That's what John liked so much about his wife; she didn't hold grudges, she said her piece and then let him reflect on it. Which is entirely what John did. Paula noted the anxious look on John's face.

"What's the matter? You look troubled."

John sat down, Paula gave him a cup of tea and then said, "Right, are you going to tell me what's wrong or do I have to guess?"

John groaned. "It's work."

Is it ever anything else? thought Paula.

"What's happened now?"

"That's just it, nothing's happening, we are no closer to solving the murder of Shirley Delacot despite that her father is an eminent South African Diplomat. Did I do the right thing going back to work? Only I don't seem to have my edge anymore."

"Well, that's up to you, darling, but ask yourself, would you have been happy just staying at home all day, or would you prefer to be out solving crimes?"

John didn't have to think about this for long as he already knew the answer. Louie gave a little bark as if to let John know that he approved.

*

Billy Haskins was afraid of Francis Delacot. It had been like that for many years and he had come to live with it. He was afraid of what Delacot might say if he didn't deliver the bear. It was a long time ago, but Delacot was one to hold grudges and not forget and certainly not forgive. It hadn't been Billy's fault; the girl was in the wrong place at the wrong time. This was Delacot's other daughter, the one they never spoke about. To the outside world Delacot was a widow with a young daughter, but there was another daughter. She had died in tragic circumstances. Delacot had had an affair whilst married to Shirley's mother, and the result of that affair was his love child. He provided for his daughter, but never acknowledged her, that was until she came looking for him. She wanted to extract money from him, believing it was her right. At the time Billy Haskins was working in South Africa as a personal bodyguard to Francis Delacot. One of the questions he was asked before being hired was, "Can you keep your mouth shut?"

Billy assured the other man that he could. One day Delacot had taken him to a tattoo parlour and demanded the tattooist to ink a teddy bear onto Haskins' arm. Haskins was very annoyed; he didn't want a tattoo inked onto his arm. He felt as though he was being branded. Tattoos invariably hurt and sometimes they went bad and festered. He tried to protest, but Delacot wasn't listening.

"My security, you understand," Delacot had said.

Haskins had very reluctantly succumbed as he was getting a huge sum of money for protecting the other man.

The accident had happened when he was trailing Avril Behan on the instructions of Francis Delacot.

Avril and her daughter had been crossing the road, and then it happened. Billy had panicked; he needed to get out of South Africa as quickly as possible. He knew Delacot could be quite ruthless, he had experienced this on other occasions, during his time guarding him. Wanting to avoid a scandal, Delacot had told Billy to go home and he would be in touch. He assured Billy that his secret was safe if he did what Delacot wanted. Every so often Billy would get a reminder that he still "owed Delacot".

All these years he had been a free man building his own corrupt empire, but not on the same scale as Francis Delacot. Delacot believed he was untouchable as he had diplomatic status, and he had run his corrupt affairs accordingly.

Now as Billy tried to think of a way to find the Emerald Bear, he seemed to be running out of options. He had tried to intimidate Paul Plumpton and scaring him and wounding him to within an inch of his life, but all that had done was drive Plumpton to go underground and it appeared that he had vanished completely. It was now imperative that Billy found the bear and handed it over to Delacot, but where was he supposed to start looking? Things were getting more precarious for Billy as the local police under the direction of DI Clueless seemed to be closing in.

*

"Sir, after lots of scanning the internet, I have

finally found out about the teddy bear tattoo."

Margaret was quite breathless with excitement.

"Well, Margaret, don't keep it to yourself, let us all in on it."

"Well, sir," Margaret began, "at first there was nothing and then I stumbled on a page about Francis Delacot and he was talking about his extensive bear collection and how valuable it was. He was also talking about the valuable paintings he had hung in his house."

"Yes, yes, Margaret, get to the exciting bit about the bear tattoo." Bora was becoming a little impatient.

"It turns out there are only three tattoos in the world, with that particular bear on them. They are all accompanied by numbers in the catalogue."

"So how do we work out who has which number?"

"I'm sorry, sir, I don't know."

Bora's mind was working overtime; he had been told by DS Lockhead that Billy Haskins had a bear tattoo although it was very faded. Were the bear tattoos received willingly, or had the recipients been in some way forced to have them, a little like a branding iron?

Now they knew who the three tattoos belonged to, but were there any more? Any more that perhaps no-one knew about? The third one was the dead girl. They needed to know if there was another person with a tattoo and then maybe there would be some kind of clue as to who killed Shirley Delacot. They knew the Emerald Bear was the most desirable and expensive in the world, but who actually knew where it was?

"Margaret, you have done well, but can you find from the catalogue who was assigned each number? Or if the people who owned the bear tattoos had ever been involved in any kind of police matters, or civil proceedings come to that?"

Margaret blushed a little. "Thank you, sir, I will do my best to try and find out about the numbers."

Margaret left the Inspector's office. She knew he was a married man but that didn't stop her admiring him from afar; she liked his mannerisms and his good looks. *If only,* she thought.

"Christine, have you found anything else out? Margaret has done a sterling job finding out about the tattoos, now we just have to do some extensive checking and see if anyone on any of our databases has an inked tattoo of a bear then maybe that will lead us to the killer."

Christine felt as though the DI was chastising her for not realising about Billy Haskins sooner, although he wouldn't come out and say it. She felt uncomfortable as she sat in her chair slowly drinking her coffee.

She was drinking coffee in the DI's office and a few miles away a scared Billy Haskins was drinking coffee in his front room, wondering where to go next to try and track down the bear. It was no use asking Lennie or Midge because then the whole sorry story with Delacot would have to come out and that was not a risk he was prepared to take. He knew Delacot would only keep quiet until it suited him and if he didn't get the bear then…

CHAPTER 10

Steve was driving John home. It had been a particularly wet day and at the crossroads the car lurched forwards and stopped. Steve needed to check if the engine was firing properly; he knew how to check for faults on cars, as before he had become a policeman he was training to be a mechanic. Getting out of the car and pulling the collar up on his jacket against the wind as the weather had turned very cold, very quickly he saw on the signpost four numbers. After he had checked the car over and was satisfied that the only reason the car had stopped was because it had a bit of water in the engine due to the torrential rain, earlier that day, he climbed back into the driving seat and said to DI Bora, "Sir, I have just seen something very strange on that signpost, I'm sure it has never been there before. As you know we travel up and down this road every day, but it was strange."

"What were the numbers?"

"A seven, a three and two ones."

Weird, thought John. *Could this be anything to do with*

the tattoos? Was it some kind of code that the tattooed people were able to follow to find the bear? He quickly dismissed the idea though, thinking, *Why on earth should four random numbers mean anything to anyone?*

Billy Haskins had agreed to meet Lennie and Midge in the Goose C. He couldn't discuss his dilemma with them, but he could discuss with them where they thought Paul Plumpton might be.

"Well, any ideas?"

"No, boss, not seen him since that night we had our little game with him."

Billy grunted as he picked up his pint. Now it wasn't just a little game, it was a matter of life and death, mainly his, if he didn't find the bear.

"No ideas at all, have neither of you seen him?"

"No, boss," they said in chorus.

"What we need is a plan. We need to find Plumpton before the police or anyone else does. Is that clear?"

"Yeah, boss, but where are we supposed to start looking?"

"You can start with that office of his in town, ask around see if anyone has seen him recently and if they have, where?"

Lennie and Midge didn't really want to start looking for Paul Plumpton. After all, if he did go to the police, both men would be incriminated and possibly charged with kidnap and causing grievous bodily harm.

Reluctantly Lennie and Midge agreed to go and investigate Paul Plumpton's office. When they arrived there they noticed that the shutters were down and there were bars on the windows. It was obvious even to Lennie and Midge that no-one was there.

Out of ideas, they rang Billy to tell him.

As the phone shrieked out Billy nearly jumped out of his skin; he wasn't expecting it to ring. Surely it couldn't be Delacot yet, surely he was going to give him more time to try and find the bear. He picked up the receiver cautiously.

"Hello boss, dead end, place all locked up, doesn't seem like there's any sign of life."

"Lennie," Billy roared. "Don't ever phone me on the landline again, have you got that? Never. I repeat, never."

"Okay, boss, keep your fur on, I only phoned to ask you what you wanted our next move to be."

Billy was fuming with Lennie. "Go 'ome and we'll meet up at 6:30 in the Goose C tonight."

"Oh, okay then."

*

Inspector Grieves had had a boring day. How he wished he was back at the Met, instead of pursuing a wild goose chase. He was staying in a small B&B just outside the town centre. It was quite a cheerless place and the landlady was very stern; she didn't really approve of single men, especially when they brought women home.

Nate Grieves and Christine Lockhead were definitely what you would call an "item", though, and Nate comforted himself that there was at least one good thing in this godforsaken place. They arranged to meet at the Goose C before travelling into town to a restaurant.

Christine busied herself choosing her outfit and deciding whether she was going to wear her hair up or down. Odd, really; she felt a little nervous, that was why she was making such an effort. Considering the men she had been out with before, she was taking extra care over her appearance tonight for this man. Make-up applied, taxi ordered, she took one last look in the mirror.

Nathan Grieves was dressed in a casual suit, no tie and no socks. Christine thought that was pretty radical, given the way he dressed for work.

"Hello, you look nice. Shall we sit over there at that table?"

They were having a quiet drink when three men walked in, all raising their voices and swearing. They ordered their drinks at the bar and then proceeded to find a table at the back of the pub. The men hadn't seen the two officers, and weren't aware of their presence. Even so, they probably wouldn't have recognised them, thought Christine.

"Now listen to me, we have to find Paul Plumpton so any ideas 'ow we do it?"

Midge smirked. "Suppose we could put an ad in a paper, you know, cryptic like."

"No, Plumpton is too clever to fall for that."

"We could ring his number and say we want a house viewing."

Haskins thought about this. "No, that wouldn't work, didn't you say that 'is office was all shuttered and barred, like no-one was there?"

The men ordered another round. This called for some serious drinking and serious thinking. Haskins had started to sweat profusely and decided to remove his jacket. Just at that moment Nate Grieves decided to use the bathroom; he brushed past Haskins' chair and mumbled an apology, not before noticing, however, the four numbers written on Haskins' now bare arms. The numbers were 7311.

*

Grieves was sat in Bora's office. "We were sat in the Goose C when Haskins and his cronies came in. They didn't recognise us so they walked on and found a secluded table near the back of the pub. I needed to use the bathroom and that was then that I saw it."

"Saw what, man? For goodness' sake spit it out what you saw."

"Okay, okay, John, all in good time. I heard him refer to his cronies as Lennie and Midge, none of the party seemed happy and they looked like they were trying to drown their sorrows."

John was becoming more and more impatient with this man; he thought him a buffoon when he first arrived at the station and his opinion of him had not changed.

"Bloody Hell, man, get to the point. I don't want to know their life stories, I just want to know what it is you saw."

"The numbers on Haskins' arm, isn't that what you have been going on about for the last two days?"

John was trying very hard to keep calm. And what were the numbers?"

"Seven, three, one, one."

"Have you any idea what these numbers mean?"

"No, have you?"

"This meeting has been really useful, not. Send in DS Lockhead if you can bear to tear yourself away from her for two minutes."

Nate Grieves stormed out of Bora's office, slamming the door viciously behind him, nearly taking it off its hinges. The cheek of the man. Just because Christine and he were seeing each other!

"Now DS Lockhead, we need to bring Billy Haskins in for another chat. What have we got on him to date? What grounds have we got to bring him in?"

"Well, we could call his bluff and tell him that we have evidence that he has tried to kill Paul Plumpton on two occasions."

Bora thought for a moment. "Yes, well I suppose that might work, the only problem is that bent brief he has. We don't want to be referred to the IPCC for harassing a member of the public who we can't prove has committed a crime."

"I think we could risk it, sir."

"Very well, bring him in again and treat him a person of interest."

Christine was sat in on the interview as Bora started asking questions.

"Would you like a cup of tea, Billy?"

"No, Clueless, I don't want nuffink off you."

"Billy, I keep telling you, it is Detective Inspector Bora to you."

Bora needed to proceed cautiously, try to lull Haskins into a false sense of security by pretending to be his friend.

"Now Billy, we know about Paul Plumpton, would you care to fill in the other details about him?"

"Bloody crook," said Billy.

DS Lockhead noticed the look on the Inspector's face, she thought the same. They were both villains, the question was who was the biggest one?

DI Bora asked again, "Billy, do you want to tell us more about Paul Plumpton?"

"No comment."

DI Lockhead stretched out her long legs and

moved closer to Haskins.

She was aware of her striking beauty and she knew that men usually co-operated with her, being in such proximity. In fact, you could say she was the police's secret weapon. She needed to win him round and get him to start talking.

"That's a fine tattoo on your arm, it looks a bit faded though, will you have it re-inked?"

"No, I bloody won't. It 'urt like 'ell the first time, why would I want it done again?"

"And can you remember when it was that you had it done?"

"Course I bloody can, what do yer take me for, an idiot?"

"No, Billy, not at all. I just wondered when you had it done."

"Well, nosey copper, mind yer own, as I don't want to tell yer."

"It says here that you worked for a time in South Africa as personal bodyguard to our Mr Francis Delacot."

Billy started fidgeting nervously in his chair and there were little beads of sweat beginning to form on his brow.

Louie barked. Haskins kicked out his leg, just missing the dog.

"Get that mangy mutt outa 'ere, I don't like it."

"Well I'm sorry, Billy, but the dog stays."

Billy grunted again. "Bleedin' dog."

Christine Lockhead was scrutinising Billy closely, when she noticed part of his little finger was missing.

"What happened to your finger, Billy?"

"A dog bit it clean off, that's what."

DS Lockhead grimaced. "I bet that was painful. Was that when you were working for Francis Delacot?"

"No comment."

The Inspector was growing tired of Billy's games and "no comment" answers.

"Now are you going to tell us about Paul Plumpton?"

"I give 'im 'is first proper start, and that was 'ow 'e repaid me."

Now they were getting somewhere, thought Bora.

"What do you mean, that was how he repaid you?"

"Bloody scammed me out of fifty grand, that's what. 'Im and 'is so-called friend, and that Ryan Evans got no better than 'e deserved in my opinion."

"Ryan Evans committed suicide."

"Yeah right, Clueless, if that's what you want to believe."

Bora had read the Coroner's report thoroughly and discussed it with Lockhead just in case he had missed anything. They had both agreed that Ryan Evans' death was suicide just as the Coroner's report had found.

Bora needed to look at the report again and he

would ask DI Grieves to take a look, but that was for later; in the meantime they had Haskins and they didn't want to miss an opportunity to ask him more questions.

"What do you know about Ryan Evans?"

"Nuffink except 'e was a little shit, said he could get me somethin' I wanted, but told me it would cost me. I paid 100 grand only to be scammed by 'em both."

"What was the something they promised you? It must have been worth a lot to you for you to pay a hundred thousand pounds? If you thought you had been defrauded out of so much money why didn't you come to us?"

Billy had an incredulous look on his face.

"Come to yer? Yer gotta be joking, Clueless. Yer can't even find 'oo killed that lass in the farm'ouse."

"Did you know her, Billy?"

"No."

"Did you know she was Francis Delacot's daughter?"

Billy did not answer, he just shrugged his shoulders. Even the name Francis Delacot bred fear into Billy.

"Billy I will ask you again, did you know Shirley Delacot?"

This time Billy felt compelled to answer.

"I knew 'er a bit as she was Delacot's daughter, but I didn't see much of 'er. She didn't like 'im very much."

"Didn't like who, Billy?"

"'Oo do yer think, Father bloody Christmas?"

"So to recap, Billy. You got to know Francis Delacot well when you worked for him in South Africa?"

"S'pose."

"Did he pay you well, Billy?"

"'E didn't pay anyone well if 'e could get away with it."

"Does Delacot have a bear tattooed on his arm?"

Billy visibly flinched.

"'Ow the 'ell would I know?"

"I think you do know, Billy, and you are evading the question."

Bora had now established there was definitely some history between Delacot and Haskins.

Bora decided to turn the conversation around. He knew Billy was visibly rattled, but that would keep for another day.

"Have you been terrorising Paul Plumpton?"

"No comment."

"Only I heard his wife left him a few weeks ago and took their young daughter with her."

At this point a smile crossed Billy's face. "Bloody good riddance to 'er if yer ask me."

"I heard you wanted to make Plumpton jealous by starting an affair with his wife."

"Worst thing I ever did, she was so demandin'. I'm

glad she's buggered off somewhere."

"Well we know about her and now you do too, but what have you done to Paul Plumpton?"

"I ain't done nuffink to 'im an' you can't prove that I 'ave."

"Oh we will find out, Billy, rest assured about that. If we find out that you have been terrorising him and using threatening behaviour towards him, we will charge you with assault."

"Heh, try it, Clueless. You can't pin nuffink on me and yer know it."

"Well, I'm so glad we had this little chat, Billy, but don't try and leave the country as I may want to speak to you again."

Billy got up and as he did so Louie started barking.

"Bloody mangy mutt." And with that, he practically ran out of the station.

This time Clueless had got too close for comfort for Billy; he obviously knew about the bear tattoos, but he didn't know what the significance of the tattoos was. Billy was not going to enlighten him, as he feared for his own life and at the moment his life was very precarious. He knew Delacot wouldn't wait much longer for the bear, and now Delacot's daughter was dead the whole thing had become so much more of a mess. He feared that Delacot would blame him for the death of his daughter, even though he hadn't killed her, or at least that was the version he would tell Delacot. The Emerald Bear meant so much security and guaranteed the owner lifelong immunity from hostile entities.

*

Shirley Delacot had been to England on a previous occasion; she was twenty when she first arrived in England. Although she travelled on her own passport as soon as she was settled, she changed her name to Denacot. Nobody quite knew why. For a few years she had lived a quiet life, outside London; she was a secretary in a charity office, that was where she had met Jorge. Jorge was from Paris and he, like her, had come to England to start a new life and she hoped this would be the start of a new life for her. She had quarrelled again with her father and that was why she decided to take herself away from the situation in South Africa.

She had the teddy bear tattoo inked shortly after arriving in London. She was fully aware of its symbolism, but as far as she knew there were only three others like it in the world. Although she had quarrelled with her father, this was about being part of something very special, something that only a handful of people knew about.

Jorge had often asked her about the tattoo, but each time she would just smile sweetly at him and change the subject. The fewer people who knew about it the better. That way neither her life nor anyone else's would be put in danger.

She remembered the day well when she had been summoned back to South Africa. She was twenty-four, old enough to make her own decisions and yet when they came calling for her, she felt obliged to go. It was not really a request, it was a command. She had packed up her belongings, given back the key to her flat and then she had to tell Jorge. What was she going to tell Jorge, though? She felt she owed him some sort of explanation, but she couldn't tell him the truth as to why she had been summoned back to South Africa so abruptly. She thought hard about the problem; she would tell Jorge that her father was ill and needed her to help with his affairs.

As she prepared to meet Jorge for the final time, she dressed carefully as she wanted him to remember her, when they had been happy together. Shirley had thought that they may eventually marry and have children, but this was not meant to be. Now she was losing the man she loved, and she couldn't tell him why. There were times when she despised her father and everything he stood for and especially the Emerald Bear.

She arrived home to find her father admiring his latest acquisition; it was a painting. He looked his daughter up and down.

"Hmm, you've put weight on since I last saw you."

"Thanks for that."

Being away from her homeland for four years had made it very difficult to come back, and here was her father, being his arrogant self as usual. *No change there then,* she thought.

"What was so important that you had to drag me away from the life I was trying to make?" she yelled.

Francis Delacot looked his daughter in the eye and said, "Business, dear girl, business."

She hated him when he talked like that to her, it reminded her of the way he talked to the people he thought were his inferiors.

"I want you to take the Emerald Bear to England and place it in the safe deposit box with the number I give you."

She looked at him incredulously. "You must be joking, do you realise what you are asking me?"

He looked at her in a calculated way. "Yes, I know."

"Why me? Why should I risk my life?"

"Because," he began, "no-one will be interested in a young woman who is going to be a language teacher."

"What did you say?"

"Yes, I have it all arranged, you are going back to England and you will work in a private language school in the North West. I have met with the Principal of the school and he has agreed to take you."

Shirley was furious.

"More like you found a dodgy person and told them some story about me and you agreed to pay them a lot of money for taking me on."

He gave a little cough. "Well yes, something like that. You will need to take two bears," he continued, "one with the emerald in and another to act as a decoy. Don't let them out of your sight, and I will send you the instructions on how and when I want the bear depositing. This is a very dangerous job, my dear, but I don't think you will come to any harm as there will be people watching out for you. Once the bear is firmly delivered to the safe deposit box, then we can both sit back and enjoy a very opulent life, the two of us."

He wasn't thinking of her; all the time he played the devoted father, but the only thing he was devoted to were wealth and greed, she thought. However, the bear would offer them both some security and she might eventually be able to recognise her dream of setting up an organisation, where she could charge rich people huge sums of money for attending her seminars.

This was where Ryan Evans came in. Francis Delacot had been reading The Washington Times, when he came across the story of Ryan Evans who had been convicted of teddy bear fraud on a grand scale. On his release from prison in the United States he had come back to England and started his own language school. He had spoken to Evans a few times and agreed that it would be a good idea for his daughter to become a teacher there. He had told

Evans that he was prepared to pay him a huge sum of money, but he was not to divulge his daughter's identity, although he had never given a reason why.

Ryan Evans was a greedy man and not one to be taken advantage of, so he had agreed to take Delacot's daughter but he wanted the money up front. Francis Delacot wasn't pleased with this arrangement, but what choice did he have? Ryan Evans had a gambling addiction; he needed money to pay his creditors and to keep his school open.

Delacot had given Evans just enough information about his daughter, he had also asked him to find her somewhere to live.

A few days later saw Shirley Delacot head for Shrewsbury, with Ryan Evans in tow acting as her chauffeur, after introducing himself as the Principal of the Brewmans Language School.

"I wish to be known as Miss Denacot."

"Very well, I shall tell everyone that is your name."

She hadn't met Paul Plumpton, but had told Ryan Evans of her plans to open a centre. Evans had looked through businesses and had found a flat for rent that he thought would be ideal for Miss Delacot. The developer's name was Paul Plumpton; he had wasted no time in getting a flat sorted for her. He had also mentioned to the Plumpton Development Agency, that this woman was looking for a run-down property that she could bring into a state of repair to house a charity organisation, she wished to set up. Paul Plumpton knew of the very place, it was an old, deserted, dilapidated farmhouse. He saw the opportunity for getting the farmhouse renovated to a good standard, without him having to pay out any money; and after all, if she changed her mind or wanted to move on he would have a reasonably good building to sell on, without having to do all the costly repairs. This was looking to be a very lucrative proposition.

*

Billy Haskins was aware that Shirley Delacot was in the country. The only reason for her being here, he thought was to do with the Emerald Bear. At last, after all these years it would be payback time for Delacot. The that still terrified him, but he would hold the power if he had the bear. He needed to devise a plan but he could not be seen to be involved with anything. Then very inconveniently the girl had been murdered and the bear was missing. He needed to find that bear before Delacot realised it was missing. He had heard on the local news that a young woman had been murdered at the Fallons' place; although they were unsure who it was, he felt sure it was Shirley Delacot. If it was her, he knew that she would have the Emerald Bear with her.

Now she was dead and her true identity was revealed, Billy Haskins knew he had to act. He had found the number of a Ryan Evans, who was listed as Principal of the Brewmans Language School. This information about where she was supposed to start work had been released by the police in an attempt to find her killer. He set about convincing Evans that he could make him very rich if he found a particular teddy bear that the murdered girl had in her possession. Evans was unscrupulous and decided to go along with the plan as his ever rising debts were beginning to encroach on every area of his life. He was getting desperate for money, although the school was paying its way.

"I will give you £50,000 if you find the bear and bring it to me." He was to recruit a Paul Plumpton also. He knew Plumpton would be struggling for money, especially as he had withdrawn his teddy bear collection along with his money to fund Plumpton's lavish lifestyle. One hundred thousand pounds seemed a little amount if he had his hands on the Emerald Bear. Besides, he didn't intend to be out of pocket for long; he would double cross the two saps as soon as he was able to. Then he would have the money and the bear. Delacot would be mad when he found out, but Haskins had a plan where he would take the money and simply disappear. Illegal jewels were always so hard to detect as they involved many people, sometimes quite influential ones stretched over many continents. He would sell his own teddy bear collection at one of those auction houses were they operated behind closed doors, because of the huge amounts the collectors' items went for. He would be literally "quids in", he thought. Things hadn't worked out for Billy though. He had been scammed by Paul Plumpton, who he was convinced now had the bear. That was when he came up with the plan to have an affair with Plumpton's wife, but even that had backfired. Haskins was still convinced that Plumpton had the bear; he had threatened him twice and Plumpton had given him no real information. Even the affair with Plumpton's wife hadn't yielded any success at finding the bear. He was no nearer to finding the bear, than when he first found out about Shirley Delacot's death. Who had the bear was a mystery. Was it Delacot? No, it couldn't be because Delacot had rung him and threatened to expose him if he didn't surrender the bear. Was it Paul Plumpton? If it was, he had more brains than Billy had given him credit for. Billy sat in the pub, not knowing what he next move could be; he was running out of options to find the bear and Paul Plumpton had not been seen anywhere. He must be in hiding, he thought.

DI Bora was sat in his office asking himself the same questions. He needed answers. He felt Billy was the key, but he just didn't know how he fitted in with Delacot and what hold Delacot had over him.

John arrived home that night. Paula noticed he was more tired than usual.

"Are you sorry you went back to work so soon and into such a high-profile case?"

John thought about this for a while. He had been doubting himself for a couple of weeks now. When he was sighted things had been so much easier. He had been able to spot clues instantly; that was what had earned him the nickname of Razor. Now he felt more of a blunt knife than a razor. His instincts hadn't really helped him so far during this case and he had to rely a lot more on Christine Lockhead. She was a good officer as long as she was focussed and at the moment John thought her mind was on other things than police work. She had to have a life outside work, he chastised himself, just because he didn't. Paula, though, was becoming more and more frustrated as he lived for his police work. They never did anything together anymore. When John had first lost his sight, they had gone out for long walks, they had spent hours talking and now all John wanted to talk about was the ongoing murder case. Something he felt he could not really discuss with his wife, arguing that she wouldn't understand.

CHAPTER 11

Jake Barnes lifted a doll off the top shelf and began to dust it. He regularly cleaned all of his toys. His toyshop was the boast of Allerdale. He had been providing the people of Allerdale with their toys for many years. Johnny's birthday. Sarah's Christmas, birthdays and Christmases too numerous to mention. In fact his shop was so successful, he told his customers, that he ran a Christmas Club and practically all the village had an account with him. Jake was always first to buy in the new trends in toys and his customers expected him to do that. His father had owned the shop before him and when he had died, he had passed the toyshop on to his son.

The shop had been successful and the people of Allerdale still believed that it was, but that was far from the truth. The bills were mounting as more customers turned to digital games and computers. He had used some of the Christmas Club money to pay off the debts. By the time the residents of Allerdale had realised what he had done he would be long gone and the shop would be closed. He had been planning this for months, realising that the shop was becoming more and more unprofitable.

Jake Barnes was a loner; he had always regarded himself as a misfit. To his customers he was always jolly and obliging, but in reality he was a mean-spirited man, who believed in taking calculated risks. As he pulled the shutters down on the shop for the last time he looked furtively around to ensure none of the villagers were about to spot him. He checked his watch; the taxi was on time. With a last check to make sure he had his passport he heaved the bag into the car and sped away to the airport. Once on the plane he afforded himself a wry smile, imaging the looks of horror on the villagers' faces, when they realised he had buggered off and took their money with him.

He didn't really care; his father, he thought, had been a weak man and far too generous. He had made changes when he had taken over the business, but because of his father's reputation the villagers had remained loyal. *Stupid people,* he thought.

The air hostess poured another whisky, which he quickly drank, then settled down in his seat and went to sleep. He didn't really like flying but thought that a couple of drinks calmed his nerves, so that was why he had consumed the whisky. He saw the plane as a means to an end, to be boarded, to take him to a new life.

*

Jake Barnes had grown up on a farm; his parents were hard-working farmers, but Jake had other ideas. At school he had been bullied, that was until he started to stand up to the other lads. He realised that if he could get things that they wanted they would leave him alone and he became handy with his fists, so his peers no longer bullied him. After leaving school he signed up to join the army. This seemed like a logical step for him. His mother was upset at the time but she eventually reconciled herself to the fact that her son was to be a soldier.

His father was now fulfilling his dream about owning a toyshop due to an inheritance from a Great Aunt. He always hoped that he could pass the shop onto his son, when he died.

Unmarried, Jake toured the world as a soldier, he lived off his wits; women didn't particularly interest him. His final campaign had seen him injured with shrapnel in his leg. He was not a hero. He had struggled to move, but had left his other comrades to die, when he could have helped them. As a result of his injuries he was declared unfit for duty and returned to civilian life. His parents were overjoyed to see their son returned to them and his father hoped he would take his rightful place working alongside him in the toyshop.

During his time in the Army, Jake Barnes had

become mean spirited; working as part of a team was alien to him so eventually all his army colleagues left him alone. He wasn't invited to any of the social gatherings that they held, but he wasn't bothered, preferring his own company. During his last tour of duty he had met a young South African soldier, by the name of Francis Delacot. Delacot told him that someday he would be a great man, someone that others would look up to and revere, even fear him. Barnes had met soldiers like him before, all talk and no action. It was many years later that the name Francis Delacot came to his attention. The headlines read:

"Eminent South African Diplomat to fly to London to broker an exciting new trade deal."

*

John Bora sat in his office. He was feeling quite miserable, it had been weeks and there hadn't seemed to be any breakthrough on the murder of Shirley Delacot.

Chief Superintendent Cole had voiced his dismay with John, indicating that they had spent a huge amount of their budget trying to find the killer and they hadn't so far managed to solve this case.

"I need this case solved as quickly as possible, John. Do you think you came back to work too soon?"

John resented that comment. Who was he to judge whether he had come back to work too soon?

"No, sir, we are working flat out to try and catch

the killer."

"Well I hope to see some results soon. How you getting on with your dog?"

"Louie is fine, sir, he is a confident dog and very intelligent."

"Good, good. Well, I will let you get on."

He bent down to stroke Louie, who lifted his head and growled.

John couldn't help stifling a wry smile.

"Thank you, sir." John pulled on the dog's harness and they left the office.

"John, I have a name for you."

John Bora wasn't really interested in Nathan Grieves' power of deduction; so far he hadn't seen anything about Grieves that impressed him, but he was getting desperate for some kind of breakthrough, so he decided to listen. Inspector Grieves poured himself a coffee and sat down.

"Well, what's the name then?"

"Jake Barnes."

This was a new name to Bora, and now he was becoming interested.

"Well, it seems that Jake Barnes shut up his toyshop and buggered off with all the Christmas Club money. I have been doing some more digging and found out that Jake knows Francis Delacot."

"Hmmm." Bora stroked his chin. There was the name again, Francis Delacot. It seemed that he had a wide circle of friends, or maybe they were enemies, who knew too much about him.

"Is there a connection between Delacot and Barnes?"

"Yes, they both served in the army together."

"Do we know anything else?"

"Barnes was injured, during his last tour of duty, where he met Francis Delacot. That was before he became a Diplomat."

"Do you think this Barnes knows something?"

"It's possible, from all accounts our Mr Francis Delacot is not all that he seems."

"Well done, Nathan."

It was the first time Bora had actually acknowledged that Grieves had a first name.

"Let's see what else we can find out either about Jake Barnes or Francis Delacot. I shouldn't have thought a high-flying Diplomat would want to be associated with a lowly toyshop seller."

It was a proven fact that when people became upwardly mobile that they tended to leave persons that they viewed as of a lower status behind. Delacot was no different, from what Paul had seen. He expected results and only associated with people who could further his career. To John he seemed like an arrogant greedy man. As yet though, John had to keep his suspicions to himself as there was no positive proof of anything, either with Francis Delacot or Jake Barnes.

It was a puzzle that needed solving and John Bora loved a good puzzle.

"Margaret. See if you can find anything out about a Jake Barnes. It might say he was a war hero. That's B-A-R-N-E-S. Owned a toyshop in Allerbury and absconded with all the villagers' Christmas Club money."

Margaret blushed slightly, not that Inspector Bora could see her and that was a good thing, she thought, then there wouldn't have to be an awkward exchange.

"Yes sir, I'll see what I can find out."

"Oh and while you're checking him see if you can find a link to Francis Delacot, there must be a link somehow."

Margaret put in her password and fired up her computer. She wanted to impress DI Bora and show him how efficient she was. Two hours had passed and Margaret had uncovered nothing. The only things she found were headlines about Francis Delacot sealing some trade deal or other.

Louie was getting restless; John buzzed for Steve. "I think we should call it a night. Are you ready, Steve?"

"Yes sir, won't be a tick."

It was a warm night and John could think of nothing else except going home and having a cool beer. It had been raining in the day, but now the weather had cleared and it was quite warm. Steve drove with the windows down so John could smell the air. He enjoyed the ride home with Steve and the windows down; since becoming blind all his other senses had been heightened. He could smell the diesel of the car engine, he could smell the fresh air as they rounded the corner towards his house. Suddenly a thought hit him; was there a smell in the farmhouse, he had missed?

"Steve, was there a smell in that farmhouse, where the murdered girl was found?"

Steve thought carefully. "Not that I can remember, sir."

"I want to be taken to the farmhouse tomorrow, with Louie. If we have missed anything, Louie might find it. He's such an intelligent dog. Goodnight Steve, see you tomorrow."

"Goodnight sir."

John sat down and Paula poured him a beer. Louie lay down beside him and fell asleep. John awoke with a start. Paula was getting ready for bed.

"John, I hardly see you at the moment and when you are here you seem in a world of your own." John grunted and went to bed.

*

Steve had a restless night. His baby was teething and he had been taking it in turns with his wife to comfort the child. He was late going to collect Bora.

"Sorry I'm late, sir. Been up all night with the baby. He's teething."

"Right, let's get going then. I'm not expecting to find anything, but we live in hope."

The drive up to the farmhouse was in silence; Bora didn't seem to want to talk. Steve wondered if the job was getting too much for him. Louie sat quietly in the back. They slipped quietly into the farmhouse, Steve pulling up the tape that said "Do not cross" to allow DI Bora to move forward. Louie began tugging on his harness. "What's up, boy, what have you found?"

Steve quickly stood beside the dog and looked around. He couldn't see anything. The dog changed position and then sat down again. "Louie. what is it?" At this point the dog started to bark' it was unusual for Louie to bark as he was very highly trained, but John thought there must be something wrong, for the dog to behave in such a way. Steve was on his hands and knees desperately trying to find something, but he couldn't. then suddenly, he pulled out a wool fibre obscured by a floor board. He opened a bag and popped in the fibre.

"Well what is it, man? Have you found something?"

"Yes sir, it seems to be some sort of fibre."

"Excellent work, Louie, good boy."

He bent down to pat his dog.

Steve was a little dismayed; he hadn't acknowledged that he was the one who had found the fibre and put it safely into an evidence bag to preserve it.

Back at the station, John was, with the help of

Steve, able to add something to the timeline. He hoped that the other officers were also able to give some positive information.

Inspector Grieves was looking very pleased with himself.

"Sir, I've managed to track down that boyfriend of Shirley Delacot, when she first came over here when she was twenty."

"Excellent."

DI Bora felt that they were now getting somewhere. A wool fibre and now a name of a previous boyfriend of the dead girl.

"His name is Robbie Monks. My friend Aspey did some digging and found out that they were an item back in the day. He knew her as Shirley Denacot, apparently, they were in a serious relationship. Then one day according to him she just disappeared. No reason, no forwarding address. He had been devastated. They were making plans to get married."

"Good work, Inspector, can we bring this Robbie Monks in for an interview?"

He still lives in London, sir, so maybe the Met should handle it."

Bora thought for a moment.

"No, definitely not your part of the Met. Can't you bring him in and I will travel up to London with you?"

"Well you know, John, that's not really the right thing to do. You need to let the local force handle the interview."

"Very well, we need to send the info to London, but I want you to take the lead on the interview."

"Be reasonable, John. You know I would have to clear it with my superior."

John frowned. *God, this man is so negative,* he thought. What would it take to get him motivated? John could see why the Met had gladly seconded him to their force.

"Go tomorrow. As the senior investigating officer I will ring your station and talk to your superior. Is it still Marcus Raines?"

"Yes."

Grieves didn't particularly like Chief Inspector Raines. He found him to be arrogant and pompous.

"Marcus, John Bora here."

"John, I thought you had been invalided out of the force when you got shot. I heard you lost your sight."

John gave a small cough. "Yes that's right, but I have not been pensioned off yet, in fact now I am DI Bora."

There was silence on the other end of the phone. Then Marcus began slowly.

"But if you are blind how are you managing?"

"Well I have a good team around me and then there is Louie."

"Who is Louie?"

"Louie is my guide dog. The force provided him for me. He's excellent."

Marcus Raines clicked his tongue. "Only you, Razor, could get away with that."

At this John started to laugh; he hadn't been called Razor for a long time, not since he and Marcus had been local officers on the beat. Marcus had moved to London and been promoted quickly first to Detective Inspector, then Detective Chief Inspector.

"About Grieves."

"Oh yes, lucky you having Grieves seconded to you."

Bora grunted.

"I need him to come back to you and conduct an interview with an old acquaintance of the murdered girl that we are investigating."

Bora heard a moan on the other end of the phone.

"Very well, John, if you insist. As soon as he has done the interview though he is getting on the train and coming straight back to you."

"Thanks, Marcus."

Inspector Grieves set off for London. Christine was in a bad mood; she didn't think that Nate should be travelling to London to interview someone, when they could have brought the person to Shrewsbury. Besides, she worried he might meet up again with his former girlfriend who he had dumped for her. He might just do the same to her; no, she wasn't happy.

DS Lockhead stormed into John's office. "Really, sir, did you have to send Inspector Grieves back to

London?" she demanded.

John raised his head and said, "Yes, and I will thank you not to question my decisions, DS Lockhead." Christine felt suitably chastised.

"I wouldn't have sent him back to London if I didn't think it was necessary, but I think this person might give us a clue as to why Shirley Delacot was murdered."

"Has there been a development then?"

"Yes, we found a wool fibre at the farmhouse a couple of days ago."

"Why wasn't I informed?"

"Because," began Bora, "it might be something and nothing, but your detective boyfriend found the man who Shirley Delacot was supposedly going to marry, so I thought that was at least a lead worth following up."

Inspector Grieves sat down and studied the file in front of him.

"Well it's very good of you to come in, Mr. Monks."

Robbie Monks shuffled nervously in his seat. He had a couple of criminal convictions, but that was a long time ago, in his youth.

"So, you and Miss Delacot were planning on getting married then, is that right?"

"Yes, but I didn't know her as Shirley Delacot, she always told me her name was Denacot. I arrived home from work one evening and there was no letter and no sign of her."

Inspector Grieves wasn't impressed.

"Did you look for her?"

"Of course, I did."

"Did you report her as a missing person?"

Robbie Monks hesitated and then said, "No."

"And why was that? Surely you thought it suspicious that the woman you were going to marry had just simply disappeared."

"I began searching for her, but then three days later I received a handwritten note that said, 'Don't come and look for me, have had to go back to South Africa, father very ill.' That was the last I heard of her. I went back to the flat and noticed her passport and most of her clothes were gone."

"And you didn't think that was suspicious?"

"I didn't want to get involved in anything."

"What do you mean?"

"Well I loved Shirley dearly, but she did have a dark side to her, and she did have secrets."

"How do you know she had secrets?"

"I caught her one day, having quite a heated row with someone and when I asked her about it, she just shrugged and said it was nothing for me to concern myself with."

"Can you remember who the person was or what they were arguing about?"

Robbie Monks began to wring his hands nervously, he could feel the palms of his hands starting to sweat.

"It was a man, but I couldn't make out what they were saying, they seemed to be talking in a foreign language."

"Can you remember anything about the conversation, or how the man looked or how he was dressed?"

"He was quite tall with a small greying beard. At one point he looked as though he was shouting at her. When the man left, Shirley was practically in tears. I asked her about it but she wouldn't say. A few days after receiving the note, I bumped into a neighbour that told me that two men had come and escorted her away in a car."

Grieves shuffled the papers in front of him. Was this really leading somewhere, or was it just a waste of time?

"Well thank you for your time, Mr. Monks."

Robbie Monks alighted from his chair with a relieved look on his face; at last his ordeal was over. He knew that he should have told someone at the time, but as time went on he decided he was better not knowing what had happened to Shirley. The next time he had come across her name, was when he had read about the murder of a diplomat's daughter called Shirley Delacot. He knew that it was Shirley, but he was still too scared to afford the luxury of knowing why she had changed her name and why she was leading the life she was.

Nathan Grieves had returned to Allerdale without anything concrete to offer DI Bora. As far as he was concerned it had been a wasted journey.

Christine Lockhead was pleased to see him and relieved that he hadn't met up with his former girlfriend, or at least she hoped he hadn't.

She strode into DI Bora's office clutching a local newspaper. She poured herself a coffee and sat down. She began to read. 'William Haskins, a local money lender, was badly beaten last night. He was taken to hospital where he remains having suffered a massive heart attack.'

Bora clicked his tongue. "Money lender, bloody loan shark more like. It seems like he has upset someone. Well he won't be getting into mischief for a while. Christine, go to the hospital and see if you can find anything out."

"On it, sir."

"And send DI Grieves in. I hope he has some news for me."

CHAPTER 12

"Well, Grieves, what did you find out?"

Nathan Grieves seemed uncomfortable. He began, "Well John, I'm afraid I thought it was all a waste of time really."

"What do you mean?" Bora was losing patience with this officer, who he viewed at best as incompetent; now he would be adding lazy to his opinion of him. How did he ever make DI?

"The man, Monks, I interviewed, seemed to be frightened of something, but he wasn't telling me what. He just said he didn't want to get involved. He is happily married now with a child on the way."

Bora sat in his office and wondered why he wasn't further on with this case. Every avenue led to a dead end, surely there must be a breakthrough soon.

DS Lockhead walked into the hospital ward, the young sergeant looked up.

"Hello, DS Lockhead. It doesn't look good for the fella in there."

DS Lockhead glanced over into the room and saw

all the wires attached to Billy Haskins.

"I'm afraid he's totally out of it, Sergeant, you won't be able to get a statement from him for a while, if he makes it, that is."

Christine left the hospital. As she was driving back to the station, *That's another suspect out of the frame for Shirley Delacot's murder,* she thought.

"Yes, thank you."

John turned to Christine. "Billy Haskins didn't make it. Now we have a murder and an attempted murder on our hands. Any ideas who might have beaten Billy so badly?"

Christine thought for a while. "No, sir."

*

Francis Delacot picked up the paper; he had the local news sent to him on a regular basis, no matter where in the world he was. He just happened to be in London. He liked to keep an eye on local news. When scanning the headlines he read, 'Local man badly assaulted and dies in hospital. Police are treating it as attempted murder.'

He continued to read the article and was frozen to the spot when he read the name Billy Haskins. He needed that bear, but how was he going to get it now that Billy Haskins had died? He felt sure Haskins had been on the brink of giving it to him and he was planning to have a meeting with Haskins later that week. He was outraged that someone else had got to

Haskins first.

Did he have the bear?

Who else knew about the bear?

If someone else knew about it then who were they?

More to the point, where was the bear now?

Was it the group that had kidnapped him?

Ever since he was supposed to meet Paul Plumpton in the hotel he had been keeping tabs on him, even instructing Haskins to frighten him into revealing where the bear was. This plan hadn't worked though, or had it? Had Billy managed to beat it out of Paul Plumpton and get him to reveal where the bear was?

Or had Plumpton outwitted them both and he still had the bear? Delacot needed to know. He tried to phone the Private Investigator who he was paying handsomely to follow Plumpton, but there was no answer, just a message saying that the number was no longer in use. He had to go to Allerdale, he had to see Billy Haskins for himself, but how if he was in the mortuary? Francis Delacot snook into the hospital, donned a white coat, put a stethoscope around his neck and claimed to be a doctor.

"Ah, Nurse," he quickly looked at the nurse's name badge, "Nurse Grimes, isn't it?"

"Yes, Doctor."

Nurse Amelia Grimes had been on the ward for

only two weeks and she was still getting to know the doctors.

"William Haskins, is he still in the mortuary?"

"Yes, they won't have released the body yet as the pathologist needed some more information. Besides, no-one has come forward to formally identify him yet."

Delacot nodded. "Yes I see, dreadful business being badly beaten and then suffering a fatal heart attack."

Delacot walked down the corridor following the signs for the mortuary. The first bit had been easy, but now what would his excuse be, to look at Haskins? He had to think quickly.

"I've come to formally identify William Haskins." The pathologist looked Francis up and down. "Haven't seen you before. What did you say your name was?"

Delacot suddenly realised that he wasn't wearing a name badge.

"Dean. Francis Dean."

"How come they have sent you to formally identify the body?"

"I er, remember him slightly from years ago when I treated him at another hospital."

The pathologist was suspicious. What had he been treated for? Stab wounds, a bullet wound? There were certainly signs of old injuries on his body.

"What was it you treated him for again?"

"I can't really remember off hand, I do see a lot of patients you know. Maybe it was a superficial wound, yes, that was it."

"Must have been a bloody big wound for you to have to treat it."

Delacot could feel the sweat beginning to run down his back and start to soak his shirt. He needed to check the body and then get out of there as soon as possible.

He pulled the sheet back, and pretended to slip on the floor, landing across the body. He quickly felt around, no, there wasn't anything on the body. He quickly regained his balance, and said, "Yes, that's him."

Damn, he thought. He would have to go back to that new nurse and quiz her about Haskins' belongings and what he was brought in with.

"His belongings are in a bag in the Sister's office," she ventured, "as no-one has claimed them. I'm not sure what they do with them."

Delacot gave the nurse his best sickly smile. "Of course, thank you Nurse Grimes."

He hurried off towards the Sister's office, hoping to slip in unnoticed. Fortunately everyone including the Sister were busy, so he had no trouble locating the bag with Haskins' belongings in. He quickly rifled through the bag – wallet, keys, an assortment of pieces of paper containing phone numbers, but definitely no bear!

Now he needed to slip out of the hospital unnoticed so he discarded the white coat and the stethoscope and walked out as a visitor. Nobody had suspected anything, as they had all been busy. The problem was though, now where was he to look to try and locate the bear? It seemed as though the Private Investigator no longer owned the phone number that he had been given and the cheque that he had paid the Investigator had already been cashed. He needed to gather his thoughts as he was travelling back to London. Where was Paul Plumpton?

*

"I need you to go and formally identify Billy Haskins please, Christine, and while you're there pick up his personal belongings if no-one else has claimed them. I am very interested to see what Billy was up to."

"Wil do, sir." With that, Christine swept out of the Inspector's office. She liked getting her teeth into a good mystery and she definitely thought this was one. No witnesses to Billy's beating, in fact no incriminating evidence, but she was determined to find something.

As she walked towards the hospital mortuary she was met by the pathologist.

"I've come to formally identify our Mr. Haskins."

The pathologist gave her an odd look.

"Too late, I'm afraid."

"What do you mean 'too late'?"

"Well some doctor has already formally identified him, he claims he was a patient of his years ago. Was most insistent about identifying him."

This was interesting, who was the doctor?

"Have you a name for this doctor?"

"Yes, it was Francis Dean."

"Are you sure about that?"

"Yes, quite sure, but he didn't have a name badge on, which I thought was odd."

"Did he take anything from the body?"

"No. I thought he was rather clumsy though as he slipped on the floor, lost his footing and ended up bent over the body."

"Thanks, Peter. I'll go and collect his belongings then."

Peter waved; he quite fancied the attractive DS.

Christine went to find out if there was an actual doctor called Francis Dean, and just as she thought, the man was an imposter. He, whoever he was, had been posing as a doctor. She scoured the doctors' names a few times, just to make sure she hadn't missed it, but no, there was no such doctor on the roll. So who was he, and more to the point what was his interest in a lowlife like Billy Haskins?

Back at the station, Christine was looking through

Billy's belongings and shouting out phone numbers to DI Bora.

"Stop. That number sounds familiar. I wonder where I have heard it before."

Bora was racking his brains; wasn't that the number for the South African Embassy in London?

What business would Billy have with the South African Embassy? Then he realised, it wasn't the embassy Billy was interested in, it was the visiting Diplomat Francis Delacot. Now it all made sense, Billy was going to contact Francis Delacot, but something happened and Billy was badly beaten, so the meeting between him and Delacot never took place. A quick look through Haskin's belongings confirmed Bora's suspicions. Christine shouted to him that there was a return ticket to London for the 2nd of the month. That seemed ages away from when Haskins was killed, but ever the miser he had bought the ticket well in advance, as it was cheaper. So was the meeting with Delacot arranged a month previously and how did Billy know Delacot's whereabouts, unless he had been in contact with him?

Was it Delacot that had come down to Allerdale to identify Haskins? That seemed rather strange, but there seemed to be no other explanation.

Billy Haskins' funeral was set to be a solitary affair, but at the last minute an anonymous donor had stepped in to pay the funeral costs.

"Get down to the cemetery, Christine, and see if there is anyone at the funeral that you recognise."

This was an easy task as there were only three mourners at the funeral, but one of them was a woman.

"There was a woman at Billy's funeral, sir."

"A woman, well, do we know who she was?"

"There wasn't really anyone to ask, but the gravedigger seemed to know her. When she had gone, I went over to him and asked if he knew any of the mourners personally. 'The woman,' he said, 'that was Billy Haskins' sister Mary.'"

"Sister? I didn't know Billy had a sister. Well, did you find anything else about her?"

"Nothing really except the gravedigger said she moved out of the area ten years ago."

"Well where did she move to? Get Margaret on the case to track down all the Mary Haskins on the electoral roll within a fifteen-mile radius. I would like a chat with Miss Mary Haskins."

*

The Goose C seemed remarkably quiet; the old oak beams emanated years of smoke and grime. The corner where Billy Haskins and his cronies always sat was eerily empty, as was the rest of the pub. Christine and Nate had gone in there for a 'quick one' after work, hoping to glean some information from Billy's associates. Disappointed that there was no-one in the pub that they could have eavesdropped on, they quickly finished their drinks and headed home. Christine was convinced that this was the real thing and was ready to commit to Nate Grieves. After all the affairs and flings she had had over the years, she finally felt that this was the man that she wanted to settle down and spend the rest of her life with. She couldn't quite believe it herself, her, Christine Lockhead, the person who had always been a free spirit was talking about commitment.

Inspector Bora was sat on a chair in the meeting room. Louie was beside him. Inspector Grieves was poised at the whiteboard ready to record any information that had come to light to further the murder inquiry.

"Right, I want a thorough search of Billy Haskins' house, from top to bottom. Every piece of paper, every phone number, and all the money. He was a loan shark, people, I am sure if we look hard enough we will find money and other expensive items, I need them all bagging for evidence and I want this as soon as possible."

The officers set to work immediately, they recovered three bin bags and £25,000 in notes.

This was the time that Bora really felt frustrated about not being able to see. He had to rely on Steve or Christine to shout out phone numbers or every scrap of paper.

"Sir, here is a sheaf of invoices, they all refer to the sale of teddy bears."

Steve looked at DS Lockhead and grinned. "Yeah right, Sarg."

"Excellent work, Christine, what do the receipts say?"

"Well they all seem to refer to an auction house called Sunderlands. The prices are staggering. Twenty-five thousand pounds, thirty thousand pounds, forty-five thousand pounds."

DI Bora let out a large whistle. "So where are the bears and where is the money? I want every bank account of Billy Haskins' scrutinised. I want to know more about these bears, and if there were any more."

"Sir, I have traced a Mary Haskins to just outside Allerdale, it gives her address and where she works."

"Well done, Margaret, I knew I could rely on you."

"Thank you, sir." And with that, Margaret put down the phone.

"Well, we seem to be uncovering more and more information about our friend Billy, it seems he wasn't just a criminal and loan shark. The question is, did his extortionate loans finance the teddy bears, or was the money from the teddy bears stashed somewhere?"

The officer showed the woman into an interview room. She was a thin, gaunt-looking woman with grey hair and a rasping voice.

"Detective Inspector Bora, finally we meet."

"It is very good of you to come in, Miss Haskins."

"Come off it, Bora, we both know why we are here. You want information about those confounded bears that my brother had. I was the brain behind those bears. As you know, my brother wasn't the sharpest tool in the box. I arranged the auctions, I arranged the buying and selling. When Billy died I went to the house and took the existing bears to my house. After all, they were partly mine anyway."

"What do you mean, partly yours?"

"Well when we first started collecting them we split everything down the middle, the bears, the money. Billy was useless at managing money."

"Come, Miss Haskins, surely you knew what his main line of business was. He was a loan shark."

"Inspector, I prefer money lender, he would always give a struggling person a helping hand."

"Where is the money? There must be thousands."

"No comment. I think I would like to have the presence of a solicitor now. My solicitor."

"Very well, you are allowed one phone call. I suggest you do that now."

Mary Haskins got up from her chair and proceeded to use the telephone.

"Right, Inspector, my solicitor will be here shortly and then we can get this mess cleared up. As I have said before I haven't done anything wrong and you have no proof that I have."

Inspector Bora took the opportunity to ask her about Francis Delacot before her solicitor arrived.

"Do you know a Francis Delacot?"

Her face physically paled, observed DS Lockhead.

"No comment."

"Can you tell me about the suits hung up in your brother's wardrobe, some with the labels still attached?"

"Come, come, Inspector, surely you have worked that bit out by now. My brother wanted to pay back Paul Plumpton as he felt deceived and betrayed by him. I came up with the idea for him to have an affair with Plumpton's wife as I thought that would be the ultimate humiliation. I chose the suits for my brother because all his life he never had any dress sense."

"Well that figures, I suppose."

Bora wanted to revisit the question as to whether she knew Francis Delacot, but the woman was having none of it and just repeated, "No comment."

"Why didn't you formally identify him at the hospital when you knew he was dead?"

"No comment."

This interview was not going well and Bora was losing patience.

A knock came on the door and a smartly dressed man in his forties walked in. Louie gave a small growl. Noel Smythe had recently defended two high-profile cases and was regarded highly in his profession.

Immediately the solicitor spoke DI Bora knew who it was, he was just as slippery as most of his clients.

"Now Inspector, if you have no evidence of wrong-doing then you cannot charge my client and I suggest you release her."

John Bora had to admit that they had no evidence of any wrongdoing to keep the woman there.

"Just don't leave the country."

The woman and her solicitor swept out of the interview room, threw a look of scorn at the desk sergeant then strode out into the warm afternoon.

"That was close. Did you tell them anything?"

"No, of course not."

"Good, because we don't need it to be public knowledge that we know Francis Delacot. The police will find out soon enough, but by then, my dear, we should be out of the country."

Mary Haskins smiled a smile, but the smile never quite reached her eyes. Although she was in love with Noel she had been let down badly by a man in the past and therefore she was suspicious of all men, even the one who proclaimed his love for her.

They were planning a trip to Hawaii, but Mary had started to have misgivings. Was he just after her for her money? Besides, that nosey Inspector had told them not to leave the country and she wasn't sure whether he meant it or whether it was just said in jest. She needed to check her offshore accounts and make sure no more money had been taken from them. She had known about her brother's arrangement with Francis Delacot, but she argued, that was for her to know about and for him to find out about. Francis Delacot could be totally ruthless, as her brother had found out to his cost.

"Odd, that," deduced Inspector Bora. "Why wasn't she down as next of kin? No wonder we couldn't trace her, it's as though she doesn't exist. She didn't seem unduly upset about her brother."

"She visibly paled, sir, when I mentioned Francis Delacot."

"Yes, why was that I wonder? I need you to go back to the mortuary and take a picture of Francis Delacot with you and ask what's-his-name if it was the same person that identified the body."

"Ah, Inspector Grieves, just the man."

Grieves shot Bora an icy look; it was just as well that he couldn't see him. As the days passed the two men seemed to be more antagonistic towards each other. Did Bora know how close he and Christine Lockhead had become, and the fact that they were talking about marriage? Grieves didn't care either way, what Bora thought.

"Have you heard of Sunderlands Auctions?"

"No."

"Only I thought with you being based in London that you would have heard of them."

"Well I haven't."

Bora thought that Grieves was being particularly obtuse. He continued, "Sunderlands is a private auction house, where all the auctions take place behind closed doors. They are not open to the general public, attendance at these auctions is strictly by invitation only."

"What's the point of it being an auction if the public can't attend?"

"Well that is exactly the point, that is what I want you to find out."

"You mean you want me to go back to London and check this place out?"

"That is the general idea," Bora said sarcastically.

Grieves was in a bad mood, he had plans for the next few days for him and Christine, now he would have to spend a few days in London.

DS Lockhead was in a bad mood when she swept into Bora's office. "I see Nate is going to London for a few days," she growled.

"Yes, that's right. I want him to check out Sunderlands Auctions."

John could have asked her to go with him.

"Did we get a positive ID on that doctor?"

"Yes, Peter said it was definitely him."

John stroked his chin. "Hmm, I thought as much, but why did Delacot need to see Haskin's body so urgently?"

"Do you think Billy's beating had something to do with Delacot?"

"It's a possibility, but knowing that arrogant twit he wouldn't have got his own hands dirty, no, he is far too clever for that."

"So are we looking at any suspects for Billy's beating?"

"My dear girl," Bora said in a condescending tone. Christine hated it when he used that tone with her. "Billy Haskins was a crook and a loan shark, I imagine there were any number of people wanting to give him a good hiding. It's our job to try and sift through his acquaintances and see if anyone fits the profile."

*

Christine and Nate were in the pub. They had decided to go there before Nate went away for a few days. The Goose C was practically deserted. The tables where Haskins and his cronies usually sat drinking pints and plotting people's downfalls were distinctly quiet. There was no raucous noise coming from any of the tables. Christine looked up at the old wooden beams that were a feature of the pub and read on a plaque high up, 'Smile, Jesus loves you.'

How ironic, she thought. Here they were discussing a man's beating and the plaque said that. She loved the atmosphere of the olde-worlde pub, but Nate wasn't impressed. "A dark hole," he said.

The evening passed without any incident or event

happening. None of Haskins' cronies had ventured into the pub. Were they all scared about what they could reveal about each other, or were they scared of something else, and that is why they weren't at the pub? Even the landlord had remarked on how quiet the pub was and the fact that he had not seen Haskins' cronies since the day of the beating.

"Have you got CCTV, then? It might give us some clue as to who beat Haskins up."

The landlord took his time before answering. "Well I do have CCTV but I wiped the tape yesterday."

Brilliant, thought Christine. The only thing that might have given them a clue as to who attacked Billy Haskins and the dozy bugger had erased the tape.

*

Francis Delacot was a desperate man and he was becoming more desperate as the days went by. Where the hell was the bear? Had he made a mistake entrusting it to his daughter? Had she deposited it somewhere before she was murdered and now he would never find out? That bear he felt belonged to him, he had gained the prestige to own such a valuable commodity. His paintings and other works of art would pale against the emerald, but the question was, where was it? Now that Billy Haskins was dead there didn't seem to be any other openings for him to discover where the bear was.

His thoughts turned to Paul Plumpton. Was he really a family man, or was he something more dangerous and did he have the emerald? Delacot felt Paul Plumpton to be inferior to himself; he wasn't particularly bright, or was that just an act and he had everyone worked out, without trying too hard? Had he rumbled Delacot's lifestyle and did he know too much? He must be found and he must be stopped, but not until he had divulged where the bear was. They had done a good job on Haskins, but why did the idiot have to go and die? Delacot hadn't finished with him and he had thought up many ways to keep the intimidation up on Billy Haskins. He felt he was so close to a breakthrough, with Billy ready to tell him everything and then he died.

He looked around his opulently furnished apartment. The South African Embassy in London certainly knew about style. This apartment was nearly but not quite, he thought, as elegant and expensively furnished as his apartment back in South Africa. Francis Delacot didn't know who had attacked Haskins, but he wasn't really concerned about that, all he wanted to know was where the bear was. Had Haskins found the bear? Had someone else known about the bear and if they had, was it them that had attacked Haskins to steal the bear? That wasn't concerning Delacot now, he had to prepare for the auction. He changed into a black suit and donned a false beard; glasses completed the look. He was heading to Sunderlands which was a grand building on the high street.

From the outside Sunderlands looked like a large Victorian house, it was quite plain on the outside but inside the beautiful high ceilings reflected décor not of the Victorian period, but of the Renaissance period. The corridors were long and dark, except for the room at the end of the house, which should have overlooked the magnificent gardens, but it didn't. Instead the room was partitioned off with heavy oak doors with velvet curtains. Behind the doors lay a square box where the attendees sat. The attendees would book a box and stay there for the whole auction; names were never used, the heavy oak doors just displayed numbers. There was no bar, or anywhere to have refreshments, just a jug of water and a glass on the shelf of each box. None of the attendees ever met each other but from time to time the 'regulars' began to recognise each other's voices although the auction was conducted secretly with the purchase of the most expensive teddy bears. No money ever changed hands at the auction, all payments were made to offshore accounts, or Swiss bank accounts, neither of which were identifiable. Each attendee had a number tattooed on their forearm; they would hold it up to a pad situated above the door of the box and they would then be registered to bid.

Grieves had hoped to get an invite to the auction, but unfortunately his application was denied; without revealing who he really was he would have to be content with waiting outside and observing from a distance. Poised with his camera with a telephoto zoom lens attached he observed from his car. Each attendee was carefully photographed before entering the building through a side door. Each of the men looked inconspicuous dressed in dark business suits; they were all clean shaven and bareheaded, all except for one man. Grieves quickly took a succession of shots, there was something odd about this man, he was wearing a black suit but also a hat that Grieves identified as a Jewish hat known as a Kippah. Before he entered the building this man looked around, as if checking not only to the left and right of him, but spending a few seconds looking up and down the high street. With one final look he slipped into the building. Something about this man, thought Grieves, seemed to be familiar, although he couldn't place what it was or if he had seen the man before. If he had seen the man before he certainly hadn't looked the way he did now. Grieves began racking his brain. Where had he seen this man before? Perhaps when he developed the photographs it would become clearer to him.

He waited in his car; he was getting rather peckish

and he was thirsty. As he was about to move off a blacked-out sedan shot past him and parked outside the side door of the Victorian house. There were four chauffeur-driven cars in quick succession that swept past Grieves. They all seemed to form a line outside the Victorian house and again so as not to arouse suspicion, each of the cars filled up and then they were gone. He had tried to see the people as they came out, they looked to be the same people as had gone in hours earlier. One man was missing though, the man with the beard and the Kippah; had he missed him, or was there another door he could have come out of? Grieves waited another ten minutes to see if he could see the recipient of the beard, but he came to the conclusion that he was nowhere to be found.

Francis Delacot had ditched his disguise once he had signed in and put his forearm on the pad. He had quickly proceeded to change out of his disguise and blend in with the rest of the bidders. He was actually furious; the bear he was hoping to claim, didn't even seem to be at the auction. So had he made a wasted journey? He was about to leave his box, when he spied another man going past. He couldn't be sure, but he thought it looked suspiciously like Paul Plumpton. He had never credited the man with much common sense or business acumen, he saw him as a greedy little man, who was just out to get the best price he could for the bears, but here he was at this prestigious secret auction. Was he a conman or a very clever individual? Delacot was still pondering over the other man when he bumped into another attendee.

"Watch where yer bloody going, will yer?"

He now needed to be out of the building as soon as possible for fear of someone recognising him without his early previous disguise.

*

Sat in his hotel room, he played the pictures back on the TV. Everyone seemed pretty unremarkable except the man with the beard. As Nathan lifted his glass of lager to his lips, he finally remembered who the mysterious man with the bear and Kippah might be. Yes, it was Francis Delacot, he took the small picture from his jacket pocket and began to highlight the similarities. Remove the beard and the hat and glasses and yes, it was Francis Delacot. Once again that name had come up, not just because it was the dead girl's father, but he seemed to remember that Francis Delacot had impersonated a doctor at the Allerdale Hospital. Nathan felt sure that this man was Francis Delacot, but he couldn't arrest him because for the time being, as Grieves was aware, he hadn't committed a crime.

Inspector Bora was building up a clear picture of Billy Haskins; he was a prolific criminal with many activities. Bora was puzzled how this man could undertake so much and not be caught. He was interested in Mary Haskins. *There's something not quite right there*, he thought. Was she the mastermind behind Billy's illegal activities? Was she the one that instructed him on what to do? On further investigation would they uncover money stashed away somewhere? Bora had so many questions that he wanted answers to. After investigating Billy's bank accounts, he found large amounts of monetary transactions, proof that he was running an illegal money lending business. Bora had every bit of paper scanned and transcribed into Braille so he could scrutinise his affairs more. This was a painstaking business as Bora didn't want to miss anything but having to read Braille made the whole process more difficult. He needed to talk to some of the people that Haskins had loaned money to, but he knew that would be hard as most of the people who owed Haskins money would be afraid to talk because of possible repercussions. He needed to find out as much as he could about Haskins' activities, and he realised the only person who may have information was not forthcoming.

"I want Mary Haskins bringing in as she is now 'a person of interest'."

"Yes sir, I'll get right onto it." Christine Lockhead was in a good mood today as her boyfriend Nathan Grieves was returning from his trip to London and she anticipated a nice romantic evening ahead, with a nice meal, some wine and then the inevitable sex.

"Inspector Grieves, Nate, how was your trip to the big smoke and what did you find out?"

Grieves poured himself and Bora a coffee, sat down and proceeded to recount what had gone on in London. "So, I'm definitely sure it was Francis Delacot at the Sunderlands auction. I took a few pictures from the safety of my car where I was well hidden, by the bushes."

"I hope you weren't spotted by anyone," interjected Bora.

"No, I used a very powerful zoom lens camera, office issue."

"What I don't get is why he used a disguise to go into the auction, then it had been discarded when he came out.

"Hmm, perhaps he wanted to be perceived as two different people, we know he is good at impersonating others if he feels the need. Was he carrying anything at all when he came out? A brown package perhaps or maybe something concealed under his coat?"

"No, I observed him carefully, he wasn't carrying anything that I could see. I did note though that he was irritated. He bumped into someone as he was coming out of the building and was quite rude when he barged past them, not stopping to apologise or even look up. It seemed very odd."

"I want you to find out as much as you can about Francis Delacot, whether he has any Jewish relatives, etc., etc. It seems quite bizarre that he used the disguise of a Jew going into the auction. I feel there is much about this Francis Delacot that we don't know and is it bringing us nearer to finding the killer of his daughter or are we beginning to uncover something much bigger than just murder?"

At that moment the phone rang. "Sir, Mary Haskins has moved from the address we have and no-one seems to know where."

Damn, thought Bora. *That's a blow.* They would have to spend more time and man power now, trying to track her down and she could be anywhere. Once she realised the police would come after her she had bolted.

"You better return to the office then and we can discuss the next steps."

"Righto, sir. Will be there as soon as."

*

Christine Lockhead looked in her mirror, applied fresh lipstick and strode into the office expecting to see Nate and Bora. She could hardly contain her excitement at seeing him again, but she took a deep breath and told herself she had to remain professional.

"Hello, Inspector Grieves," she beamed. Inspector Grieves gave her a warm smile.

"Grieves has been bringing me up to speed about our friend Francis Delacot, it's a pity we have gone no further in bringing in Mary Haskins. Does no-one have any idea where she has gone? Did you speak to the neighbours?"

"It's quite a rundown area, sir, and everyone was staying tight lipped. It was as though they were scared of something."

"What hold does this woman have over people, I wonder?"

"I couldn't say, sir, but they definitely seemed scared of something, even to the point of saying that they didn't really know her."

"I want her found. Start with the electoral roll and see if there are any other Mary Haskins registered, then I want you to go and talk to each one of them. See if there is anyone else on the roll called Haskins and go and talk to them. Inspector Grieves and I have work to do, good luck and see you later."

Christine was dismayed, she thought she would be spending the rest of the day in the office near Inspector Grieves and now she would be out for the rest of the day probably on a wild goose chase. Sometimes her boss could be impossible. However, she knew like him that she was single minded when it came to criminals, so once again she set off.

Inspector Grieves shouted after her, "See you tonight."

Huh, little chance of that, she thought, unless she miraculously had some kind of breakthrough this afternoon.

Inspector Grieves had been delving into Archives; he had read all the news about Francis Delacot and his diplomatic status and the fact that he was always seen at high-profile gatherings. As he was dismissing much of the information he was reading as unimportant, he stumbled upon a news article about Delacot when he served in the South African army. The article read:

'Francis Delacot was hailed a hero when he saved two men from hostile enemy fire. The brave young soldier had spotted five men hidden in the undergrowth. He had alerted the others, who had retreated as the insurgents had started to fire. They had reached their tanks in a matter of minutes and were beginning to advance. Two men had remained behind and Delacot had acted as a shield, before leading the three of them to safety. The insurgents had fled for fear of being captured. The two men with Francis Delacot were named as Billy Haskins and Jake Barnes.'

That was when Delacot had first come to have knowledge about the Emerald Bear. He was reading a newspaper that referred to it. He just knew that he wanted that bear. The years had progressed and Francis Delacot had worked his way up to being a diplomat in South Africa. He had never given up his dream of owning the bear and becoming one of the richest and most powerful men on earth.

Grieves came up from the archives; he needed to see Bora urgently. Apart from the information about Francis Delacot, he had found a very old clipping referring to an Emerald Bear, the owner of which would be untouchable by any government and no-one really knew who owned it at present or what it looked like. Over the years several pictures had emerged, but no-one was able to identify it completely and because of its value and what it represented no-one wanted to be seen actively pursuing it.

The Inspector, however, was not in the office, he was with the Superintendent who was again asking why there hadn't been much progress on the murdered girl case. Bora had told the Super that it was a very complex case and the more they looked, the more they were uncovering.

"I pushed for you to come back, John, as you know, as you are a fine officer, but I wonder if I have done the right thing, and have you come back too soon?"

John resented these comments but resisted the urge to tell the Super where to go. Instead he just said, "I think we are getting quite near to finding out who killed Shirley Delacot, sir, but I think her father has something to do with it."

At this point the Superintendent became interested. "You mean the Diplomat Delacot? Have you proof of this?"

"Not yet, sir, but at this moment Grieves is down in the archives finding out as much as he can about Francis Delacot."

"Why is that?"

"As you know, sir, Grieves went to London to find out about the Sunderland auctions, the secret ones where they buy and sell expensive teddy bears. We thought maybe the Emerald Bear might be up for sale and perhaps Delacot would want it."

"Tread carefully, John, Delacot is a very dangerous, influential man, he could make lots of trouble for our government."

CHAPTER 13

"John, I think that Delacot had something to do with his daughter's murder."

"Don't be absurd, man, it was his daughter."

"Yes I know, John, but I think something went wrong and that was why the girl was killed."

"What do you mean?"

"Well years ago in 1946 there was an emergence of a bear, that contained the biggest emerald in the world, and it was said that the bear would be coveted by many organisations. I think Delacot heard about the bear and knew that he wanted it. I think maybe he enlisted the help of Billy Haskins to find it, knowing that if Haskins didn't co-operate he would report him to the authorities. Billy Haskins admitted working for Delacot many years ago and when the tragedy happened I think Billy fled back to England."

"That still doesn't explain why the girl was murdered or who by."

"I know but I think the Emerald Bear and Francis Delacot are in some way connected. Why would

Delacot go to a secret auction dressed as one person, then emerge a few hours later as someone else?"

Bora scratched his nose, it was a puzzle.

"I have combed the area for forty miles and no-one has heard of a Mary Haskins. I need a coffee."

Louie stirred and lifted his head; he liked Christine as she always gave him a treat.

"Oh Louie, I wish you could talk, maybe you could have smelled out Mary Haskins."

Bora surveyed the evidence they had so far which was relatively nothing.

The girl Shirley Delacot had been murdered. Did it have something to do with the Emerald Bear?

Did she have the bear on her person, when she was murdered, and the murderer ripped it from her?

Was she being used as bait to lure in something else really big?

Through their ongoing enquiries they had found out that quite a few influential people all over the world knew about the Emerald Bear. They had not managed yet though, to work out Delacot's or Haskins' connection to the bear. Had Delacot been hoping that the bear would be at Sunderlands and that he would be finally able to get his hands on it?

*

Mary Haskins had been difficult to find, but eventually DS Lockhead had located her. As she knocked on the final door she hoped that this would be the one. A man in his early twenties answered the door.

"I'm looking for Mary Haskins, does she live here?"

"'Oo wants to know?"

"My name is Detective Sergeant—"

Before DS Lockhead had finished the sentence the door had been firmly closed. She needed to try again. She lifted the letterbox and said. "I need you to open this door, I need to speak to Mary Haskins."

After a short while Mary Haskins came out.

"You again, copper, what do you want now?"

"I would like us to have a little chat down at the station."

"Get lost."

"I could send a squad car for you to officially accompany us to the station. The choice, Mary, is yours," she said emphatically.

"George, don't just stand there, get me coat."

The young man picked up a dirty coat and gave it to the woman.

"That's better, Mary, glad to see you co-operating."

Mary Haskins pulled a face.

*

"Ah, Miss Haskins, so pleased you could join us." This was Bora at his best, thought Christine. "I would like you to answer a few questions for me and clear up a few things about your brother."

"He's dead, that's all you need to know. Have you found the bastards that beat him up yet, or are you just going to 'arass me some more?"

He may not be able to see, but Bora detected fear in her voice.

He continued, "Do you know Francis Delacot?"

"No comment."

He would try another avenue. "Have you ever met Francis Delacot at Sunderlands?"

"No comment."

"Miss Haskins if you persist in this way, I will charge you with obstructing the police."

Mary Haskins started to wring her hands. She couldn't be arrested, she was flying out to South Africa with her solicitor later that day. She needed to think quickly. What was she going to say?

"Very well, Inspector, if you must know, he was friends with my brother. I don't really know him."

"Miss Haskins, Mary, I may not be able to see, but I am not stupid. I know you know Francis Delacot, now are you going to answer my questions or do I have to formally charge you?"

She looked at her watch nervously.

"Going somewhere are you, Mary, or is there somewhere you need to be?"

She hated that nosy DS. She didn't miss anything.

Always able to think on her feet, Mary had to concoct a story that was believable and hopefully one that would stop the police delving further into her private life.

"Okay, I met Francis Delacot years ago. He was at a teddy bear auction in London."

"Sunderlands by any chance?"

"No, somewhere just outside Piccadilly, he struck up a friendship with my brother, seems they were both interested in teddy bears."

"I thought you said you were interested in teddy bears?"

"I said I had them. I didn't say I was interested in them."

"Do you know what the Emerald Bear is and what it looks like?"

"No."

"Did your brother never tell you about the Emerald Bear and how much it was worth?"

"No."

"Come Mary, I think you know Francis Delacot and about the Emerald Bear."

"No comment."

She really did need to leave the police station as she was cutting it very fine for her flight and Noel would be waiting for her at the airport. Bora had his suspicions that Mary Haskins was likely to leave the country. Once on board a plane she would be out of his jurisdiction and he wasn't prepared to let that happen.

"Where's that fancy solicitor of yours?" the DI asked sarcastically.

"He's on holiday if you must know, not that it is any business of yours, nosy copper."

"Well I'm sorry Miss Haskins, I'm going to charge you for withholding information."

"You can't do that," she screamed.

"Oh, but I can. Charge her with obstruction and take her to a cell."

Mary Haskins looked at the clock on the wall; they had taken her shoes and her watch before putting her into the cell. This wasn't how she had envisaged her escape, she had thought it would be nice and easy, just packing a suitcase and meeting Noel at the airport. At least the police hadn't discovered her suitcase, or so she thought. Without Noel's help she was not sure how long she would be in the cell. Noel would be furious left waiting at the airport; after all, they both knew it wasn't for a legitimate reason that they were flying out to Cape Town. They had hatched a plan to get Francis Delacot alone then quiz him about the Emerald Bear, hoping that if they applied so much pressure on him he would crack and pay them the money they had demanded. Now all this, though, seemed to be going wrong.

"Sir, two officers have just come back from Mary's house and guess what?"

"Don't tell me, she had a suitcase packed and she

was going away."

"Yes sir, but how did you know?"

"Call it instinct. Do we know where she was headed?"

"Cape Town, sir."

"I thought as much, now I wonder if she is ready to talk."

*

Noel Smythe paced up and down and checked his watch; if she didn't arrive soon they would miss their flight and then their connecting flight. They had paid for a room in Dubai, they would lose the room and their money, he didn't like losing money. How would he explain to Delacot why they were late? Delacot would be on his home soil now after his trip to London. This was going to be tricky. Where was that blasted woman? She had set it up for them in the first place and now she wasn't anywhere to be seen. He tried ringing her again, there was no answer. That was the fifth time he had called her. It hadn't occurred to him that she might have been taken to the police station for more questioning. He had thought they had dealt with that matter the last time he was there.

The custody officer gave a quick glance at the vibrating phone in Mary Haskins' belongings and dismissing it as unimportant he carried on with his report. He didn't like writing reports and viewed the ringing phone as a distraction.

Noel Smythe tried her mobile one more time and received no answer. There was nothing else for it, he would have to travel to Cape Town on his own and hope Delacot would understand. This wasn't a problem as so as not to arouse any suspicion they had both purchased their tickets independently but hoped to meet up at the airport then they could have travelled together. He looked around the airport anxiously one more time then walked to the boarding gate; there was no sign of her. *The bitch*, he thought. *I hope she hasn't double-crossed me.*

Mary was beside herself, she knew that whatever time the Inspector decided to release her now she would have missed her flight.

"Sir, I don't think we can hold her much longer, we need to bail her."

"What time is it?" asked Bora.

"5.30 p.m., sir."

"Very well. bail her and then kick her out. She won't be getting a flight to South Africa today. I want her followed."

Mary Haskins stormed out of the police station; she checked her phone. Six missed calls from Noel. *Bugger*, she thought. She had missed her flight. She wondered whether Smythe had gone without her and what Delacot would say when she didn't arrive. There was nothing else for it, she would have to try and rebook a flight for later in the week; she knew

Delacot would not be pleased as he was expecting her to be there. He had re-arranged his schedule to accommodate them both. She knew Delacot had a temper, but she couldn't prove that it was his men that had attacked and half killed her brother. She was not naïve enough to think that Delacot didn't have men everywhere. England, Germany, America to name a few. Her dilemma now was to slip out of the country unnoticed, but that was going to prove difficult as the police were watching her every move. She had avoided them before and kept all her businesses out of the spotlight, so as not to arouse suspicion. She at least needed to get out of Allerdale but where to go was the problem. She knew Delacot would be furious that she hadn't arrived after he had gone to the trouble of rescheduling his timetable. He was not a patient man, and from other experiences she knew he didn't hesitate to wreak vengeance on someone he thought may have double-crossed him. She knew of numerous other people that had crossed Delacot and they almost always paid the price, or they remained indebted to him for life. She knew he could be totally ruthless and he was a trained killer, although supposedly he was a military hero. She had her doubts about that though because she thought he was a coward and bully.

He had manipulated her brother, because he was weak. He knew he should have stood up to him when the tragedy happened in South Africa but because Delacot gave him the option to flee the country, he knew he would always have to pay the price. Although in theory the teddy bears belonged to Billy Haskins, he was only holding them for Delacot. Mary Haskins had demanded her share of the proceeds of the sale of the bears, unaware that although her brother seemed to be getting a lot of money for them, Francis Delacot was taking a huge share and leaving Billy with the rest, although it seemed like a huge amount at each sale. When Billy returned to England he wanted to put his past in South Africa behind him, but Delacot wasn't going to let him do that. Immediately Billy had set foot on British soil, two men were there explaining what they wanted him to do. That was when he was introduced to the teddy bears. Although they just appeared as expensive bears they were auctioned at a special sale because of what they contained. Sometimes it was drugs, sometimes it was precious gemstones. That is why the auctions were held in secret. She remembered him showing her the tattoo and the numbers on his arm; he had been reluctant to have it done, but the two men insisted and threatened him what would happen if he didn't get it done. Once the numbers were tattooed onto his arm the two men explained what the numbers were and how the auction worked. There was no going back now for Billy. Although Billy was authorised to bid for the bears, he rarely knew what they contained and he had to find a safe place for them to be held until such time as when Delacot wanted them back. That is why he recruited Paul Plumpton; he knew Plumpton from when he had loaned him some money. Although he felt his lifestyle wasn't extravagant (apart from the gambling and fast cars) he enjoyed being the one feared which made it easier to carry out his illegal business of money lending. At one point he was doing so well that he set up an offshore bank account. The money kept rolling in, and if the customers couldn't afford to pay then there were always consequences.

Mary Haskins knew it was just a matter of time before the police found his bank accounts and she worried that it would just be a matter of time before they found hers, now she was under close scrutiny. She needed a plan; she was always so good art forming plans, she had got her brother out of many scrapes and difficult situations by forming a plan. The thought of Francis Delacot and his rage made Mary not only scared, but unable to think straight as the day of the South African Sunderlands auction loomed ever closer. She could hire a car and drive to France where she might be safe for a short time, but she was a nervous driver. Besides, the police had now confiscated her passport. She would have to buy a forged one but that would take time and unfortunately she didn't have much time. She weighed her options; be arrested and put into prison to await trial or take her chances outside and become a sitting duck for Delacot's men. Should she give herself up and go to the police station and admit to her crimes or should she at least try to get away? She had been successful at living quietly while still undertaking her illegal businesses, maybe she could slip under the radar and do it again. She was a resourceful woman and used to reinventing herself, it was her survival mechanism, but this time she was out of ideas. Then it came to her, it was very risky but she must try. She would obtain a false passport and travel on this to South Africa then she could prove to Francis Delacot that she had not double-crossed him. She contacted an associate of her late brother's and told him of her dilemma. He agreed to help her, but it would come at a huge financial cost to her. She had taken precautions, but on the day that she was supposed to pick up the forged passport she opened the door and there stood a uniformed police officer.

"Ah, Miss Haskins, I would like you to accompany me to the station, there are a few things we need to clear up."

Mary Haskins felt trapped. Should she try and run past the officer and out towards her new life? The officer looked very lean and fit; she knew that this would be futile as she wasn't very fit and she would be unable to outrun the officer. Still, she needed to try. She turned away from him and started to run through the house and towards the back garden, only to be stopped by an officer waiting for her to come out. *Clever buggers*, she thought. *They have thought of everything.*

This time Bora was determined to keep her in a cell for as long as possible before charging her with numerous offences and advising the judge to refuse bail. He knew that without her fancy solicitor she would have no chance of getting off lightly, and then perhaps he could get to the bottom of why her brother was beaten so badly and what connection he had, if any, to the Emerald Bear. He wanted her to explain the tattoos and the numbers and the connections with Francis Delacot, as he was sure there were.

CHAPTER 14

Paul Plumpton had arrived back in Allerdale having been hiding in Spain, for the last month. He had lost weight and was sporting a sun tan. His hair was grey and he sported a goatee beard. He yearned to see his daughter, not particularly his estranged wife but his daughter, he felt like it had been an age since he last saw her. The problem was he didn't know where to start looking for her. That flighty wife of his would and could have moved onto someone else whom she saw as a meal ticket with lots of money. Although things had been good between them at first, eventually she had tired of him, but not before giving him a beautiful daughter, that was what had compelled him to come back now after having recovered from his heart attack. He had gone into the Goose C and was told that Billy Haskins was dead. He felt so relieved; perhaps now he could get on with his life and put the whole sorry affair with Haskins and his cronies behind him. He still looked over his shoulder though in case someone from Billy's crew wanted to get him. The bar man told Paul that no-one connected to Billy had been into the pub since his death. Paul began in earnest to try and find his daughter. First he rang his wife's parents who were not very co-operative at first, telling him that they hadn't seen them for at least two months, but they had later relented and told him they had an address, if it was any use to him. Paul went to the address given to him by his wife's parents; there was a little girl playing in the front of a very grand property that was double fronted.

"Daddy, Daddy, I mean Uncle Mark, come and look at the snails, they are moving."

"Yes princess, I'm coming, but remember what Mummy said and don't get your pretty dress dirty before we go to Granny's."

Paul remembered the tinkling laughter of his little girl's voice, he had missed that so much. In the time he had been away she had changed, her long blonde hair had been cut into a bob that fell just below her shoulders. He resisted the urge to rush straight up to her and give her a hug. He needed to find out more about what was going on and the set-up there.

He parked the car and proceeded to walk up the drive, his daughter had gone into the house.

"Hello mate, can I help you?"

He looked at the younger man stood before him clad in expensive designer clothes.

Paul swallowed and said, "I'm Paul, Emily's father."

The other man swallowed hard then said, "You can't be, he's dead."

"I assure you I'm very much alive, now are you going to let me see my daughter?" He pushed past the man standing at the door, who still couldn't believe it.

The moment Paul was in the room his daughter dashed up to him and shouted, "Daddy, Daddy! Mummy, it's Daddy."

Julie came out of the kitchen looking visibly pale.

"I thought you were dead," she stuttered. "I thought after that heart attack that you had died."

"Well sorry to disappoint you but I'm very much alive and I want to see my daughter."

Carl had now entered the room. "He's says he is your husband, but you told me he was dead."

Julie felt uncomfortable. "Yes, yes I thought he was dead."

"This changes everything, Jules. I'm not supporting another man's kid no matter how cute she is."

"Wait, Carl, listen."

Carl sped out of the drive, realising he had been duped by this enchanting avaricious woman.

"Why did you have to turn up and ruin everything for me?" she screamed.

"Is this another one in your long line of

boyfriends? Is he mega rich and has he proposed?"

Julie didn't know what to say; she thought she had been rid of him, when she started an affair with Tom.

Paul jeered, "First Tom, then God knows who else. Well let me tell you I knew all about Tom, his real name was Billy Haskins."

Julie was puce with embarrassment. He had known all along and kept it from her.

"You bastard, you knew."

"Yes, but I decided to teach you a lesson. It backfired on you though, didn't it, because when Haskins found out how money grabbing and manipulative you were, he backed off. Now I think I'll be with my daughter. Come along, Emily, do you want to go on a ride with Daddy?"

"Yes, yes," the little girl squealed with excitement.

Paul drove away and out of Julie's life forever. He knew she wouldn't contest custody as she had always been so self-centred and looking for her next get-rich scheme in the form of a millionaire. No jury in the land would allow her custody even if she tried for it. As soon as it was possible he would go into town and start custody proceedings, and also divorce proceedings. So far he had managed to keep his own affair a secret. Now though he would have to up his game and pretend to be the wronged husband. Laura he felt sure would understand then, and who could resist his adorable little daughter? He knew custody and divorce proceedings were both going to be very costly, he was determined not to ask Laura for help, although he knew she would have gladly given it to him.

As he drove up Allerdale High Street, he thought he recognised Lanky Lennie and Midge, they were always together. Memories of his torture came flooding back. Were they still working together now that Billy Haskins was dead and did they know any more about the business with the bear? He began to panic. Just as he turned into the drive of the house he was renting, the two men passed by.

He needed more money; applying for custody and a divorce would cost a lot of money. There was no money left from Billy Haskins, his wife had seen to that, so the only thing he could do was sell his business. He would contact the agent immediately and put it up for sale.

*

With Mary Haskins still being uncooperative Bora decided to rethink his strategy.

What did they know?

Shirley Delacot was dead (murdered).

Ryan Evans was dead (committed suicide).

Billy Haskins was dead (heart attack probably brought on by a severe beating).

"I don't like it, Christine. I think we are missing something. What is the single factor tying all these people apart from our friend Mary together?"

Christine thought for a while before answering. "I think it's Paul Plumpton, sir."

Bora stroked his chin. "Hmm, could be."

John Bora needed to start putting the pieces of the jigsaw together.

"Come on, Louie, time to go home."

"What do you think, Steve?"

"I don't know, sir, it's a baffling case, but I don't think that Francis Delacot is innocent. I think he has something to do with it."

"He wouldn't have his own daughter killed surely?"

"Not unless something went wrong."

*

Paula was sat on the sofa dozing; she'd had a stressful day. "Good day, John?"

"No, not really, we don't seem to be making any headway with this murder case."

"Oh, I noticed that the lettings agency in Allerdale High Street is up for sale."

John stopped mid-mouthful of his meal. "What did you say?"

"The letting agency called Plumptons is up for sale."

At last things were starting to make sense for John.

He reached over and gave his wife a hug.

"What's that for?"

"You, my dear, are a genius, I always knew you were when I married you."

"What did I say?"

"Paul Plumpton's letting agency is up for sale, the man must need money."

"Well that's usually why people sell their businesses, but I noticed it has had the shutters down for months now, so I'm not surprised it's being sold. I don't suppose many people would want to frequent a letting agency knowing that a girl who was supposed to be viewing a property was murdered."

John went to bed, but he tossed and turned all night. He couldn't get Paul Plumpton out of his mind.

DS Lockhead and DI Grieves were sat waiting for DI Bora. He had summoned them for an early morning briefing. Grieves had complained to Christine that he didn't like to get up so early, and couldn't Bora sleep?

"Paul Plumpton. I want him brought in as soon as possible for a chat."

"Is that all?" Nathan Grieves said tetchily.

"All, all, is that all? Yes it bloody is. I think Plumpton could be our murderer. Now go and organise it. Not you, Christine. I want to talk to you."

Christine helped herself to another coffee and braced herself for a lecture from her DI.

"I've been thinking all night about Paul Plumpton. He knew all the other people, he was desperate for money to keep his money-grabbing wife in the style she expected. He had to pay private school fees for his daughter, and the house was heavily mortgaged. Now even if his business was doing exceptionally well he could still be struggling. Don't you agree?"

"Yes sir."

"He never really gave us a satisfactory explanation as to why he slipped out of the country to America and then pretended he didn't go. He never pressed any charges the couple of times he was beaten up and then after his heart attack he just seemed to disappear. I want to know where he went and with whom."

Now this case is getting interesting, thought Christine.

It could be Plumpton, thought Bora. All the signs pointed to the fact that it could quite possibly be him. He thought about a case he had worked on years ago where the perpetrator came over as a very popular likeable man, a family man and generous to his friends. Then one day his friend's daughter went missing. She was eighteen and she was found strangled at the bottom of a deep quarry. It took nearly two years to convict the man, because he had to have psychiatric done; he initially denied all knowledge of the murder, then one day quite by chance someone overheard a conversation about himself and the murdered girl. He was convicted and sent to jail. The whole community was in shock and disbelief as no-one thought him capable of such a heinous crime. The judge in his summing up had called him a clever, devious criminal that was a danger to society. Could the same thing be played out with Paul Plumpton? The family man who doted on his small daughter, the businessman, who took the high moral ground regarding weapons and especially guns.

"Mr. Plumpton, would you like a coffee? DS Lockhead will make you one if you would like. I hear you have your daughter living with you now, I bet you're pleased about that. Are you going for custody of her?"

Paul Plumpton was tempted to tell the DI to mind his own business, but he just looked at DS Lockhead and said, "Ye, that's right."

"And what about that wife of yours?"

"We are separated."

"Not that it is any of my business," said Bora, "but are you starting divorce proceedings?"

Paul Plumpton was getting really irritated now. "I don't see that it is any of your business."

"I'll take that as a yes then."

"Hmmm. Custody proceedings and divorce proceedings will probably cost you a huge amount of money. Is that why you are selling the letting agency?"

Paul had to be careful how he answered that question; he didn't want the tax man poking around in his affairs, he just wanted a quick sale and then he would be rid of the agency and he could concentrate on his daughter and gaining custody of her. They still needed somewhere to live and Emily still had to go to school, and he had no doubt that Julie would gain as much as she possibly could from the divorce. He knew he would have to employ a good solicitor, one that could prevent her from taking every penny. The money from the sale of the business could go into a trust fund for his daughter, the rest of the money would be deposited in a secret account, one that his wife was unaware of. He might even invest it in teddy bears.

"You never really explained why you went to America and came back so quickly, would you like to tell us about it now?"

"I went on a business trip, but it didn't really work out."

"And why was that?"

"Which company?"

Plumpton was at a loss to make up the name of a company. He had to think quickly.

"Denacot Properties."

"I haven't heard of them. Have you, DS Lockhead?" Christine shook her head.

"Now Mr. Plumpton I know that isn't the truth so stop wasting my time and tell us the real reason you went to America."

Paul Plumpton simply said, "No comment."

Bora felt despair, not another suspect struck dumb.

"Are you proposing to charge me with something? Because if so I want legal representation."

"Now Paul." Bora always used this tactic to make the interview seem as though it was more of a friendly chat. Christine smiled to herself; he was so good at this and she felt that they would have a confession within the hour.

Bora decided to try another angle. "When you were attacked by Billy Haskins' men, why didn't you report it? I heard you had taken a vast amount of money from him, but he didn't report it either."

"Do you like to collect teddy bears, Paul?"

The questions were coming at Paul at an alarming speed, he needed time to think.

"Haskins and I had a business agreement and he turned nasty when I demanded my money."

"Yes but you have to admit £50,000 was rather a lot of money. What was the transaction for?"

"It was for property, yes, that was it, for property, but the sale fell through and he demanded his money back."

"Known Billy long, had you?"

"Yes, he gave me my first break, when I was a struggling electrician." He had so far avoided answering the question about teddy bears. He hoped the Inspector had forgotten about that question.

"I will ask you again, Paul. Do you like teddy bears?"

"Inspector, I have a young daughter who adore teddy bears, so what is there not to like about them?"

"Tell me about the ones in the cabinet, that you kept for Billy Haskins."

Shit, he thought. *How the hell did he know about those?*

"As you have just rightly said, Inspector; they weren't mine. I had an arrangement with Haskins to mind them for him."

"Were you never tempted to look on the internet and see how much they were worth? Because apparently Billy had quite an expensive collection. Did you double-cross him, Paul, and claim a bear for yourself? Was that it? Was that why his henchmen decided to teach you a lesson? Oh yes, Paul, we know all about it."

The colour had drained from Paul Plumpton's face. Was his secret going to be exposed at last?

Bora was clutching at straws, but he wasn't going to let Plumpton know that.

"Do you know Francis Delacot?"

"No, I don't think I do."

"Come on, man, you either know him or you don't."

"It is the murdered girl's father, isn't it? I can't say I have ever met him. Ryan Evans set up the meeting for the girl to have one of my properties and it was him that paid me."

Paul saw this answer as a safe bet, because they

couldn't really ask Ryan Evans as he was dead. Bora had to muster all his strength to try and keep his patience if he was going to get a confession.

"Well if you've done nothing wrong then you have nothing to hide."

"Where were you on the night of March 23rd?"

"Did you know who the girl was?"

"No, I hadn't met her personally, my admin assistant dealt with this particular letting."

"Why wasn't the appointment for the farmhouse recorded in your appointment book?"

"I think it must have been an oversight."

"Some oversight, an appointment to potentially offload a property that needed full renovation without you incurring any cost. Come off it, Paul, I think the girl knew too much, was it the fact that she knew too much about you and that is why you lured to the farmhouse and killed her?"

"No, no, that wasn't how it was."

"Then how was it?"

"When will my solicitor be here? I'm not saying anything else until he arrives."

DS Lockhead looked on the roster. The duty solicitor was Graham Gaines. She rolled her eyes at the thought of the slippery weasel. "I'm sure Mr. Gaines will be here soon."

Graham Gaines, bloody hell, could Bora's day get any worse? He couldn't stand Gaines. He needed to get some questions over with before Gaines arrived in the hope of extracting the truth from Plumpton.

"Well Paul, have you ever heard of the Emerald Bear?"

"Inspector, my client, doesn't have to answer that question."

The Inspector continued, "Have you ever seen the Emerald Bear?"

Plumpton gave a loud cough. "No comment."

Oh God, we're on this game again. Bora felt sure that Plumpton knew about the Emerald Bear. Is that why he killed Shirley Delacot? Had he followed her into the farmhouse, spoken to her and then decided to kill her when the information or item he wanted wasn't forthcoming? Had he done the deed then gone back to his office and completely erased the appointment booking from his diary? The weather had been terrible, he could have driven there, spoken to her and then killed her, knowing that they wouldn't be able to trace tyre tracks as the torrential rain would have washed them away.

"What make of car do you drive?"

"It's a black Range Rover. Oh no, you are not going to pin this girl's death on me. I had nothing to do with it."

Bora, although he couldn't see the man, could sense the fear the other was feeling.

"DI Lockhead, arrange to have the car brought in

for forensic examination as soon as possible please."

"Wait a minute, you can't do that. I've done nothing wrong. Besides, I don't own the car now."

"Well that is interesting, because on the night of the girl's murder a black Range Rover was set alight and completely burned out. It was found the day after close to the entrance of Fallows Wood. Would you like to tell me about that, Paul?"

The Inspector continued, "Where were you on the 23rd March? We know you had an appointment with the dead girl."

"No, wait, I told you I didn't go to the farmhouse that day, I was running late due to a Planning meeting and I texted Shirley explaining to her that I was unable to make it and that she should make her way home and we could arrange the viewing for another day."

Bora was not convinced. Was this man very clever or very devious or both?

"Where were you that afternoon?"

"No comment."

"Did you go to the farmhouse knowing it would be deserted except for you and the girl, and when you challenged her she would not give you what you were looking for, so you decided to kill her?"

"No comment."

"Inspector, you can't make accusations like that, you know you can't without having firm evidence to back them up."

"All in good time, Mr. Gaines. I feel we shall have all the evidence we need very shortly."

"I want my client, either arresting or bailing."

"All in good time, Mr. Gaines, as I have already said. Paul, you either start telling me the truth or I will arrest you for the murder of Shirley Delacot. Now would you like to tell me where you were on March 23rd?"

"I was in a Planning Meeting."

"And did anyone see you?"

"Course they did. I told you it was a Planning Meeting."

"And where did you go after that?"

Paul wasn't going to answer that, it would cause unnecessary pain to someone and he didn't want that.

"No comment."

"Paul Plumpton, I am arresting you on suspicion of the murder of Shirley Delacot. DS Lockhead, read him his rights."

"Now see here, Bora, you can't arrest a man without hard evidence."

It was the solicitor talking. What did he know? He was still wet behind the ears.

"My daughter, she will be home from school shortly. Who will look after her?"

"I will inform Social Services and someone will be there to meet her and take her to a place of safety."

"But she is in a place of safety, she's with me,"

Plumpton protested.

"Take him to the cells."

Bora was deep in thought. When he had mentioned the Emerald Bear, he had gained no response. Odd though, now Plumpton was being uncooperative. Had they found their killer? It seemed Plumpton was unwilling to divulge information about where he was on that fateful afternoon. Was he protecting someone?

"Paula, did you ever meet Paul Plumpton in a professional capacity?"

"I seem to remember I met him once years ago, when I first came to Allerdale, he was the one I rented my flat from."

"What did you make of him? Could he be a killer?"

"What an odd question to ask me, John. I don't know, I only met him briefly, I mostly dealt with his admin assistant when it came to signing the contract for the flat."

"Well Paul, you said in a previous statement, that you didn't kill anybody. But I'm wondering if that is the truth. You can see things from my point of view. We need to know what you were doing in America and whether you met anybody."

Paul took a deep gulp; he knew things were getting serious now. He had been held overnight in the cells and he knew they couldn't hold him much longer without proof. And the sooner he was released, the sooner he would be able to see his daughter again. Social Services had called his wife and she had picked her up. He wondered whether Julie would still be at the address he had gone to previously. He would have to get in touch with her somehow, but he wondered what the point was if he was going to be convicted of murder. He smirked to himself; the less they knew the harder it would be to convict him, that was what his solicitor was for, to get him out of this nightmare. Would he divulge that he had agreed to meet Francis Delacot in America, or was it too dangerous? He didn't know who had assaulted him in that hotel room in America, but it was obvious that someone knew he was there. Was it all staged, he wondered, and was it Francis Delacot that had attacked him by hitting him from behind? He wanted the bear, but wasn't prepared to pay for it. He could have been waiting in any of the rooms. He remembered losing consciousness and then waking up; the intruder had gone. The room had been ransacked; whoever it was that wanted the bear wanted it desperately, but they had fled empty handed. Paul had taken the bear safely back to England, he still had it in his possession, he intended to advertise it in Sunderlands and sell to the highest bidder. He had discovered Sunderlands when he was surfing the dark web. What had happened to him? He had been totally consumed by wanting as much money as possible without thinking about the cost to his family.

"Did you take something from the body when you killed Miss Delacot?"

"No comment."

If he said no it would be an admission of guilt. If he said yes it would prove that he took something from the girl, the police would get a warrant to search his premises and find the bear. He had been clever and devious up till now, but when Bora said they would get a search warrant, he panicked. Would they find the bear and then would all his hopes of a new idyllic life with his precious daughter be destroyed?

"I'm disappointed in you, Paul. I thought you were a man who could be trusted, so far I think everything you have told me has been embellished. You know what that means, don't you? Not telling me the truth. We will obtain a search warrant and search your premises. I wonder what we will find. In the meantime we will bail you. You do realise that if you are convicted of murder, that it would be very difficult for your daughter to see you."

Paul suddenly didn't feel brave, he was in a dire situation and he hoped the solicitor would be able to help. If the bear was as valuable as everyone said, he was sitting on an absolute fortune, but if he engaged a top barrister that would definitely be an admission of guilt.

Paul shuddered; it wasn't a game. He breathed a

sigh of relief.

*

Bora had obtained the warrant to search Plumpton's premises. His adrenaline was pumping; at last he hoped to solve the murder. "Steve will drive me, I want to be there when we find the bear, maybe it was the bear that the girl was carrying and somehow Plumpton found out about it. This Emerald Bear appears to be an enigma, maybe we can expose it.

"Come on, Louie, we are going on a Bear Hunt," at which the other officers laughed.

The room contained many boxes and it was a painstaking task opening all the boxes and checking the contents. Eventually one of the officers found the bear.

"Sir, I've found the bear."

"Excellent work, Sergeant, put it in an evidence bag and we'll transport it back to the station along with anything else that might incriminate Plumpton."

Back at the station Bora was feeling pleased with himself; he could go to the Super and tell him the good news that he had solved the murder case. *Well Razor, you haven't lost your touch,* he thought. The right man in custody and the evidence they needed. A gems expert was coming down from London to verify the emerald or emeralds and he would be escorted back to London via a very secure security van. After all, if the gems were real there was no way that the fact wanted to be broadcasted.

"Excellent work, John, I knew that you and Grieves along with the rest of the team could solve the murder." John felt his nose put out of joint, bloody Grieves had been as much use as a chocolate fireguard, but here he was getting the praise and the glory along with him.

"Christine Lockhead, how has she done on this case?"

"She has performed very well."

"Good, good. You need to encourage her to go in for her Detective Inspector exam, I think she is an excellent officer."

Bora inwardly winced. There was that word again, excellent, it seemed to be the Super's favourite word, when he wasn't bawling John out. John gave Louie a slight tug on his harness. "Come on, boy." The dog got up and proceeded to guide John back to his office.

There was much excitement in Allerdale Police Station as the gems expert was about to arrive from London, flanked by two burly security guards.

"Hello Jones, now where is the bear?" He instructed the two burly security guards to stand on either side of him. The bear was handed over and the whole station was hushed in anticipation to see what was about to be revealed. Jones took out his knife and began to slit the fur; to everyone's amazement there was nothing at all in the bear except stuffing.

"Bloody hell, you got me down here to look at the most expensive bear in the world and there is nothing, nada. This bear has never contained gems of any sort, I don't know why you thought it would. A complete waste of my time. Your station will be billed for this."

Bora was disappointed. Was his watertight case about to fall apart? He still thought Plumpton had killed Shirley Delacot but now what was the motive? If it wasn't a bear, but Plumpton believed it was the bear, that would be a good motive for greed. The question remained though, who thought it was imperative that something was snatched from the victim's body? The victim's hands looked as though they had been grasping something and there was still that wool fibre that they had found at the farmhouse.

CHAPTER 15

John Bora was feeling very glum and dispirited. His murder case was in danger of collapsing. He began clutching at straws; maybe Plumpton would confess when faced with life imprisonment. It must have been Plumpton, as he didn't have an alibi for any time in the afternoon or the evening of the 23rd.

Christine Lockhead had waltzed into his office she was carrying the local newspaper.

"Sir, I'll read this to you, it's about Mary Haskins."

Bora groaned; he was feeling particularly tired after a bad night.

"Mary Haskins was given a sentence of eighteen months suspended for two years for illegal money lending."

"Huh, bloody great, all the things they could have said and yet it was just the one charge."

"I know, sir. Would you like a coffee?"

"Yes, two sugars please." He needed to get some energy from somewhere.

A knock came on the door and Bora shouted,

"Come in."

"Sir, a lady wants to talk to you, she says it is important."

"Good grief, man, isn't there anyone down there that can handle it?"

"No sir, she insists on talking to you."

"Very well, send her down then. Christine, stay."

A woman in her forties entered. Bora couldn't see her but he would know that perfume anywhere, it was his wife's favourite and very expensive it was too.

"Please sit down. I am Detective Inspector Bora and this is my Sergeant, DS Lockhead."

The woman gracefully sat down.

Christine was puzzled. What was a well-dressed woman like her needing to visit a police station for?

"Would you like a coffee or a tea perhaps? DS Lockhead will make it."

"So you're the famous John Razor Bora. I didn't realise you were blind."

She gave a small cough. "I'm sorry, I do apologise, that remark was uncalled for."

Bora just smiled.

"Now, Miss er."

"Actually it's Mrs, I'm a widow."

"Well Mrs…" He hesitated.

"Greenhalgh, Laura Greenhalgh."

"How may I help you?"

"It's about Paul Plumpton."

"Madam, you do know he is on a suspected murder charge, don't you?"

"Detective Inspector I'm quite aware of that. Why do you think I'm here?"

"I've no idea."

"Paul has an alibi for when that young woman was killed."

"How do you know?"

"Because he was with me all afternoon and all night, only going home about 7.30 a.m."

"Is there anyone that can vouch for that?"

"Yes, we had an evening booking at Henricos in Shrewsbury. He came straight from a Planning Meeting and I got him to change his clothes before we went out. He hates wearing suits all the time, he likes to be a bit more casual."

"Hmm, that's all very interesting, but can Henricos verify this?"

"Oh yes, I have the receipt for the meal here. Look, it says the time and the amount." She was now showing it to Christine.

"We will have to have this verified, you understand."

"Yes of course, only try and keep my name out of things for Paul's sake."

"Why?"

"Come, Inspector, isn't it obvious I'm having an affair with him?"

Bora had a surprised look on his face. Christine nearly choked on her coffee.

"That wife of his is a complete witch and she never shows him any affection, if you ask me the only good thing to come out of that marriage was his beautiful daughter. He hated her being with Emily even though she is her mother. He says she never really showed her much affection, she was more interested in what the neighbours thought, and she constantly scolds the little girl, well, for simply being a little girl. It's always been Paul that has taken her on adventures and showed her real love and affection. Oh she comes across as the fine lady with lots of money, but actually the money is always her husband's. She has a foul mouth when she is angry and the reason Paul wanted to get away and take his little girl with him, was because he realised it was having a bad effect on the little girl, the constant toxic atmosphere."

"You seem to know a lot about Paul's personal life."

"Well of course I do, I've been the one he's turned to sometimes almost crying with frustration at the antics of his wife."

"Well I must say this puts a very different slant on things. It explains some things but not all."

Laura thought for a moment. "Oh, you mean the black Range Rover."

"Yes, the very one that was found burnt out not far from the farmhouse the morning after the murder."

"That wasn't Paul's, it was my brother-in-law's and he came to pick it up the next day."

"Pick it up from where?"

"Why from my house, of course."

"Did your brother actually pick up the Range Rover from your house?"

"Yes, of course he did, he would have been very upset if it wasn't there. So you see, Inspector, I'm afraid the Range Rover you found burnt out was not my brother's."

"Let me get this straight, you are saying Paul Plumpton spent the afternoon and the evening with you. You went out for a meal and then came went back to your house."

"Yes, that's right."

"Why was Paul driving your brother-in-law's Range Rover?"

"He was having engine trouble with his and I didn't want him to start messing with it, especially with his good clothes on. So I phoned my brother-in-law and he said he would look at Paul's car and in the meantime, we could borrow his. My brother-in-law is a mechanic, that's why he agreed to have a look."

"You do realise all this needs to be checked out and if it is found to be false, we could charge you with wasting police time."

"Oh please, Inspector, do you think I would make up a story like that?"

"Well thank you, Mrs. Greenhalgh, we'll be in touch."

"Thank you, Inspector." She nodded at Christine and was gone.

"Well what do you make of that? The sly old dog, having an affair under his wife's nose."

"I'm sure she was doing the same," Christine interjected.

"Have you forgotten the Billy Haskins affair, where she thought she was going to be a rich daddy's plaything, only to find out that he had other plans and it was just a revenge for Paul Plumpton double-crossing him? He couldn't keep up the act for long and soon became bored of her and trying to be something he wasn't."

"Yes." Bora gave a little laugh. "You know the first time he was going to meet Plumpton's wife he had it all arranged. I bumped into him going towards the Goose C and he recognised me and said, 'Look out, Clueless.' I could tell that voice anywhere and of course I couldn't see him, but I could smell his awful aftershave, which he had seriously overdone. I remarked on the fact that he was wearing aftershave and no doubt he was spruced up. He volunteered that yes, he was wearing a new suit, because he was going to see a lady.

"Well you could imagine my surprise. I just said, 'I hope she appreciates the effort you've made, Billy.' Billy walked off and I proceeded to the pub with Louie."

"It seems they're all at it round here," said Christine, laughing.

"Sir, I've checked out Henricos. He was able to vouch for Plumpton. He said they were regulars and came in at least once a week."

"Well it's going to make us look pretty stupid if we say we've charged the wrong person."

"Yes sir, right away."

"I'll come to you, Bora."

"What are you doing, John? It looks like we'll have to release Plumpton now. The Area Commander is very annoyed. It makes it look as though we can't conduct a murder investigation properly. John, are you sure you are up to this, or do you think you have come back too soon? I could refer you to Occupational Health and you could be invalided out of the force on a good pension. You need to think about it, John, a nice cushy retirement, you would be able to keep Louie of course."

Why did it seem like everything in this investigation was wrong? John wished he'd never heard of the Emerald Bear. Every lead they followed seemed to lead to a dead end. First there was a bear, then the bear they found turned out to be worthless; surely there was more to it than this and where did Francis Delacot fit into it? He was sure he did. They had never found who had beaten Billy Haskins. Was he playing away with someone else's wife and got a beating for it? If the perpetrator wasn't Paul Plumpton, then who was it? Bora had been sure they had the right man. Henricos was known for doing business that wasn't completely legitimate. Could someone have threatened him and used 'gentle persuasion' or something more sinister? Could Laura Greenhalgh be believed? She came across as believable but had someone put her up to it? Laura Greenhalgh had been polite, well-mannered and charming. If her story was true John could see why Paul Plumpton had started an affair with her, she was obviously giving him the love and affection that he didn't get at home. John thought about his own marriage; he had been neglecting Paula recently, he would make it up to her.

"Steve, stop at a flower shop and buy me a nice bunch of flowers there for my wife."

John arrived home with a big bunch of flowers for his wife.

"John these are lovely, but what have I done to deserve them?"

"For just being you," he said.

He ate his evening meal and then settled down

with Louie at his feet. He thought how attached to this dog he had become; Louie was part of the family.

John was very quiet after their meal. Paula sensed that there was something wrong.

"John, speak to me, tell me what is wrong."

"I screwed up the murder investigation. Sykes has intimated that maybe I should retire from the force and enjoy my retirement, he seems to think the Occupational Health therapist would push through my application to retire unchallenged. Told me I would get a good pension."

No wonder Paul was feeling down after his operation, he knew he wouldn't be able to see again and had become depressed knowing that he would never be a police offer again, then the force had thrown him a lifeline and he had taken his second chance, but now it appeared that it would all come crashing down. Paula was worried. Although John displayed leadership qualities at work, she knew he could still be quite fragile.

"Let's sleep on it, John, and you can make your decision with a clear head. Did the Area Commander give you a time to make up your mind about retirement?"

"No."

"Well take your time to think about it and don't rush into things. I'm sure whatever you decide we will manage."

John went into the office the next day. It was as if Louie sensed there was something wrong, and he patiently sat by his master, giving a little growl every so often to reassure his master that he was still there.

Inspector Grieves walked into the office. "Morning John, you OK?"

John wanted to shout, "No I'm bloody not." But he just acknowledged Grieves politely.

"Did you get a rocket as well over Paul Plumpton? The Super is furious."

"I know."

He started to discuss the case with Grieves and was quite surprised how insightful he seemed to be. He had never exhibited these qualities before. Had he had a wake-up call, John wondered?

"If it isn't Plumpton then who else could it be?"

"Do you remember anything more about your observations at the Sunderland?"

"No, but I took a sneaky picture of a poster one of the men was holding as they came out of the building."

"Now he says. Well what did the poster say?"

"I wasn't near enough to get a close-up of it but if I examine the camera photo again I'm sure I can decipher it."

"Well what are you waiting for, man? This could save both our skins."

Was there a glimmer of hope on the horizon?

They certainly needed one and right now. John had been thinking about his position on the force; he wanted to go out in a blaze of glory, that's what he had always wanted. Now that pleasure could be cruelly snatched away from him, invalided out of the force!

Inspector Grieves searched his camera and began to panic; had he inadvertently deleted the picture and dismissed it as of no consequence, especially when they had charged Paul Plumpton with the murder?

Oh please God, I hope it's still here. He began furiously thumbing through the pictures. *Ah, found it,* he thought.

"John, I've found it."

"You took your time."

"Yes but I have it here now."

It said Sunderlands, but in very tiny print 'Gough Hall November 12th.'

"Where is Gough Hall?"

"It is in New York but not in the fashionable part, away from the main area."

"How do you know that?"

"I went there several years ago with a girlfriend, when we went to New York."

"Think, Nathan. Was there anything unusual about any of the men you saw?"

"No, can't say there was apart from that Francis Delacot fellow, if that's who it was."

"I was talking to my friend Aspey yesterday. He was asking how the murder investigation was going. What could I tell him? I said it was not going well."

"But haven't you arrested someone for her murder?"

"Sounds dodgy to me, Nate. Do you remember ages ago I told you about a Jake Barnes?"

"Yes, I remember you said you didn't know much about him except he had asked for a teddy bear tattoo."

"Yeah, that's right. Only the name came up recently. I was out in London and someone said about this dodgy geezer that had run off with all the town's Christmas Club money. Well I thought nothing of it, if he wants to do a runner that's up to him, but then I heard the name Jake Barnes and well, I thought you might want to know, it might help clear up your crime rates and all that. Someone said he come from Allerdale, just thought you'd want to know."

"Margaret, find out all you can about a Jake Barnes, there must be something on the internet. He was the one who ran off with the town's Christmas Club money. See if you can find out where he lived."

"He lived in Allerdale, sir, there is a picture of him, I'll print it out and give it to Inspector Grieves."

"Yes Margaret, and thank you, you have been a great help and you are always so efficient. Thanks again. Right, Grieves, we have work to do."

"Yes John."

"Do you think this Barnes might have skipped the country with the money?"

"It's possible."

"Teddy bear tattoo auction in Sunderlands in America. Do you think he could have gone there for some reason? He clearly has some interest in teddy bears to have had a tattoo of one inked on his arm."

"Is your friend Aspey reliable?"

"I think so, just as much as some of the other people I know."

Was this failed investigation going to be turned around into a success after all, wondered Bora?

"Sir, I have been trawling through lots of databases and I have come up with something you might find interesting."

"Well Margaret, let's have it."

"It seems that in 1946 a South African miner found an enormous emerald. He concealed it on his person and took it home. He lived alone, but he had a childhood teddy bear and he sewed the emerald into the bear for safe-keeping. He intended to sell it to the highest bidder at a secret auction," she continued, "but before he could take it somewhere, the miner and the teddy bear completely disappeared and neither have ever been found. Francis Delacot felt that it was rightfully his as he said the miner was his uncle, but that has never been proved. Over the years lots of people have looked for the bear, but with no success."

"What about Sunderlands, Margaret? Have you found out anything about them?"

"No, not yet, sir."

"Thank you, Margaret, you have done really well."

Margaret blushed. "Thank you, sir."

Bora was intrigued. So Delacot felt he had some connection to the Emerald Bear, but surely he wouldn't have had his own daughter murdered.

Christine Lockhead had walked into DI Bora's office.

"Margaret has been in, she left this information, she read it all out to me, but there are the notes."

Christine picked up the papers and began to read.

"Oh, this is interesting. Did we find out anything else about the fibre found at the crime scene?"

Bora shook his head. "No, but maybe we can assume it was from a teddy bear. If it was from a teddy bear did the murderer take the teddy bear and is he or she the one that has the bear and the emerald?"

"I think we should try and find out more about Sunderlands. Is Margaret on it?"

"Yes, she has done sterling work at this point, the jigsaw is coming together. Now we need to find out what Francis Delacot is up to and who else knows about it."

The investigation was becoming more intriguing. Francis Delacot, Paul Plumpton, one very dead Billy Haskins, nobody arrested for his beating. This case was escalating on an international scale, but Bora knew that he had to tread carefully where foreign diplomats were concerned. It wasn't called diplomatic immunity for nothing.

Margaret was working hard; she felt that she was onto something, now if she could only find out more about Sunderlands. She was an ambitious officer and was hoping that eventually she would be promoted.

DI Bora and DS Lockhead were discussing Margaret's latest findings. Inspector Grieves was not present as he had rung in sick. *A likely story,* thought Bora, *either too much alcohol, or too much sex last night more like.* He had quizzed Christine about it, but all she had said was that he was feeling 'under the weather this morning and was going to ring the doctors.'

Having no choice, they had had to let Paul Plumpton go, but Bora was still not convinced that Plumpton was innocent. He was a very shrewd operator. *Maybe he could have bribed those people to give him an alibi. Still, back to Margaret's findings,* he thought.

"Sunderlands it seems is a very secretive place. Does it operate under the name of Sunderlands, or does it change the name to where it is being held?"

"Apparently, there are branches all over the world, but each time the name is changed. We have only

THE EMERALD BEAR

been able to track it as Sunderlands, because it always has the same type of auctions."

"The auctions work a bit like a poker game, there is usually a £50,000 buy in."

"Sounds like something out of an Ian Fleming novel, next you are going to tell me there are international spies involved."

Christine gave a laugh. "No sir, not spies, just very rich businessmen, or very greedy ones."

"Well do we know how it works then? Get to the interesting bit."

"Each participant is invited, if you don't have an invite you don't get in. The bears are put up for auction and the bidding starts. Nobody knows anyone else and the participants can't see each other, they are all behind screens. In order to bid on a bear you have to put your arm on the plate located just outside the box, the plate reads the code and you are allowed to bid."

"Are all these people bidding on the Emerald Bear?" Bora asked.

"No, the way the bidding works is that people bid on the bears and if theirs is the winning bid then they take that bear."

"So, the Emerald Bear is always up for grabs then?"

"No sir. Once the winning bid has procured a bear they are entitled to go to the next auction. They are

307

given a number for the next auction and so it moves up."

"What moves up? I'm confused."

"Well sir, the Emerald Bear has a number and is a specific bear and so far no-one at any of these auctions has been able to track down the bear or the number. People from all over the world are looking for it, but they can't be seen actively looking for it. That is why the auctions are kept secret. It is a shrewd move on the auctioneers' part, because each time a bidder is invited they get £50,000 and either it is a scam on a massive scale or Sunderlands really do have the bear and they are making it into some sort of game for the bidders. As long as people keep turning up to these auctions, the more money Sunderlands get. However, there is a risk involved. Each time a bidder procures a bear, not only do they have to pay the price for the bear, but they also have to smuggle it out of the country where the auction is held. That's because these bears contain either illegal drugs or precious stones. Once they have accumulated enough bears and enough numbers then they are invited to bid on higher amount lots, in order to get closer to the Emerald Bear."

"Well it seems that this is an international affair, not just a local investigation."

"I need to inform the Super and they may get Interpol involved."

"Will it still be our case?"

"I hope so."

The Inspector's imagination was really fired up now, he felt the old Bora, the one who was ruthless and determined. His adrenaline level was high. *Quitting the force, I don't think so,* he thought. Not with such a juicy, intriguing case to be solved.

"Do you still think Plumpton is involved?"

"Yes I do. He has motive, that is greed, he had opportunity owning a rental letting company and I think he is a shrewd person, that is laughing at us and thinking up new ways to outwit us."

Christine agreed.

"He also travelled to America with a bear I presume, he definitely came back with a bear. Was it the same one or was it a different one? His visit to America was unexplained and he came back battered and bruised. Did he get into an altercation over the bear, or did he hide it ready to smuggle back into the country? Did someone find out he had the bear and decide they wanted it? Was Francis Delacot in America and was there a Sunderlands going on? Has anyone been able to establish whether Francis Delacot has any connection to the Jewish community?"

"No Sir, we are still working on that. What we did find out though, about Mr. Delacot, was that he was a man used to getting his own way and he has acquired quite a few works of art and amassed other things including precious gems."

"Where did he get the money from to buy these things, I wonder?"

"Well if he had been frequenting Sunderlands auctions, he must have been bidding on the more expensive bears in the hope of finding the Emerald Bear."

"Yes, and he could have been smuggling illegal drugs when he cut the bears open and selling them to the highest bidder. I am sure there would be quite a few drug cartels interested in the drugs."

"He could have bid on bears with precious gems inside and sold them to the highest bidder. That would account for his accumulated wealth, I suppose."

"He must have had enough money to buy the paintings outright, because these types of paintings do not come up in ordinary art auctions."

Bora had more questions than answers. It seemed as though every avenue they followed turned up something new and they were not really any nearer to finding the young girl's killer, but at least now they had possibly established a motive. It was all a mess, but one that John Bora was determined to untangle to get justice for the murdered girl. It seemed she had put herself in danger, to carry out something. Did Francis Delacot knowingly place his daughter in danger? Had he coerced her or had she done it of her own free will? They needed to get Francis Delacot and interview him, but that was proving practically impossible as he was away "travelling". Being a diplomat meant that he didn't have to disclose his whereabouts or his business and the South African Embassy were remaining tight lipped about him. Was he an embarrassment to them, Bora wondered? Did they know about his illegal dealings and turned a blind eye?

Delacot had been a diplomat for quite a few years. Having returned from the South African Army a hero, he had been able to easily enlist to become a diplomat. He actually enjoyed the Kudos; he wore expensive suits and drove expensive cars, many ordinary people wondered how and where he managed to amass such a fortune, but it appeared if someone crossed him, they would pay the price. Is that what had happened to Billy Haskins? Had he thought Billy had double-crossed him and had arranged for him to be beaten up? This was all speculation at the moment, but it was becoming clear that Francis Delacot was a powerful man and not above manipulating the law to get his own way.

Grieves had seen him in London wearing a disguise; was he impersonating someone else, and if so who and why?

Wearing a Jewish Kippah and sporting a false beard hardly said inconspicuous, in fact it said the very opposite. Had he bid on a bear, then cast aside his disguise when he had procured the bear he wanted and then attempted to slip out of Sunderlands hoping not to be noticed. Grieves had done well photographing the conspicuous man, but without any other evidence the picture alone presented no real clues. Bora started putting things together; first it was the disguise in London, then he had impersonated a doctor in a hospital to get near Billy Haskins. Bora wondered if it was a matter of time before the diplomat slipped up and showed his real hand. He still could not believe though, that Delacot could have had his own daughter killed. That was a step too far. Maybe he had planned something and it had gone wrong. Now that was more plausible. The thing that had been ripped from his daughter's hand was probably a teddy bear, but if so, how come they had found one in Paul Plumpton's things and on further investigation it was found to be just an ordinary bear with stuffing in? Then there was Paul Plumpton; had he travelled to America to take part in the auction? He had been handed £50,000 by Billy Haskins. He had twice been beaten up and nearly died, but he would not report his attackers, then the woman had shown up, saying that he had spent the evening and afternoon with her. He had no grounds to disbelieve her, especially when she produced a receipt for the restaurant they frequented. Plumpton had been used to good living and had made money with his letting agency, but the fly in the ointment was his wife. Was

that why he had sought solace from another woman?
Was the affair going on before his wife had embarked
on an affair with Billy Haskins? Had he some inside
information about the bear when he returned from
America and had he risked a lot by being beaten up
for a bear? Was that why he had decided to confront
Billy so that he would confess? This, however, didn't
happen and Billy sustained a heart attack. How had
Plumpton felt about that? Annoyed, disappointed?

Then there was the case of Ryan Evans who had
committed suicide in mysterious circumstances. Had
Evans got too close to the truth about the bear and
Plumpton had murdered him and made it look like
suicide?

"Margaret, get me the file on Ryan Evans. I want
to know what the Coroner's findings were again."

Margaret dutifully found the file and took it to
Bora.

"Sit down, Margaret. Would you like a coffee?"

Margaret blushed even though she knew Bora
couldn't see her.

"Er, yes sir, thank you. Would you like one?"

"Yes please, two sugars."

She felt her knees going week at the sound of his
deep masculine voice. *What a shame,* she thought, *the
best ones are always married!*

She proceeded to read the Coroner's report to
him. Bora stroked his chin. *Nothing unremarkable there,*

he thought. Evans had debts, maybe they were too overwhelming for him, or maybe someone whom he had cheated previously had threatened to blackmail him, or Paul Plumpton had become greedier, wanting to keep the bear and the money for himself. Maybe he had threatened Evans. Although there were no signs of an altercation or a fight on Evan's body, it still seemed strange, that he had taken his own life. The Coroner had written it up as suicide though. And as far as that was concerned the case on Ryan Evans would be closed. Bora thought though that if he searched hard enough he would see the school being signed over to Plumpton, but there was no evidence of this. Had Plumpton so far outwitted everyone, playing the scared victim to Billy Haskins and then waiting for his moment to pounce? Had there been one bear, or more than one bear and did Plumpton know about the bear or bears all along? They had found a bear in Plumpton's possessions, but what if there had been another bear, one that he had ripped from the murdered girl's person, and had there been a number with it? Had he taken the expensive bear and hidden it somewhere to take to America? Had he found the number that was with the bear? That would explain the position they found the girl in. Had he discovered Delacot's secret and gone to America to do a deal with him, but the deal had backfired?

Christine had remarked that Plumpton's

appearance had changed. When he had first come into the station, he was well dressed and well groomed, then over time his features had changed, he had become gaunt looking and dishevelled and his clothing was dirty and worn. Was that the stress of trying to keep up a mistress and a young daughter: or was he genuinely down on his luck since his wife had left him? His mistress Mrs. Greenhalgh had vehemently defended him and spoke about his suits and his good clothes, but there hadn't been any evidence of expensive suits or good hardwearing clothes, the last time he had been in the police station. He hadn't left with Mrs. Greenhalgh but seeing her pass the cell he was being held in, he had shrunk back into the wall, hoping that she would not see him and the mess he looked.

They had found a knife, but it had been wiped clean, there was no DNA on it whatsoever, apart from the victim's. So that was another reason that Plumpton had been able to be released. There was no DNA match and no fingerprints on the blade. If it had been Plumpton he had been meticulous and thought of everything, but Bora knew that if he was the murderer, sooner or later he would make a slip and then he would be caught. Bora had seen this all too often in his career — a suspect had a watertight alibi and then suddenly the whole thing had blown up in their face, revealing the crime they had committed.

Bora felt it was only a matter of time before Plumpton would do something that would reveal his true hand. Bora drank his coffee; he was lost in his own thoughts and then he suddenly remembered that Margaret was still sat there.

"Well Margaret, thank you so much, it has been very helpful going over Ryan Evan's file again." Was now the time to broach the subject of promotion with her? "How do you think you are doing, Margaret? Do you enjoy the work you are doing?"

"Yes sir."

"Well maybe it's time we looked at a promotion for you."

Margaret thought her heart would burst. This was what she had longed for. Maybe she wasn't destined to be a gofer and an intel officer all her life, maybe she could do some actual police work on the beat as a constable. Up until this point, although she worked in the police station she was a civilian officer and now Inspector Bora was talking about her becoming a police constable.

She left Inspector Bora's office with high hopes.

CHAPTER 16

Jake Barnes stepped out of his apartment into the pouring rain. His leg was aching; it always ached when the weather was bad, but he had to admit since coming to America his leg hadn't been quite as bad as the fresh air and warm sunshine seemed to be doing him good. He hadn't been particularly phased uprooting himself from Allerdale and he didn't have a conscience about the money he had stolen from all the 'gullible villagers'. He had bided his time and played his part well, although he despised every minute of it and the village. His father, though, thought that after leaving the army working in the toyshop would be the best thing for him.

"You will get to meet all the lovely villagers and this is such a nice place."

He had worked in the shop dutifully and when his mother had died several years previously it was then that he had become interested in international affairs. He had been to America before when he was in the army and thought that it would be a good place to settle. He would have a base and he didn't particularly have to worry about money as his mother had transferred her savings to him before she died. Then he had the sale of the house. He knew he wouldn't have the sale of the toyshop because he would be wanted for theft. So he wasn't bothered, he would let the toyshop go into administration and then let the creditors fight it out between themselves as to who would get what. Besides, the time wasn't right, he needed it to have the maximum impact and this was definitely not the right time. He began to settle into his new life; America was a big place and if someone wanted to get lost then it would be virtually impossible to find them. He had found himself a good apartment just on the outskirts of Manhattan and had bought himself a car to enable him to get round. It was an automatic car, much less strain on his leg. At first he had found driving round Manhattan slightly difficult as he tried to manoeuvre past the parked cars, but eventually he had got the hang of it. He kept himself to himself and was only on nodding acquaintance with his neighbours, he preferred it that way. Then there would be no nosy parkers or busybodies wanting to know about him or his business. If anyone ever asked him what his profession was he would say simply 'retired toyshop owner.' If people questioned him further he would say that he had come out here to get away from the

English weather. That seemed to satisfy most people, although he tried his best to stay away from people, preferring his own company.

"So John, like I said, I have found out the next Sutherland auction is in America."

"Can you be sure of that?" John was sceptical. He didn't want members of his team going all the way to America on a wild goose chase, and the Super would have to okay it first.

Christine Lockhead was excited; she had taken two weeks leave to accompany Inspector Nathan Grieves to America. Although Bora didn't approve, he couldn't really stop her spending part of her annual leave in America.

"You know, Christine, Inspector Grieves won't be there on holiday, he will have serious business to conduct."

"I know, I know." She was getting tired of the Inspector repeating the same thing over and over to her. However, she did hold out the hope that when Nate Grieves and she arrived in America they could go to Las Vegas and get married in the little chapel, stood next to a life-size model of Elvis Presley. She had liked Elvis ever since she had been a young girl and her dream wedding was to go to the little chapel in Las Vegas. She didn't want a big wedding with lots of people there, that would come later, she thought, when they were back in England. She packed carefully and wrapped the new dress she had bought for the occasion in tissue paper, so it wouldn't get damaged.

As they came in to land, Christine became excited.

"Well Christine, you know this isn't a holiday for me, in fact we may hardly see each other."

Christine felt crestfallen. Wasn't he going to sweep her off her feet after-all and marry her in the little chapel? They hadn't really discussed this. As they sat in the airport lounge waiting for the taxi to take them to their hotel Nate suddenly blurted out, "I've seen my ex a couple of times and she wants us to get back together."

At this revelation Christine was absolutely gutted, she was nearly crying with rage and frustration. She told herself she had to hold it together, or it would be a very unpleasant trip.

"What did you say? What did you say?" she demanded.

"I told her I needed to think about it."

"You needed to think about it. What about me? Or don't I matter?" She could see what she had planned as their romantic holiday slipping away from her. She had accepted that he would be working, but hoped that they would spend at least some time together, when he proposed to her.

Inspector Grieves looked into her eyes; they seemed cold. "We are in separate rooms, you know."

That was another blow to Christine. After these

last couple of months spending time together in the same bed and making mad, passionate, love, was he now going to throw her over for his ex? This was not at all turning out how she had expected it to.

They arrived at the hotel jet-lagged and after checking in they went to their respective rooms. Christine felt miserable. She hung her clothes in the huge wardrobe, gently taking the tissue paper from her special dress, which she had hoped would be her wedding dress. *No such luck,* she thought. Had he been using her all along and still seeing his ex? He had only been back to London though once, she reasoned, so how could he? There had been a few days, though, when he had been missing, but she knew that he was on secondment form the London Met, so she just assumed that when he wasn't there with her he was involved in Met work.

Shortly she heard a knock on her door. "Christine, I'm going to a casino, do you want to come?"

She shouted through the door without opening it. "No, I think I'll stay here, thanks anyway."

"Suit yourself, I think it will be a good night, but if you don't want to come then it's fine by me."

Christine felt like telling him where to go, but she was too much of a lady to tell him to get stuffed although that was what she was thinking.

Nate Grieves arrived back at the hotel at four a.m. looking a lot worse for wear. He had a six o'clock shadow and he looked dishevelled. He needed a shower and a shave to liven himself up, as he needed to be in work for eight thirty; he was to report to the local police for them to share any knowledge they had about Sunderlands. Grieves liked to gamble and he had lost heavily at the roulette tables. He had kept his obsession under control while in England, but as soon as he had come out to America he had started gambling again. He was sure Bora knew, but he had never said anything, besides, he didn't have any proof and he could hardly report him to his superiors without concrete proof. He quickly showered, shaved and put on a clean shirt and tie. He hailed a cab to take him downtown to the local police station.

"Ah, Grieves, it's good to meet you. We've heard a lot about you from the Met."

Nathan Grieves hoped that what they had heard was good. Introductions over and after a short briefing Grieves found himself on the boardwalk desperately searching for the address he had been given. The local police force weren't really very co-operative as they pointed out to Grieves that it was his case and outside their jurisdiction as no crime had been committed that they knew of. As he checked out the avenues looking for the address, he wondered whether he had been too brutal with Christine and whether he had been insensitive to her feelings. He was regretting telling her about his ex; maybe he should have saved that bombshell for when they were back in Allerdale. He had a slight twinge of guilt. He thought of the good times they had shared, and the amazing sex; he was engrossed in his thoughts when a car horn blared at him and the driver shouted, "You idiot. You nearly got yourself killed then, for fuck's sake don't jaywalk. You're lucky I didn't report you."

Jake Barnes was in a foul mood and to make it worse he had nearly mown down some idiot jaywalking. He had received the letter that morning, so someone knew where he was, but Sunderlands always had a way of finding out where prospective bidders were and in what country. He had checked his finances this time buy in wasn't £50,000, it was £75,000. He had the money, but was he going to risk it just to be a participant in Sunderlands? After weighing up all the odds, he decided he would participate, he knew the prize was almost certainly within his grasp. He couldn't afford anyone else taking his place, the stakes were too high.

Francis Delacot was preparing for his trip to America; it was important that it seemed as though he was on a diplomatic mission. He had given the South African Embassy a very sketchy itinerary and hoped they wouldn't question him too much. They had insisted that he travel with a bodyguard for his own safety. He loathed this idea, because the guard may become suspicious about his business and the last thing he wanted was a scandal or an investigation into his private life. He knew that the more people were aware of his comings and goings the harder it would be to procure what he wanted. Seeing him accompanied by a six-foot bodyguard would undoubtedly put off some of his prospective clients. He preferred to call them clients, although he knew he would exhort money from them in one way or another. He had no scruples and was not beyond blackmailing someone to achieve what he wanted. All his 'clients' owed him something and for that reason they were all scared. They knew his temper as some had already crossed him, he was definitely not a man to be crossed.

This was the second time he had been to America in the last four months. He thought of Billy Haskins and how he had double-crossed him and then that no good sister of his hadn't turned up, leaving him with the useless Noel Smythe. Smythe wasn't really a player, he had just tagged along on Mary Haskins' apron strings hoping to make a quick buck. *So much for that*, he thought. It had gone horribly wrong and now the bear seemed out of his reach. Especially when he thought he was so close to obtaining it.

Grieves eventually found the address and with his camera slung over his shoulder he pretended to be a tourist sat on a bench opposite the tall dark-coloured building. He screwed the telephoto lens onto the camera and waited. Shortly, men in dark-coloured suits began to file into the building. It looked as though they were having to show either some identification or say some sort of password. He wished he had a recorder that would have picked up things being said, alas, he had only been issued with a camera. This was his big chance to make a name for himself within the English police force and he was determined not to sabotage his chance. He began snapping away at the front of the building, taking care not to reveal himself. None of the people looked familiar to him, he thought that no-one from the London Sunderland was there, then out of the corner of his eye he spotted a man with a beard wearing a Kippah. Yes. It was Francis Delacot, he was sure of it. He began furiously snapping away, when a burly man came over. Grieves was a tall man, but this man was even taller and he had a look of malice in his eyes.

"What you doing here taking photos?"

Grieves had to think quickly. "It's my first time here in America and I thought I would just take some pictures of the wonderful buildings that surround this beautiful park."

The other man eyed him up and down and then decided he was satisfied with his answers; after all, he did look like a tourist. No idea how to dress in such heat. The tourists, especially the British ones could always be spotted wearing open-necked shirts, sunglasses and a camera slung over their shoulder. As he moved away the man issued Grieves with a warning. "If I see you take any pictures of things that I think you shouldn't I will personally wrap that camera round your neck. Got it?"

"Yes I will be careful what I take pictures of from now on. My girlfriend back home will be so pleased to see the pictures of the wildlife in the park and the magnificent buildings."

The other man shrugged and walked briskly off in the direction of the grey and black building.

Phew, that was close, thought Grieves. He needed to be much more careful about taking pictures. He was still curious though about Francis Delacot. Would he come out as he had done in London without the trappings of a Jewish man? Grieves waited and waited till well into the afternoon; there had been no action now for several hours and he was getting hungry. He would get himself a hotdog and a strong cup of coffee and then resume his watch. It was late afternoon, before the big oak door swung open and people began to silently file out. Most got into waiting cars that sped off at speed. Once again Delacot came out of the building without his disguise. *What is this man up to?* thought Grieves. That had been the second time he had come out of a building minus beard and Kippah.

It had been a long hot day and when Inspector Grieves got back to his hotel room all he wanted to do was sleep.

Christine had been out most of the day sightseeing, but she had to admit that it wasn't much fun on her own. She was now sat in the hotel bar sipping on a cocktail.

Grieves had awakened from his sleep and decided to go down to the bar.

"Christine, you look gorgeous in that dress, the colour is so you." He felt he had to make an effort after dropping such a huge bombshell on her previously. Although Christine had donned her make-up, Nate could see that she had been crying.

"Thank you, Nate, that's nice of you to say so," she said in a cool tone. "Did you have a productive day?" She wasn't really bothered whether he had or he hadn't but nonetheless, she would still make small talk with him, especially if they were going to be in the same hotel. She felt used by him and it wasn't a feeling that she was used to; usually it was her that called the shots, not the other way round.

Previously they had discussed cases together but this time in this place it seemed different. He decided not to tell her about the threatening man or Francis Delacot. He sensed that there was something going on in this town and for her safety, the less she knew the better. She never pressed him for more details, she just turned back to her drink and then ordered another one as soon as she had finished.

"Woah, slow down, Christine. Those cocktails can

be quite lethal."

She turned to him and answered in a sarcastic tone, "And what business is it of yours? You don't own me."

Christine tottered unsteadily back to her room; she didn't feel so good. Nathan had followed her to make sure she didn't fall, as she was quite drunk. She must have passed out, because the next thing she heard was someone shouting, "Ma'am, housekeeping."

She looked down at herself and discovered she was still wearing the same clothes from last night. She felt a mess.

"Can you come back in an hour please?"

"Very well, ma'am."

She needed to get in the shower and wash off her makeup from the night before and wash her hair that felt slightly sticky. Everything was done in slow motion as she felt she had the hangover from hell.

Presently she heard another knock on the door. *Damn,* she thought. *Who is this now?*

"Christine." It was Nate. Would she let him in or was she going to let him stew?

"I'm busy," she lied.

"Oh, that's a shame. I was going to ask you if you wanted to come on a sightseeing tour of the town with me."

Christine thought about his offer momentarily then answered quite bluntly, "No."

Nate was trying his best to make it up with her, but she wasn't having any of it.

*

Francis Delacot was beside himself with rage.

"What do you mean a tourist was taking photographs?"

The bodyguard shrugged. "Just seemed like a tourist."

"Well what do I bloody well pay you for, chatting to tourists or keeping me safe?"

"Would you know him again?"

"Suppose so." The bodyguard seemed uninterested.

"He might be in the park today, said something about his girlfriend liking wildlife and he was taking pictures of the park and surrounding areas."

"I want you to go to the park and see if you can spot him, wait there all day if you have to. If you spot him follow him back to where he is staying and find out who he is."

The bodyguard was not happy; it was an extremely hot day and he didn't want to be waiting around in a park for someone who might or might not show up.

"John, it's Nathan Grieves here. I just wanted to keep you updated about where I am up to in my observations. I took some more photographs yesterday and guess what, our friend Francis Delacot seemed to be using the same disguise that he had used previously. I nearly got caught, I think it was a bodyguard of Delacot's but I managed to persuade him that I was a tourist."

John clicked his tongue. "Let's hope so for your sake."

He turned to the person sat next to him, his name was DS Jackson. *Why they have saddled me with this useless DS I will never know,* thought Bora. At least Christine knew what good policing was all about. He had expressed his concerns to the Super.

"Now John, give the lad a chance, he got top marks in his promotion exam."

John was not convinced to him he still seemed 'wet behind the ears'.

The murder investigation was beginning to come together, except that Paul Plumpton had gone missing again and despite the police's best effort they had been unable to locate him. Bora had all the ports checking for him and all the airports, but up to now there had been no trace of him. DS Jackson frustrated him, he had to repeat everything to him at least twice and so far he hadn't contributed anything useful. He couldn't even make a decent cup of coffee!

"Sir."

"Yes DS Jackson, what is it?"

"Well sir, I was thinking, could DI Grieves be in any trouble if someone guessed who he really was?"

John thought about the question for a moment. "I

suppose so, but DI Grieves is an experienced officer and he would know if he was walking into a trap." Or at least Bora hoped so.

*

It was a hot day and Nathan Grieves set off for the park; he liked that park, the lush greenery, the peace and tranquillity. His camera was cumbersome so he made the decision to leave it locked in the hotel safe. As he went to sit on the bench he had sat on the day before he noticed someone lurking in the bushes. He was sure it was that man from yesterday, but he was just in a tee-shirt and jeans, maybe Grieves was mistaken. The man sensed he had been spotted and dodged deeper into the undergrowth, now completely hidden from view. Nathan spent an hour reading his guidebook and planning his next casino trip. When he arose, he was unaware that the man in the shirt sleeves was following him. As he approached the hotel reception desk a man in a blue uniform said, "Wait a minute, Mr. Grieves, I have a letter for you." And with that the receptionist handed over the letter. By this time the man in the shirt sleeves had ensconced himself firmly in the bar and was reading a newspaper, a pint of beer sat on the table in front of him. So that was his name. Grieves, was it? He quickly finished his beer and left the hotel, after first making a note of the hotel resident and the hotel. Surely the boss would be pleased with him now.

*

The man checked his finances again; he could hardly contain his excitement, to be invited to and be able to participate in another Sunderlands auction was relatively unheard of, twice in one place. He could feel the tension as he shaved and put on his suit, which had been hanging in his wardrobe waiting for this very day. Today could be the day, the day that he became one of the richest men in the world. He felt he could almost touch the grand prize, the prize that he had been waiting most of his life to acquire. He was not a forgiving man and he had tracked Francis Delacot for many years now; he knew what his fraudulent activities consisted of, how he had prayed on people weaker than himself and pressurised people into parting with their most expensive or prized possessions. How he used extreme violence to get what he wanted, but always under the auspices of diplomatic immunity. He never indulged directly in physical violence, but employed an army of men that went under the guise of personal bodyguards. He knew that they all carried weapons of some sort although they all managed to conceal them well.

*

Bora sat in his office pondering over what the young DS had said. Would Nate be in any danger? How could he be though if no-one knew he was there? He had travelled with DS Lockhead just supposedly as friends on a vacation to the States. He thought about Christine and tried to reassure himself that she was more than capable of looking after herself, should the need arise. Still, there was something that worried him although he wasn't sure what it was. He had formed the opinion that Francis Delacot was dangerous, but there was no reason to think that Grieves and Delacot were aware of each other. Suddenly he was jolted out of his thoughts, by an excited DS Jackson.

"Sir, we have found Paul Plumpton, he's living Telford way with some woman called Laura Greenhalgh."

Bora smiled. The names didn't mean anything to this new DS, but he knew exactly who they were. He thought of the well-dressed woman who had come to see him about Plumpton and thought, *Well, the sly old dog he must have wheedled his way back into her affections. Maybe they were an item after all.*

"We traced him through an estate agents. The agent said that he had rented a bedsit to him a few weeks ago."

DI Bora's face showed a puzzled expression. "Are you sure you have the right person, Jackson?"

"Oh yes sir, I showed the estate agent a picture of him and told him we needed to locate him to help us with our enquiries, the estate agent seemed only too happy to give us the information."

"Okay, thank you." He nearly called the new DS, Lockhead, that would never do. Bora was slightly puzzled; had Plumpton sold his business? If so, he would have got quite a lot of money for it as it was a thriving business. Why would he need to rent a bedsit? Surely he could afford somewhere more luxurious, unless that wife of his had taken a high settlement and used their daughter as leverage. She knew Plumpton would not refuse anything to keep his daughter with him and keep her safe and happy. Maybe he had run straight back to the waiting arms of his lover, and was why he was now residing near Telford? John felt that he still had something else to find out about Paul Plumpton; he was still not convinced that Plumpton was innocent, but it was just a matter of time before he made a slip-up and then John would be there and able to charge him with the girl's murder. In fact, you could say that John Bora was becoming more and more obsessed with the notion that Paul Plumpton had murdered Shirley Delacot. He had been told by his superior not to pursue the matter with Plumpton, but he couldn't help it. He would find the murderer and bring this murder investigation to a successful end. Then he would maybe think about retiring, or perhaps not. He missed talking his ideas over with Christine Lockhead and couldn't wait for her return and then perhaps this new DS would be moved to another department.

*

Christine had dreamed of standing in the little chapel, next to Nate and the celebrant saying their vows and them exchanging rings; now stood in front of the full-length mirror she decided to put on the soft white silk dress and pretended to be stood in the little chapel, conjuring up the memory of buying the dress and how excited she had felt about it. It had been very expensive, and she had chosen carefully realising that it would be quite hot when they reached America but she didn't mind. She hoped Nathan would look just as dashing in his cream-coloured wedding suit. It represented her dreams of becoming Mrs. Nathan Grieves.

Nate had spoiled it all and now it seemed as though her dreams lay in tatters.

She felt bereft in a strange and unknown country where the only friend she had was Nate, and she didn't really want to be bothered with him after she felt he had treated her so abominably. Before going to America, they had talked about marriage and when Nate had suggested that she came too, she thought that they would be married there. She had passed a miserable few days of her holiday, and was looking forward to going home. She had even missed DI Bora and his lectures even if they were well meaning. Christine was feeling upset and sorry for herself. She then began to scold herself, said to herself that she must pull herself together, after all she was a confident, competent, sophisticated police officer and why should she feel so down about a failed relationship with a fellow officer? She had been up that same road before. As she carefully began to take off her dress, being mindful of not spilling her tears on it and thinking about what might have been, she walked forward to adjust the tissue paper so she could wrap it up again ready for its transportation back to England when two men barged into the room. Startled, she stood frozen to the spot, dress half on, half off.

"Strip her," ordered the man to his partner, his tongue hanging out and saliva round his mouth anticipating seeing the woman's naked body. "She could 'ave it 'idden under that frock."

"No, let her get changed out of that frock. She isn't going anywhere."

She quickly pulled the dress over her head and placed it in the tissue paper.

The first man kicked the tissue paper with his heavy boot as if checking to see if anything was hidden there. Disappointed at finding nothing, he lifted his foot and proceeded to stamp on the flimsy tissue paper, leaving a dirty imprint on it and said in a derisory tone, "That won't be no good now."

"'Urry up, get someat on, whore," he yelled, while pointing a gun directly at her. They had locked the door behind them.

Christine reached into her wardrobe and pulled out a pair of trousers and a top, thankful that one of the men had refused to strip her and expose her naked body.

She was shaking; she didn't know who these men were and why they had barged into her room. There was only one other time that she had had a gun pointed directly at her and that situation she knew had been managed and contained. Now she was at the mercy of these men, no backup, no bullet-proof jacket, nothing. Who were they and what did they want with her? One of the men opened the door, the other man had a coat with a gun underneath and shoved into her back. "Don't make any false moves."

Christine knew from experience that she needed to follow their instructions as it would probably save her life. She really wished Nathan was there at that moment; unfortunately he wasn't. The hotel was quite empty and they led her down a back staircase that was a fire exit and into a waiting car. She knew struggling was pointless as she could still feel the cold steel butt of the gun in her ribs. The car's doors had been locked and the windows blacked out.

"Where are you taking me?"

"Shut up, whore. You'll see when we get there. That 'usband of yours will wish 'e 'ad never been born."

Suddenly the car came to an abrupt halt.

"Get out," said the man, still pointing the gun into her back.

She stumbled on the uneven path; she felt an arm dragging her upright.

"Who are you and what do you want with me? I'm just an English tourist."

She was led into a dark passage then into a room that was brightly lit.

"Ah, Mrs. Grieves, so glad you could join us."

"Let's get one thing straight, I am not Mrs. Grieves, my name is Christine Lockhead."

"We presumed you were already married as we saw you in your wedding dress."

"What do you mean you saw me?" she yelled.

"Well we had the camera trained on your room and that of your husband. We thought it was odd that you were just married and in separate rooms."

"That's because we had separate rooms, because we are not married."

"And where is lover-boy now?"

"How should I know? Let me repeat, we are not married."

One of the men that was in the room previously stepped forward. "If you're not married why was you seen with him when you arrived? And why was he taking pictures outside the grey house?"

"How should I know? I wasn't with him."

At that moment a man stepped out of the shadows; he was smartly dressed with a sly grin on his face.

"Right, boys, I'll take it from here. Now, Mrs. Grieves or Lockhead or whatever you wished to be called, are you going to co-operate?"

She recognised the man, it was Francis Delacot, the South African Diplomat.

"You can't keep me here, pretty soon the whole police force will be looking for me."

"I don't think so. Give me the information I need to know, and then perhaps I might show you some mercy."

"Get stuffed," was all Christine could think of to say.

"What was Grieves taking pictures of the other day in the park and where are the pictures?"

"I've no idea, I wasn't with him."

"Surely he discussed his plans with you. After all, you are both British police officers."

Christine grimaced; her ankle was beginning to throb, she must have twisted it when she stumbled on the path outside.

Delacot noticed her grimace. "Pugh, get the lady a chair. I think it might be a long night."

Christine felt completely alone. She had no handbag or mobile phone with her. She had no means of contacting the outside world.

"Why was Grieves taking photos? What did he hope to achieve? Extortion, blackmail, or did he want the Emerald Bear for himself?"

Christine thought she had better tell the irritating man what he wanted to know as she didn't know what he would do next or how he would want to punish her. There had been rumours about Delacot being cruel and torturing people, to get what he wanted, but the British police force were unable to act as it was never in England and they had no proof of any of it about him.

One of the men stepped forward. "Should we strip her and then she can experience the full force of the rod?"

She did not relish being stripped naked and despicable men ogling her naked body. The men were crowding round her like a hungry pack of wolves waiting to be thrown a morsel from their master.

Suddenly another man appeared from nowhere.

"Move back," he said to the throng of men. The men obediently did as they were asked.

"No, Francis, I will not allow it. Give the lady a drink and let's behave in a civilised manner."

Francis Delacot was not used to being spoken to like that. "Very well."

"Now Miss Lockhead, is that what you prefer to be called?"

"Of course it is, that's my name."

She was given a mug of sweet tea and she could have drunk it if her hands were not shaking so much.

"Now, Miss Lockhead. What is it that you and Inspector Grieves have really come to America for?"

This man was quietly spoken, and he seemed to have some control over the other men including Francis Delacot.

"We are here trying to track down the killer of his daughter." She pointed at Delacot. "Well, I am on holiday, Inspector Grieves is working."

"So what is your understanding and knowledge of the Emerald Bear?"

Christine needed to think how she would answer this. She couldn't accuse Delacot of underhand tricks to get his hands on the Emerald Bear. "We know it possibly had something to do with his daughter's murder, but we are still trying to put the pieces together."

"And what brought you to America?" the quietly spoken man continued.

"We heard about the auction at Sunderlands and thought that the killer may show up and claim the Emerald Bear."

"But how do you know who the killer is?"

"We have our suspicions."

Francis Delacot wanted to press her further. "And do you think you know who it is? Tell me, tell me." He began to raise his voice.

"Francis, shut up, you are not helping things."

Delacot opened his mouth to say something else, when the quietly spoken man said, "Francis, I will not tell you again."

He retreated to the back of the room mumbling under his breath. The other men in the room seemed disappointed that the quietly spoken man had spoiled their fun. They were hoping to see a glimpse of naked body, or at least semi-naked, when Delacot had started to threaten her. They had witnessed Delacot's methods of getting information out of people, but that was before the quietly spoken man had taken over. It seemed he didn't believe in violence and would not allow the others to resort to it in any form. He preferred talking and reasoning.

CHAPTER 17

Nathan Grieves was worried; he kept ringing Christine's mobile and it kept going straight to answerphone. That was puzzling. Odd, when he rang her mobile it seemed to be coming from her room. Eventually he decided to knock on her door and check that she was alright. He knocked several times and as there was no answer, he presumed she must be out. She had barely spoken to him over the last few days. He went down to the hotel reception.

"Hello, could you tell me if Miss Lockhead has gone out for the day please?"

The receptionist looked at Nathan. "No sir, I'm sorry. I haven't seen her since last evening and I wasn't on duty this morning. I have only just come on duty now."

Nate checked his watch – it was three in the afternoon. Where was she? He went back to her room and tried her mobile again; eventually he opened the door as it wasn't locked and to his surprise, there was her handbag and her mobile phone. He looked around the room and spotted a piece of what was what he presumed was tissue paper, but it had a black boot imprint across it. He undid the tissue paper and to his horror and amazement he saw the white dress, which was looking decidedly grubby now having being stamped on. *Oh my god,* he thought as the penny dropped. She had presumed that they were going to America and that they were getting married there. He picked up the dress; it looked a dirty mess with a damp patch on it, where her tears had fallen, before she had realised. But it still smelled of her perfume. Where was she and who could have destroyed such a lovely dress? It certainly wasn't her that had destroyed the dress as she was always so particular about the way her clothes looked.

There were no clues at all in the room to give an indication as to her whereabouts. Nathan was worried. He needed to tell the local police, but what could he say? That his girlfriend wasn't in her hotel room and he had found a grubby dress on the bed? Yeah right, the police force would laugh him out of the station. He wondered if her disappearance had something to do with that weasel Delacot. Manhattan was a huge place and he didn't know where to begin to look for her. Nathan found the heat very oppressive and was sweating profusely. He found himself saying, "Come on, girl, where are you?"

Had she gone to the park, or to visit the gardens?

He decided he would check the park before walking any further in the intense heat. Suddenly a man came from behind and had his arm twisted up his back. Nathan launched a punch at the man with his free hand, but the other was too quick for him.

"Listen, we have your wife and if you make any funny moves I will kill you."

"You mean you have Christine?"

"Yeah," the man taunted. "She looks mighty fine without clothes on, don't she?"

Nathan was outraged. "What do you mean 'without clothes on'? What have you done to her?" he demanded.

Suddenly the man pulled out a knife, and a car with blacked-out windows pulled up alongside them. "Move and you're dead. Get into the car now." Nathan did as he was told.

"Was it you who broke into her hotel room and destroyed her dress? You better not have raped her. I'll kill you with my bare hands if you have."

The driver of the car gave a little laugh. "Relax, no-one's raped her, I stopped that clutz from stripping her. He wanted me to strip her, to see if she was concealing anything on her person but I wouldn't, I wanted to give her time to change out of her dress, because when we walked in she was like a frightened rabbit caught in the headlights, dress half up and half down her body. He felt disappointed not to see her naked body so to get his revenge, cos I spoiled his fun, he stood on the dress and made it all dirty, so she wouldn't be able to wear it again. That's all."

"And where is she now, and where are we going? I hope you haven't harmed her."

Eventually the car stopped and Nathan was bundled out. He was led up the same dark corridor that Christine had been led up. When the room opened up and he saw all the lights, he noticed Christine sat in a corner.

"Christine, thank God you're unharmed. What have they done to you?"

Suddenly the room seemed to be filled with bodies and the body odour was overwhelming, Nathan began to gag.

He spotted Francis Delacot in a dark corner of the room; he seemed to be talking to a few other men. Then a smartly dressed man approached him. "Nathan Grieves, I presume?"

"Yes, who wants to know?"

"Well actually, I do," said the quietly spoken man. "As you can see Miss Lockhead is not harmed, apart from the unfortunate incident with her dress. Yes, I know all about it and I am sorry. Davo should not have done what he did and he certainly shouldn't have demanded her to be stripped. Oh no, that is the last thing that I wanted. Davo, sometimes has trouble following orders, that is why I always team him up with a more sensible member of my fraternity. Rest assured, Gordon would not have allowed him to strip her or rape her. That is why he stepped in and told her to find something else to wear."

"Oh, and I suppose that makes everything alright, does it? That she wasn't stripped, raped or worse?"

"Come, come, my dear Nathan, we are not all animals."

Christine had temporarily fallen asleep; she woke up with a start and saw Nathan out of the corner of her eye.

"Nathan." She was so relieved to see him. No-one had harmed her, they just kept asking her questions over and over.

"I'd like to use the bathroom if that is alright with you."

"Of course, Chrissie, I'll get Gordon to accompany you." She hated being called Chrissie and she felt that it was another tactic that her oppressors were using against her.

Gordon gently helped her up. As she put her weight on her foot she yelped out in pain. Her sore ankle had started throbbing again.

"You know he isn't a bad man, he never hurts anyone. Not like some of the thugs here, but he keeps them all in line. I wouldn't have let Davo touch you, and your dress, it was such a pretty one, there was no need for Davo to do what he did, he was just being spiteful. Was it your wedding dress?" he asked gently.

Christine felt she could talk to this man, he was the one who had shown her the most kindness. He didn't seem to be the type to be mixed up with a smelly bunch of ruffians. He dressed well and smelled of expensive aftershave and no body odour; he obviously took pride in himself, she thought. He also spoke well.

"Yes, it was meant to be my wedding dress, but I had gotten hold of the wrong end of the stick. I thought Nathan was going to marry me, but I guess I was wrong."

"Huh, that's too bad," said Gordon.

"What do you know about the Emerald Bear?" It was Delacot asking the questions, it seemed the quietly spoken man had gone away. "Why were you taking pictures of me?" he demanded.

Nathan knew he had to choose his words carefully, he couldn't say he thought that Delacot was a lying, cheating scumbag that had become rich through other people's suffering.

"We were actually trying to help you. We wanted to find out who the killer of your daughter was."

"And you think the killer would have turned up at one of these auctions? Are you trying to accuse me of causing my daughter's death?"

"No, not at all. We were hoping to flush out the actual killer though and the only way we could do this, was to take photos of the people coming in and out of the auction. I noticed that you were the only person who didn't come out of the building clutching a brown parcel, and why did you go into the auction heavily disguised and then come out without the disguise?"

Nathan was feeling fearless; he needed to prove to Christine that he did care about her after his bumbling attempt at telling her about his ex.

"Well, are you any nearer to finding out who the murderer is?"

"No," was all Nathan could reply.

The quietly spoken man had re-entered the room and both Christine and Nathan sensed that the atmosphere in the room had immediately changed.

"It seems neither of you know who Delacot's daughter's killer is and in my opinion you were just doing your job, Inspector Grieves, and you, Miss Lockhead, I believe were here just on holiday. So you are both free to go."

Nathan was puzzled. "Just like that? What was the point of bringing us here at gunpoint and knifepoint then?"

"We had to be sure you weren't trying to infiltrate our little operation. Before you go, Miss Lockhead, this is for you." He handed Christine a parcel.

"Gordon will drive you back to your hotel, and let's hope our paths never cross again."

Gordon showed them out to the waiting car.

"Take care, both of you, and if you take my advice you will leave Manhattan soon and not return. The boss is only tolerant up to a point, despite all his protestations that he abhors any form of violence."

"Thank you, Gordon, and you take care."

"Don't worry about me, Christine. I will be fine."

Nathan put his arm around Christine to steady her as her foot was very painful.

"I think you should go and get that foot seen to. We can go to the ER together."

Christine was grateful; she really needed to at least have her foot strapped. Maybe she had broken a small bone in her ankle, it certainly felt like that. She sighed. Heels would be out for at least the time being. After visiting the Emergency Room and getting a diagnosis for her foot it was clear that she had broken a little bone in her ankle. The consultant had recommended that she wore a protective boot until the bones had knit together again. She had been given a walking stick and told to rest.

Nathan saw her safely to her room and had quickly gone on before her and moved the destroyed dress out of sight. She sat on the bed and began to open the parcel that the quietly spoken man had given to her before they left. To her surprise it was a white silk dress with a note next to it. The note read, 'I hope this makes up for the one that was ruined.'

Dare she try it on? It looked her size, but how would the quietly spoken man know what her size was? She cautiously unwrapped it; it was in a box surrounded by tissue paper. The last time she had put on an exquisite dress like this, she had been broken into and two armed men had kidnapped her!

She felt the softness of the silk and decided to try it on. She laughed as it didn't really go with the black boot on her injured ankle. It would look much better with a pair of high heels, she thought. Suddenly a knock came at her door, for a split second she froze, then she shouted, "The door is open, come in."

Nathan was not sure of the reaction he might get; as he pushed the door open he saw Christine in the white silk dress.

"Wow. You look gorgeous."

Christine blushed slightly. "Don't be silly, Nathan, there's no need to be kind, I know I look absurd with a white dress on and a black boot."

Nathan began to laugh. "Well it does look a bit funny with the black boot, I would imagine the dress would look better with a pair of high heels."

She needed help taking off the dress. "Nathan, be a darling and unzip me."

Nathan duly obliged. *Funny*, he thought. *I feel decidedly underdressed stood next to this beautiful woman.* Nathan turned away while Christine proceeded to get out of the dress. He so much wanted to tell her, but he felt that now was not the right moment as she appeared slightly dopey due to the painkillers she had taken. He needed to explain to her about himself and his ex. The relationship had been complicated and for a while. Nathan hadn't really known what he wanted, but now seeing Christine in all her splendour and also seeing her vulnerability, he knew what he wanted. He had noticed that every man in the place they were taken to could not take their eyes off her. He would have ripped that animal Davo limb from limb, if he had touched or tried to rape her. It was how he would approach it though, and what he would say to convince her that it was her that he loved and wanted. Without her company on this trip he had been thoroughly miserable.

Christine had fallen asleep on the bed. He pulled the cover over her to keep her warm, kissed her tenderly on her forehead and left the room. Would he wine her and dine her on their last night, or would he wait until they were back in England and explain how he felt to her? He would make the big gesture to prove to her that he wanted her; flowers, champagne and a romantic meal for two. She had found it funny being dressed in a beautiful white dress with an ugly black boot stuck onto her foot. Nathan longed for the day when he would see her in that beautiful silk dress again and the heels to complement the outfit and know that she would be stood next to him reciting their wedding vows, all memory of the ill-fated dress and the subsequent unpleasantness etched from her mind. He wondered if she would wear the silk dress or whether she would buy another one for the occasion of their wedding. After the wedding he would whisk her off to Las Vegas for a memorable honeymoon, but in the meantime he would have to start saving as he had lost quite a lot of money at the gaming tables in during their stay.

Christine had been cleared to fly as long as she rested. On their final day with suitcases packed they awaited the taxi to take them to the airport. Christine was glad to be going home, but Nate had misgivings; they had gone to America to try and find out more about the Emerald Bear and who had murdered Shirley Delacot, instead they had unknowingly courted trouble and Francis Delacot seemed to be at the heart of it. It seemed the trip had thrown up more questions than answers. For instance, who was the quietly spoken man and what did he mean about infiltrating his little operation? Nathan knew he would have to face John but would he remain tight-lipped about what had transpired between himself and Christine or would he reveal all to John?

Christine hobbled into John Bora's office two days later. The door had been opened for her by DS Jackson, who had offered to make them all a coffee. The lad was learning, thought John.

"Christine, how are you? Inspector Grieves has told me that you have broken a bone in your ankle and have to wear a surgical boot for the time being." Bora gave a little laugh. "Won't do much for your image, you know, a stick and a black surgical boot. Look at me, a guide dog and a white stick, doesn't do much for my image. Still, never mind all that, it is good to have you back. Perhaps you could show young Jackson here the ropes. He is our new DS."

Christine scrutinised the young man; he was spotty and barely looked as though he should be out of short trousers, his hair was sticking up in all directions, his suit and his shirt both looked untidy and a little grubby. Christine would have to have a quiet word with him out of DI Bora's earshot and explain to him that he would need to smarten himself up if he was going to be taken seriously as a DS on John Bora's team. She explained to the young man as tactfully as she could that his current image wasn't acceptable for a DS. "Although John Bora is blind you will note that he always comes into work in a very smart suit with a shirt and tie. He expects the rest of his staff to follow suit and dress accordingly, as he believes in leading by example. Have you a dress suit?"

"Yes."

"Good, well I hope that is clean and pressed and at the ready as we are all having an inspection by the Area Commander next week and Bora will expect all his officers in their official dress suits."

Jackson felt miserable. He hadn't even looked at his dress suit since his graduation and from what he could remember he had spilt a pint of beer down it and it had left a sticky mark on it, and also he seemed to remember that his gloves were black as he had chased a villain over a wall on the day of his graduation before he had changed out of his uniform. He would have to go home and root out his dress suit and take it to the cleaners in the hope that it would be returned to him in time for the parade. Next, he would have to try and spruce his work suit up and find a different shirt and tie. Although he was good at his job, he didn't have much dress sense.

"What's the matter with you? You have been grumpy all night."

It was Sarah, DS Jackson's long-suffering girlfriend. "I… I met DS Lockhead today and she gave me a right dressing down about the way I looked."

Sarah laughed. "Dressing down is right, I keep telling you, you need to smarten up if you want to be taken seriously as a Detective Sergeant. Come on, I'll go shopping with you and we can choose a couple of suits and shirts and ties together."

DS Jackson agreed that this was a good plan. He would go into work in the morning dressed in a smart suit and shirt and tie and he would show that condescending DS.

Christine hobbled into Bora's office and she was stopped dead in her tracks; the young DS must have really listened to what she had said about his appearance, because here he was looking quite smart in what appeared to be a new suit and new shirt and tie.

"Well, well, DS Jackson, don't you look smart in your new clothes? Quite the DS." Jackson shot her a sickly sweet smile.

"Christine, I need someone to go down to Archives and get me the file on Billy Haskins."

"Well sorry, sir, but I can't, still having trouble using stairs, and you know how dark it is down there. DS Jackson, would you be good enough to go down and bring DI Bora the file on Billy Haskins?"

Jackson was a little dismayed although he accepted Lockhead's request. The archives were quite dusty and he didn't want to ruin his new suit, or get it dirty.

"Christine," chided Bora. "That was quite cruel of you expecting him to go down to archives with his new suit on. You could have asked uniform."

Christine laughed; she felt mischievous today.

"Inspector Grieves tells me that you came across Francis Delacot in America, but did you actually find out any more about who might have killed Shirley Delacot and why?"

"Sadly no."

How much had Nathan told John Bora? She didn't want to say too much in case Nathan hadn't told him the full story.

"I see Paul Plumpton has popped up again."

"Yes, I still think he is guilty, but I can't find the evidence to prove it. He is now living full time with that woman who came in. What was her name? Laura Greenhalgh. From what I can gather his daughter is also living with them. Apparently his estranged wife emptied their joint bank account and buggered off with all the money and she hasn't been seen since. Ah, Grieves, come in join us."

Grieves shot Christine a smile that reached up to his eyes.

"Good morning, John. Christine, how is the foot? I noticed you were up most of the night."

They were still both living together, so that was a good sign, thought John.

"Did nothing out of the ordinary happen to you when you were in America?"

"No not really," lied Grieves. "Except I was nearly mown down shortly after I arrived there because I was jaywalking. I remember this driver screaming at me."

"That was careless of you, Nathan."

"It was a bit strange though, because when he was shouting profanities at me I thought I detected an Allerdale accent."

"You're probably just imagining that," said DI Bora. "Did we ever find that Jake Barnes and the missing Christmas club money? Perhaps it was him."

DI Bora and Christine Lockhead both laughed. But the more Inspector Grieves thought about it the more he thought there was a possibility it was him. After all, he had disappeared without trace.

John, with the help of Christine began poring over the Billy Haskins file again. DS Jackson was invited to look at the file with them. After letting DS Jackson read the file thoroughly and after a period of time John said, "Well, DS Jackson, any thoughts on the case?"

"Er, sir, although it says he was a loan shark did we recover all his bank accounts? Because I bet he had more than one Swiss bank account."

Bora stroked his chin. "Well, did we find all his accounts?"

"Yes sir, I'm sure we did."

"A job for you, DS Jackson. Check all of Billy Haskins' accounts. Do as much digging as you can. If you need to know anything ask Margaret."

"Yes sir, I'm on it."

Nathan had gone off to do some research of his own. Secretly though, John thought he had gone off somewhere for a skive.

There was still a little niggle at the back of DI Grieves' mind. Could it have been Jake Barnes? He seemed to be driving quite fast. *Was he driving towards something because he was late, or was he driving away from something? I guess we'll never know.* America now seemed a distant memory to Nathan and one he chose to forget, all except seeing Christine in her beautiful dress topped off with the black boot. He had thought long and hard about when he would propose to Christine and explain about his ex; the boot wouldn't be coming off anytime soon, but he didn't care, he knew that he wanted to be with her. Pay day was coming up at the end of the month. He would book a table in a nice restaurant, order the champagne and send her flowers in the hope that she would forgive him. Even though they were still living together relations had been strained since returning from America.

CHAPTER 18

Inspector Grieves had been busy. He had contacted the local police force in Manhattan; he needed to know if a Jake Barnes had ever appeared on any of their databases. After a thorough search an officer called him back to deliver the news that all the searches had shown nothing for a Jake Barnes. Grieves was stumped. What was going to be his next move? It was like looking for a needle in a haystack. Bora and even Christine had laughed at his suggestion, now was the time to prove himself.

He had hung the blue suit back in his wardrobe and thought to himself that would be the last time he would ever have to wear it. Odd, that, he thought, how Sunderlands always insisted on their participants wearing a dark suit. It was as though it was a dress code and all the participants willingly obeyed. Besides, if everyone wore a dark suit it was harder to pick out any one person; everyone would just blend into the background. All except Delacot. He knew Delacot would have been at the auction, he also knew Delacot to be a master of disguises. What puzzled him though, was why Delacot used to dress as a Jewish man going into the auction, then come out of the auction just dressed in a dark suit, no Kippah or false beard. Perhaps he had wanted to be incognito going in, but the Sunderlands staff had insisted he discarded the false beard and the Kippah once inside. They could be quite strict when enforcing the rules and the dress code. He himself had to make sure that his suit adhered to their strict code.

Then there was the code of conduct for all participants; if this was violated then the participant was never invited to another auction. No money was ever paid out at an auction, it was always transferred to an untraceable Swiss bank account. Sunderlands were always aware of where the participants would be and would stage their auctions accordingly. He likened the auction to a very high-class poker game, except there were no glamourous dealers, no waiters serving drinks at the tables and no men dressed in evening suits. No-one knew how much money any of the other bidders had and all the bids were done in secrecy, with just the winner being told of the outcome. Sunderlands had made many men very rich, because the bears usually contained drugs, precious gems or other commodities; it wasn't the bear that was special, it was the number. Once the number had been issued then the buyer would be able to access the safety deposit box and claim the booty. No-one ever spoke to each other and no-one ever disclosed how much they had paid for a bear. Some bidders folded after the first hand and he supposed never returned, some bidders would carry on and each time a bidder moved up the scale and another bear would become available they had the chance to bid on it. He had been very frugal with his money, ensuring that he always had enough to buy the next bear.

The catalogue sent out online from an unknown email address informed the participant which tier on the scale they were allowed to bid for. After the auction was over and the money transferred then and only then were they sent the number as proof of purchase of the bear; this number then enabled them to move up to the next tier. He himself had amassed quite a fortune, but it would never be able to be traced as it was in a Swiss bank account. Some of his money was also in a bank at the Vatican. He thought that this was a good idea as it was well known that the Vatican bank accounts were almost impossible to access. He couldn't control his sense of achievement; after all this time he had finally got even. He settled down in his armchair and poured himself a beer and dreamt what he could do with his riches, he just needed the number now.

Francis Delacot was elated. Finally, he had the bear, now he just needed the number. He poured himself a celebratory glass of champagne. He would now rank as one of the richest men in the world and he wouldn't need the guise of being a diplomat, although he had to admit that it had opened a lot of doors for him. He had no qualms about 'stepping on the little people', as he put it. If they were weak, the they deserved to be taken advantage of and that was what he had done all his adult life. Lied, cheated, deceived, to get what he wanted. His own daughter knew what he was really like, that is why she had fled to England in the first place, but 'Daddy' had brought her back to South Africa metaphorically kicking and screaming. He had coerced her into helping her with his latest plan and although reluctant she had agreed. She had begun to build herself a life without him and his influence even to the point that she had a boyfriend, then all that changed when the two men turned up to take her back. Francis did miss his daughter and the killer as yet had not been brought to justice. Delacot didn't need authorities looking into his own affairs. Didn't need to find out about the extortion rackets he ran, or the drugs cartel that he was a member of, or how he preyed on vulnerable people to increase his wealth even more.

Suddenly a knock came on his door and an excited bodyguard rushed in; he was carrying a blue envelope. Delacot snatched it form the bodyguard's hand, eager to read it. This was it, this was the number. He read the letter then shouted, "No, this can't be right, it must be some mistake." He had paid the money, a very considerable amount for the bear and yet when he looked at the number it read 657592. He read the number again. The rest of the letter read, 'Congratulations on the purchase of your bear, you are now allowed to bid for the ultimate prize, this is the final tier on the scale. Instructions about the next auction will be sent to you through the email address you have supplied.' Delacot was livid; he threw the letter down in disgust, then he picked it up again and read and re-read the numbers. He was sure he had the Emerald Bear, it was in front of him, it had a little bell round its neck and a green heart on its chest. Had Sunderlands tried to cheat him out of his ultimate prize? Were they playing a cruel trick on him and having a laugh at his expense? Were they going to send the right number? He needed to speak to someone about it. That would prove to be very difficult though, as all the members of Sunderlands were unlisted in every sense, because of the nature of the secrecy that surrounded the auctions – no-one was ever given a number to call. He slit the bear up the back and began to root around inside, looking for the number. He pulled out stuffing and then more stuffing and there was no number inside the bear. Now he was worried. He had paid half a million pounds for this bear and all he had to show for it was a set of numbers. He was still in his private apartment in New York which was a stroke of luck as if he had been back in South Africa the flight would have taken much longer. He quickly called the bank that held the safety deposit boxes and arranged to fly over to open his box. He would fly to Geneva in person as he didn't trust anyone else to do it. He chartered a private plane and was on the Swiss tarmac in seven and a half hours. There had been a good head wind and the pilot had made good time from JFK Airport. He quickly hailed a taxi and instructed the driver to take him to Calle de Roux. He would make the rest of the journey on foot as he didn't want to be seen associated with any Swiss bank. If no-one knew his whereabouts then there could be no whiff of scandal or finger pointing.

He arrived at the bank and showed the cashier the number. He produced his driving licence as proof of identity and then he was shown to a huge vault that contained lots of safety deposit boxes. The young cashier had been left behind on the banking floor and now a serious-faced older man with horn-rimmed glasses was scouring the numbers on the boxes.

"Ah, here it is." The senior cashier stepped away while Delacot entered the numbers and the secret code that was also supplied on the letter. With a slight press the box lid opened. Delacot began shaking with rage; instead of expecting to see a beautiful large emerald, the box was empty. Had someone got there before him and claimed the emerald? Was it someone in the bank that had become too greedy and helped themselves? He was determined to find out.

"Who else has been down to the vault to open a safety deposit box today. Tell me. Tell me," he raged at the terrified assistant.

"No-one, sir, no-one has been down here today except you."

"How would you know?"

"Because sir, when anyone comes in to look at a safety deposit box we not only ask for ID but we also have retina recognition."

Delacot stormed out of the bank. Someone would pay for this!

He was a quarter of a million pounds down and no way of contacting Sunderlands. Was it someone from Sunderlands who had double-crossed him?

He was making a mental note of all the people he had come into contact with over the last two weeks. He had been so careful entering Sunderlands, with his Kippah and false beard, so who was it?

Was it someone from the fraternity, or was it that nosy, idiotic policeman from England? Adam didn't seem too fussed about keeping the police officers holed up to extract some information from them. He wished now that Adam would have let him loose on the officers; he would have extracted the truth from them by some means, even if he would have to have beaten it out of them. Was Adam involved in this? He had given the English woman a parcel before she left, and that Gordon, he couldn't be trusted with all his airs and graces and his smooth tongue. Delacot was now suspecting members of his own fraternity. The Emerald Bear had been all consuming for the last twelve years. He woke up in the morning thinking about it. He went to bed thinking about it and now by a cruel twist of fate or something worse it had been snatched from his grasp. He would find out who had taken the bear, his bear and the prize, if that was the last thing he did.

*

The phone rang. "Sykes here. Ah, Mr. Delacot, what can I do for you?"

"Don't be obtuse, man." Delacot was in no mood to play games. "Have you found my daughter's killer yet?"

Sykes shuffled uncomfortably in his chair. "No sir, I'm afraid not, but we are very close to a breakthrough, my officers assure me. In fact I am expecting good news about the investigation and hopefully we can wrap it up." Sykes didn't like Delacot; he found him arrogant and officious.

"What kind of tin pot operation are you running here?" Delacot knew he couldn't overstep the mark too much as he had been illegally impersonating a doctor when Billy Haskins died. As far as he was aware, nobody knew about that or ever questioned it. "I want to go down to Allerdale and speak to the detectives there and maybe then they will get their fingers out."

Sykes knew that arguing with the man would be futile, so all he could do was to ring John Bora and inform him of Delacot's imminent arrival.

"Mr. Delacot, how nice to see you again. Please help yourself to a coffee and sit down."

"Who is in charge of this murder investigation, Bora?"

"Well I think you have answered your own question, sir, it is me."

"And what is Inspector Grieves doing, and Christine Lockhead, are they both on the case?"

"Yes sir, they are."

"Well I demand to see them both now."

"I'm sorry, sir, but that's not possible, they are both actively engaged on legitimate police work."

I am not exposing two of my best officers to this demented clown for no reason, thought Bora. He began, "Mr. Delacot, I didn't realise you knew Billy Haskins."

"Of course I did. What of it?"

"Well it was just when he died an unknown doctor who claimed he had treated him years previously had identified his body. It's not usual practice when a patient dies in hospital, but he had been severely beaten before he died and we had to make sure it was him." Bora was lying but Delacot was not to know that.

Delacot was alarmed; he felt sure Bora knew it was him posing as a doctor at the local hospital. Now he couldn't get away from Bora quickly enough.

"Well, I'm sure your officers are doing a good job and I hope they catch the perpetrator soon. I am late for an appointment. So I will bid you goodbye, Inspector."

John Bora knew he had Francis Delacot rattled, but what was he hiding and was it to do with the Emerald Bear?

He needed to speak to Grieves and beat a confession out of him if he had to. He, Delacot, was not like Adam; he believed in violence and letting his fists do the talking. Only it wouldn't be his fists, he would enlist the help of one of his team to carry out the beating if that was what was required.

"Ah, Inspector Grieves. I believe you or that pretty girlfriend of yours has something that belongs to me, am I right?"

"I don't know what your game is, Delacot, or what you think you know, but rest assured neither myself nor my girlfriend have anything to hide."

"Hmm, let's see when we pick her up and then she can tell us."

Grieves would have to go along with Delacot, for

the time being, as Bora had never been told the whole story of what went on when they were in America.

"Don't worry, Christine, I won't let anyone harm you."

"Well now, Miss Lockhead, can you tell me what was in the parcel that Adam handed to you before you left us?"

Christine remained tight-lipped. "Why would you need to know that? Surely if you want to know that badly you could ask him yourself."

"I'm asking you."

"Very well, it was a dress."

Delacot gave a scornful laugh. "Come, Miss Lockhead, do you think I'm stupid?"

"It was a dress," she insisted.

"Why would he want to give you a frock? What was it, a party frock? And were there shoes to go with it?"

"No, it was a white dress to replace the one that one of your heavies ruined."

"I don't believe you."

Delacot went to raise his hand but before he could Nathan had caught it.

"Don't even think about it." Delacot was now on the back foot and Nathan was in control. "Now I believe the lady has told you what you need to know. Now leave, before I prosecute you for, let's see, impersonating a doctor, beating a man senseless, kidnapping two English police officers, running an illegal drug cartel. Do I need to go on?"

The colour drained from Delacot's face. "Right, boys, it's time for us to go, drop the officers off wherever they want to go."

"I don't think we will have any trouble from him again, but now we need to concentrate on his daughter's killer."

Christine had started to love Nathan more and more; he had proved that he had a spine and was not to be intimidated.

CHAPTER 19

Jake Barnes had been tracking the rise of Francis Delacot, ever since he had left him for dead on that battlefield. He had watched him marry and produce an adorable little girl. He himself had been denied those pleasures as he walked with a limp and felt no woman would want to look at him. Still, he wasn't bothered because he hadn't been interested in women since his army days. Looking around his apartment though, he felt there was something missing. He had the money to do whatever he liked, but somehow he felt that is was not enough. Although he had made his home in Manhattan, he still felt like an outsider and in a strange way he longed for Allerdale. He knew he couldn't go home as he would be immediately caught and prosecuted for embezzlement, or could he? That night he devised a plan.

He would change his hair colour to blond, grow a little goatee beard; it wouldn't take long as he had already started to grow one. He popped a pair of glasses on, the type with just glass in, not lenses, and then his transformation would be complete.

He needed to confront Francis Delacot, but the time wasn't quite right. He had phoned a few days ahead and got in touch with an estate agent to view a property just outside Allerdale. He couldn't return there. After all, he was known. He had obtained a forged passport in the name of Jack Ackburn and as he shut his apartment door for the last time, he felt a twinge of excitement to be going home.

He had given America a good go, but he hadn't settled as well as he thought he might. So now was the time to move on again. Life, he always maintained, was a calculated risk and he was well used to calculated risks. He had re-invented himself, with a new image and a new identity. This, he had to do. As he sat on the aeroplane he began reviewing his life. He hadn't always been a mean-spirited man, at one time during his younger days he was like the rest of the young men; although he was a loner, he still dreamed of a wife and family, but that was before he had enlisted in the army and before he had the misfortune of meeting Francis Delacot. He despised Delacot, as he had talked to people that Delacot had humiliated or acted fraudulently with. He knew Delacot's methods and he knew him to be a ruthless bully in the pursuit of what he wanted. There had been so many times over the years that Barnes had witnessed his bullying and his pointless nastiness. He had seen people badly beaten by Delacot's men and sometimes people even disappeared and were never heard of again, only to be washed up on a beach somewhere with a bullet wound to their head, or a stab wound in their neck. Delacot needed stopping but because he was hailed as an international diplomat it seemed he was untouchable. Oh yes, Barnes had read the papers on a regular basis, where Delacot was brokering some deal or other between warring factions that couldn't settle their own disputes. Publicly Delacot was hailed a hero, but privately he was reviled and feared.

Thing is, reasoned Barnes, *I haven't lived a blameless life, I became a killing machine during my last military campaign. Killing machine, that sounds so cold and heartless, but that was what it was. People just seemed to get in the way of what I wanted; and unfortunately it was very rarely a good outcome.*

He had never really learned to make friends with people and had never really had the inclination to try. He had been by his mother's side when she died, something he had never really come to terms with. His mother had always been his rock, the person he always went to whenever he was in trouble; she was the one who always covered for him and painted to the world an adoring son, knowing however his faults. However, when she became ill he nursed her. His customers at the toyshop were not aware that his mother was still alive, thinking she had died shortly after his father. Jake let people think what they wanted to, he didn't want nosy parkers sticking their noses into his affairs. It was only in the latter few years after his father had died, that Jake had discovered that his mother was a very wealthy woman having invested in stocks and shares a few years before. She had transferred all her savings to him, before she died. The toyshop though, was failing, and he didn't want to put his own money into it. Ever the dramatist, he got a thrill with running off to a different country and taking the proceeds of the villagers' Christmas Club with him. His obsession with Francis Delacot had increased over the years since his mother had died and now he spent much of his time and money, tracking Delacot.

America seemed the right place to be. All the finances were in place; he had been waiting for the last two years for the invite to Sunderlands, that was what had prompted him to go to America. Before going he had been building up his funds, ready for the call. He had bid anonymously in the past on bears, which was allowed; and then when a bidder reached a certain tier they were invited to a Sunderlands auction to bid in person in their allocated tier. Each bear that he had won, brought him one step nearer to the ultimate prize. In his suitcase was THE Bear; in his wallet were the all-important numbers. The safety deposit box for these numbers was in kept in a secure vault in London at the Bank of England.

There though, lay the problem, how was Jake Barnes to prove his identity if he had changed not only his appearance, but also his name? That remained the dilemma. He could return to the village outside Allerdale as an unknown person and continue with his life. Nobody would really be any the wiser. The police had given up looking for him, consigning his case to a lower priority as their top priority was still to find the murderer of the young girl. He thought about the problem long and hard; could he sacrifice what he had or was the overarching thought to humiliate Francis Delacot? He knew that Delacot had been wreaking havoc and distress. Once again, the newspapers were full of it. "Mystery man washed up on a secluded beach, no witnesses and no suspects." That was the way Delacot worked. He preferred to employ someone to do his killing, usually a professional assassin. The assassin would be directed by Delacot, when and where a person was to be executed. The people he employed were devoid of any conscience or scruples, they were just interested in the money that Delacot was paying them. Shootings were more messy than bodies being washed up on beaches, and Barnes presumed that these professional assassins were probably paid a lot more for their services than the men who took the people out on the boat and then drowned them. By the time the plane touched down in London, Barnes had put all these thoughts behind him. He collected his suitcase from the baggage carousel and strode purposefully into passport control. Having handed his passport over to the officer, he waited with bated breath. Had he done enough to disguise himself, by changing his name and his appearance?

The officer seemed to take an age poring over the passport as if checking every detail. Barnes had done some despicable things in his life, but he had never travelled on a forged passport. This was a whole new experience and a whole new feeling for him. His palms had become sweaty and he could feel the beads of perspiration on his brow. He must keep it together, he told himself.

"Are you warm, Mr. Ackburn?"

Jake took a tissue from his pocket and proceeded to mop his brow.

"Yes, it is quite warm in here, isn't it? I think I may be coming down with something."

The passport control officer had heard enough, he didn't want an ill passenger in his airport and waved Jake through.

"Well John, you know I said I was sure I saw Jake Barnes in America, well the more I think about it the more I am convinced it was him. He was not at the

Sunderlands auction though, I'm pretty sure of that."

Nathan Grieves had been unaware that there had been a very unusual occurrence in the past few months in America. The unusual occurrence was that Sunderlands had held not one auction, but two.

"So I'm pretty sure he has nothing to do with teddy bears, besides, I only saw him once, when he nearly ran me down."

"Have you checked any flight manifestos, to see if a man named Barnes had flown to New York any time in the last six months?"

"No, I haven't."

"Well there's a job for you. Have you heard anything from your friend Aspey?"

"No, not recently. I don't even know if he is in the country."

"Hmmm." Bora stroked his chin. His world seemed to be closing in on him. He had never taken this long to solve a murder. John Bora knew he had a good team around him, but no-one was really coming up with any answers or suggestions. Christine Lockhead was working but not to her usual capacity as she found that a surgical boot and a walking stick a bit of a hindrance. Her foot, Bora was relieved to see, was getting better but for the time being she had to keep the surgical boot on. On arrival back in England she had been advised to visit a consultant to check on the progress of her foot and it was he that had recommended that she keep the boot on for a while longer.

"You were very lucky, Miss Lockhead. Although you have broken a small bone in your foot you have damaged the surrounding areas, the ligaments and tendons. You have not snapped your Achilles tendon but nonetheless, your injury will take a while to heal."

Nathan had been wonderful with her, but he also had a job to do and feeling sorry for herself didn't help her or him.

Christine and Nathan hadn't really discussed his ex-girlfriend situation since returning from America but Nathan was going to put that right. Tonight was going to be the night, he was going to be home early and he asked Christine if she could also be home early as he was planning a surprise for her. She didn't really want a surprise, she had had enough of them to last her a lifetime, but Nathan had talked her round.

"Please, darling. I've booked the restaurant for 8.30 and I thought we could go for a drink before that." Christine really could not be in the mood for arguing, so she duly complied with his wishes.

As they sat down at the table a waiter arrived with a big bouquet of flowers for her; she blushed and read the note it said, "From your loving Nathan."

As she was about to place the flowers on the table she noticed something shiny fall out. It was a ring, a diamond cluster ring. Before she could say anything, Nathan bent down on one knee and said, "Christine, will you marry me.?"

There was no need for discussions about ex-girlfriends or feelings for them.

"Yes," she said. "Oh, yes."

Getting into bed that night with her lover beside her, Christine thought that it had been the best night of her life. Her foot was throbbing because she was tired, but she didn't care.

CHAPTER 20

"Ah, Christine, how are you this morning?"

John Bora had had a good night's sleep and was now more optimistic about solving the murder case. He had spent a long time last night with Paula talking things through. He was glad really, because they had both come to the decision that if he was unable to solve the murder case, that he would retire from the force and enjoy the retirement they were always talking about.

"Sir?" It was DS Jackson.

"What is it, Jackson?" Bora was on his second cup of coffee; he had noticed recently that sometimes he needed more than one to get him going. Perhaps he was getting old, or just tired.

"There's a man in the front office, says he wants to speak with you."

"Well surely Jackson, you are DS, either you speak to him or get one of uniform to speak to him. I don't need to. There is more than me in this station, you know."

DS Jackson opened his mouth to say something, then thought better of it. Bora seemed in an impatient mood today. It seemed as though he wanted everything done in a hurry. Jackson went away, but returned twenty minutes later. "Sir, we have tried, I have tried, the desk officer has tried, but the man is insisting that he wants to talk to you."

Bora was getting irritated. This was holding him up from the business he was trying to solve.

"Very well, show him in."

DI Bora smelled the person even before they spoke.

"God preserve us, Jonesy, you smell worse than the last time I spoke to you. Do you not believe in bathing, have you some aversion to it?"

"Listen, Inspector, do you want me information or not?"

"Well that depends, Jonesy, on how much it will cost me."

"You aint 'erd what the info is yet."

"Okay, Jonesy, what is it?"

"Would you like a coffee?"

Bora wanted to get this over as quickly as possible, but he thought if the other man had a coffee then he might go away.

Christine got up and hobbled over to the kettle.

"Thanks, miss, I'll 'ave four sugars, ta. Well I was visitin' a friend in Penkton the other day when this madman nearly knocked me clean off me feet. I told me friend and 'e said the maniac 'ad bin driving like a lunatic for the last couple of weeks. Me friend said 'e seemed to be new to the village."

"And how would your friend know that?" Bora asked sceptically.

"Well 'e said 'e'd only started seein 'im recently. Jus' seemed queer, that's all, a middle-aged man driving around the country roads like a boy racer. Now is that worth twenty quid or is that worth twenty quid?"

Bora wanted rid of the man so he opened his drawer and asked Christine to pull out a twenty.

"Now go, Jonesy, bugger off and use that twenty to perhaps have a decent meal and a shower. There is enough money there to pay for a hostel for a least one night."

Jonesy shuffled out, muttering something under his breath.

"Christine, I want you to get in touch with the estate agents in Penkton, there can't be that many of them, and see if anyone has either rented a property from them recently or bought a property from them."

Penkton was a sleepy village outside Allerdale and a maniac riding around the country roads was definitely a recipe for disaster. There was a lot of valuable farmland and livestock in the area.

Christine called on DS Jackson to accompany her; she felt it would be good training for the rookie DS.

"No, sorry. I haven't sold a house to anyone in the

last three months."

Christine wondered how these places stayed open. DS Jackson asked at a letting agency and got the same reply. Christine was about to give up; Jackson was annoying her and her foot was aching.

"Let's make this the last one. There can't be any more in this village, we are five miles outside Penkton."

"Yes, I agree." The young DS was also thinking they were on a wild goose chase.

"Yes, I remember I sold a house a few weeks ago, he paid cash for it outright. I thought it was a bit strange, but he told me he had had small windfall so I didn't question him further. He arranged a viewing and that afternoon he put an offer in for the house. I was a bit surprised really."

"And can you tell me this man's name?"

"Yes, let me see." The agent lifted a big ledger onto the counter and quickly scrolled down the names.

"Ah, here it is. A Mister Ackburn, Jack Ackburn. I have the address that he purchased, here it is. 21 Teddington Cottage, Penkton."

"Thank you, Mr. Green, you have been very helpful."

"Always a pleasure to help our brave boys and girls in blue." He winked at DS Jackson.

Christine was sat in Bora's office with her foot up trying to rest it. John did understand, she thought.

"Well, I think we have hit a brick wall and I was so hopeful, but this man is called Jack Ackburn."

"Hmmm." Bora stroked his chin. "Is it worth finding out where this man lives and visiting him and giving him a friendly warning not to drive on country roads like a maniac? Maybe he's from a big city and is not used to country life."

Bora dismissed the man as being of no real consequence. Once the officers had given him a warning they probably wouldn't come across him again. No-one liked being warned by the police even if it was a friendly warning.

*

Jack Ackburn had made a careless mistake. It wasn't like him to make such mistakes. He had been driving and taken a sharp bend too quickly and hit an oncoming pedestrian. The pedestrian had been slightly injured, but when the traffic police arrived they made him blow into a breathalyser machine and he had blown 50mg/L, well over the acceptable limit.

"Well sir, I'm sorry but we will have to arrest you for being over the legal limit of alcohol. You will have to provide a blood sample at the station. We will get someone to take your car to the police pound and you can claim it in three days' time."

Curses, thought Ackburn. How could he have been so stupid? He knew he shouldn't have had that last whisky, but he had been enjoying himself. The first time in actual ages that he had begun to relax and thought he might just be able to fit into this sleepy village.

After the duty doctor had verified that he was over the legal drink driving limit, he had his photograph and fingerprints taken and then the duty sergeant charged him and bailed him.

Had he had a lucky escape?

Sitting in his house, he thought he had got away with murder.

*

"Strange man, fancy tearing around country lanes. Doesn't he realise that there could be people and animals? I bet he was a townie." This was Christine speaking.

Bora wasn't really bothered, but Christine was looking at his file. Unremarkable features, quite ordinary really. Must have money though to have bought the house outright.

Nathan Grieves had joined Christine and John and was now studying the file of Jack Ackburn.

"I'm sure I have seen this man before," he said.

"No, I'm sure you must be mistaken. What makes you think you have seen him before? He has apparently only just moved to Penkton."

DI Grieves was scrutinising the picture closely.

"I have seen him before, I'm sure of it."

"Where do you think you have seen him, Inspector

Grieves?"

John Bora was interested.

"I'm sure it was the same man that nearly ran me over when we had just arrived in America."

DS Lockhead shot him an incredulous look, but she supposed nothing was beyond the realms of reason, given the ordeals they had both been through, which Bora knew nothing about.

"Well, he has been bailed for drink driving, but we can't really go and harass him for that. You must provide more concrete evidence if you want to arrest him on another charge. Are you sure about this, Nathan?"

"I'm pretty sure."

"So what? What makes you so sure?"

"Well it's the eyes. The hair is a different colour and he is wearing glasses but I'm sure it is the same man."

"And where do you think you know him from?"

"I need to check out a few things and then I'll get back to you." And with that, he left Bora's office.

Bora was confused. What was the DI on about, he wondered?

"Margaret, do you remember when that toyshop owner took off with the villagers' Christmas club money?"

"Yes, I remember."

"Was there a picture of him in the local paper?"

"I don't remember, sir, but I can check for you."

Margaret pulled up archives and databases. There was a picture of Jake Barnes, the newspaper report exclaiming that he had taken off with the local villagers' club money. Margaret quickly printed off the picture, it was in colour. She knocked on the DI's door. "Come." DI Bora was having five minutes; his head was aching, and he needed to eat.

"Sir, here is the picture that DI Grieves wanted."

"Okay Margaret, thanks. Can you find DI Grieves and tell him that the picture is in my office?"

"Yes sir, will do."

Grieves put the pictures side by side. Yes, that was the connection, Jack Ackburn and Jake Barnes were the same person.

"John, I think I've cracked it. Jake Barnes and Jack Ackburn are the same person."

"Are you absolutely sure?"

"Yes, no doubt about it."

"But why would Jake Barnes take an assumed name? I don't understand."

Bora stroked his chin. "Unless he has something to hide."

Whatever it was would keep until tomorrow. Bora's headache was getting worse and he needed to go home.

Steve brought the car round.

"Steve, you have lived here all your life, did you

ever come across the toymaker Barnes?"

Steve thought for a moment before answering. "No, sir, but I remember my grannie talking about Barnes's toyshop and how she bought my dad his first toy train from there and how Mr. Barnes was a lovely man, always very caring and generous. When he son was invalided out of the army, old Mr. Barnes signed the shop over to his son."

"And was there ever a Mrs. Barnes?"

"I think so, but after her husband died she became a virtual recluse, I think, and during her later years her health failed her."

"Well if she had failing health, who was she looked after by? Was she in a home or something?"

"I'm not sure, sir, but I don't think so. I think her son Jake looked after her. It was rumoured that before she died she signed over all her assets to her son and it was a considerable amount."

John had arrived home; his head was really throbbing now. Paula was in the kitchen.

"Hello John, are you okay?"

John shouted back, "Not really, I have a splitting headache."

Paula came into the room. "When was the last time you ate?"

John couldn't remember, he was going to have a sandwich at lunchtime, but he had been sidetracked and completely forgotten to eat. No wonder he had a headache.

"Really, John, you're not a child. Surely your brain tells you when you need to eat." Paula was frustrated. She placed his dinner in front of him and he began to devour it. He realised that he was really hungry. Louie was restless; he wanted feeding. John suddenly realised that he had not taken the harness off the dog. He reached down, unclipped the harness and patted the dog and said, "I'm sorry, boy, you must be starving, go and get your food."

Louie bounded over to his food and began to eat.

"Did you remember to take Louie for a walk today or were you so engaged in your work that you forgot?"

That was another thing Bora had forgotten to do.

"I suppose I'll have to take him. Come on, Louie, let's go for a walk."

When Paula returned John was asleep in the chair. He was exhausted.

Paula was worried about John; he seemed to be losing weight apart from not sleeping properly. Had the time come that John needed to retire and relax? Paula had thought he had gone back to work without giving himself much time to get over the terrible trauma of becoming blind. She knew how much work meant to him and how he had cheered up and been lifted out of his depression when he was offered a job again, but she just wondered how much of a toll it had taken on her husband. That was a discussion for another day. She gently awoke her husband and led him to bed.

∗

Elsie Cherry had decided to visit the police station. Perhaps she could help solve the murder of the young woman.

Christine spotted her as she walked down the corridor.

"Eh, dearie, what have you been doing?"

"Er, hello. It's Mrs. Cherry, isn't it?"

"Yes. That's right, dearie."

"I thought I should show you this."

Christine continued to limp towards Bora's office. "Come in and take a seat. I'm sure the Inspector will be along shortly."

"Sir, this is Mrs. Cherry. It was her that discovered the body."

"Well hello Mrs. Cherry, is there something I can do to help you?"

"Well no, not really. It's the other way round."

She produced a plastic bag with a black button inside. "I thought this might help. When I found it I didn't touch it, I just got the plastic bag round it."

"Well thank you, Mrs. Cherry. I'm sure it will prove to be useful."

Christine left the button on the desk.

"Looks like a shirt button, sir."

"Oh, okay, don't take it out of the bag. Just slip it in an evidence bag."

*

Jake Barnes had decided that now the time was right to wreak the ultimate revenge on Francis Delacot.

Francis Delacot was in London to attend a conference.

"Hello, is that Francis Delacot?"

"Yes it is, who is this?"

"You probably don't remember me, but I was one of the young soldiers that you were quite happy to let die on the battlefield during your last campaign, but you see I didn't die, I have just been left with a permanent limp where the shrapnel entered my leg."

"What did you say your name was?"

"It's Barnes, Jake Barnes, and I have been tracking you for many years to take my revenge. I am not a forgiving man, Mr. Delacot."

"Listen here, I don't know what kind of scam you are trying to pull, but I have seen them all."

"Oh I assure you, Mr. Delacot, you haven't seen this one. What does the Emerald Bear mean to you?"

Delacot stopped in his tracks.

"What do you know about the Emerald Bear?"

Barnes gave a laugh. "Well you see, my dear old man, I have it."

"What did you say? Repeat that, you scum."

"I have the Emerald Bear."

"But that's impossible."

"Oh no, believe me, it isn't."

"I demand to know where the bear and the number are now."

"Too bad, you don't get to demand anything."

"That bear is rightfully mine."

"No, I don't think so."

"Do you know who killed my daughter?"

"Maybe I do. Enjoy your conference."

Jake Barnes was feeling pleased with himself. He had taken the Emerald Bear from under Delacot's nose and he, Delacot, had no idea that his daughter would have helped the killer.

Delacot was unsettled. He needed to find this Barnes fellow. He wanted that bear and the number, and then perhaps after getting both and opening the safe deposit box, he would probably have Barnes killed.

Barnes decided to ring Delacot once more.

"Hi Francis, can we talk?"

"Unless it is about you telling me where the bear and the number is, I have nothing to say to you."

"Oh but Francis, I have lots to say to you. Who do you think it was that arranged for you to be kidnapped at the Embassy Ball? We didn't want to kill you, instead we just wanted you to know what it felt like being scared for your life and beaten practically senseless like you have done to so many of your victims."

Delacot was furious. "Shut up, you raving lunatic. I haven't got a clue what you are talking about."

"Well let me refresh your memory. You were at an Embassy Ball when you were doped and kidnapped. I was the one that arranged that. By the way, did you get your tooth fixed?"

Delacot could feel chills down his spine. So this person had tracked his every move for many years. He was dangerous and had to be assassinated. The unnerving thing though, was that he didn't know where this man was. Was he watching him now, ready to pounce from the shadows to kill him? He would have to be watching over his shoulder each time he went out. He would make sure the bodyguards stuck by his side. He needed the man to ring back so he could quiz him about his daughter; he felt sure this man knew something about her death.

*

"Well if you're absolutely sure, DI Grieves, then bring him in. I would like to know why he changed his name and appearance, I'm sure it wasn't just to do with the Christmas Club money fraud."

DI Bora would conduct the interview assisted by DS Jackson. He felt it was time for Jackson to step up to the mark and see how an interview in Bora's police station was conducted.

"Now Mr. Ackburn, or should I call you Barnes? What have you got to tell me?"

"No comment."

"I will ask you again, Jake, what is it you would like to tell me?" Using a suspect's first name always lulled them into a false sense of security.

"No comment."

Jackson pulled out an evidence bag and Bora proceeded. "Have you ever seen this button before, Jake?" The young DS held up the bag.

"No comment."

"Oh come on, Jake, I think you have seen this button before. Can you remember where?"

Oh shit, thought Barnes. It must have been ripped off his shirt in the struggle at the farmhouse and he hadn't noticed it.

"No, can't say I have seen it before," he replied.

"Do you own a black shirt?"

"Course I do, doesn't everyone? I bet you have one hanging in your wardrobe right now, don't you Inspector?"

Bora continued, "It's not about me, Jake, it is about you. We have found traces of DNA on the button. If we test yours, do you think it will be a match?"

"Shouldn't think so. The last time I wore a black shirt was to my mum's funeral."

"A black shirt, surely you wore a white shirt and a black tie?"

"Nope, can't say I did. I remember having my white shirt in the wash on the day of the funeral, so I put my black one on instead."

"I don't believe you, Jake. I think you wore that shirt on the day that you murdered Shirley Delacot, what do you say?"

"No comment."

"No you didn't wear the shirt, or no you didn't kill Shirley Delacot, which is it?"

"No comment."

Bora had had enough. This man was playing mind games with him.

"Take him down to the cells."

Turning to Jackson, Bora said, "We will have another go with him after, see if he wants to talk then."

Jackson nodded. "Coffee, sir?"

"Well Christine, what do you think, could he be our murderer?"

"I think so, sir."

"And what motive does he have for killing the young woman, do you think?"

"Revenge, greed maybe."

"Yes, I thought that, but who is he wanting to wreak revenge on?"

"It could be Francis Delacot. After all, it was his daughter who was killed."

"Yes, but why kill his daughter?"

"I don't know, maybe she knew too much about

him or maybe she had something that he wanted. It could be to do with the Emerald Bear I suppose."

"Hmmm, I suppose you could be right. I want a search warrant organised and then we can go and search his house."

"Very well, sir, on to it."

Bora sat back in his chair; alone in his office he could think the whole thing through. Suspect. Murder weapon. Motive or motives. Incriminating evidence with the shirt button. *Why, oh why did that old dear not produce the button sooner? Then we could have had the case solved sooner,* he thought.

"Sir, we have found the black shirt and it was stuffed in a corner of the attic. On closer inspection we saw that one of the buttons was missing. So we put it in an evidence bag."

"Excellent work, Christine, we'll make an Inspector of you yet," he joked. "Now though we need to see what milado has to say about the shirt and how the button came to be missing. Has Barnes' solicitor arrived yet?"

"No sir, not yet."

"Well I hope he hurries up. I would like this case wrapped up before tea." Bora was in a good mood.

Presently a tall man in a dark suit entered the interview room.

"I'm Banks, Barnes' solicitor. Sorry I'm late, only just got out of court."

"Well it looks like we might be ready to start then."

"For the benefit of the tape the people present are DI Bora, DS Lockhead, Mr. James Banks, solicitor, and Mr. Jake Barnes. Now Mr. Barnes, we have found a black shirt at your house when we searched it, and curiously it had a button missing, what do you know about that?"

"No comment."

"For the benefit of the tape Mr. Barnes is saying, 'No comment.'"

Barnes solicitor sat stony-faced listening intently to the questions being asked.

"Have you ever owned a black four-by-four car?"

"No comment."

"Really, Mr. Barnes, you aren't doing yourself any favours. Shall we start again?"

"Inspector, I would like a word with my client in private please."

Christine, will you escort me please to the canteen where we can get a drink?"

"Certainly, sir."

Christine stood up and leaned heavily on her walking stick.

"Well Christine, what do you think, is he guilty?"

"I would say so, guilty as hell. Oh, sorry sir."

"What do you think of the solicitor? Have you come across him before?"

"Well yes, actually I have. He was the defence lawyer in the case where I was held at gunpoint."

"And what was the outcome of that case?"

"The defendant got sent down for fifteen years."

"Oh, that good is he?" Bora laughed. "What kind of advice do you think Banks is giving him?"

"I don't know, sir, but if he has any sense, he will hopefully listen to the solicitor, because I can imagine he is paying a lot of money for his services. You don't get to drive a new sports car if you are on a low wage. So I imagine he is one of the top solicitors in the firm."

"Well Jake, are you ready to answer some more questions?"

"Do you know Francis Delacot? I'll rephrase the question. How long have you known Francis Delacot?"

"Since we were both in the army together."

"And was there something that happened to you in the army and that is how you ended up with a limp?"

Banks had advised his client to answer the questions and then maybe they could end up with a plea bargain, that would hopefully reduce the period of his sentence.

"We were under attack, shells were going off all around us. Delacot took two of the men with him and led them to safety. He glanced over at the three of us that were left and decided to leave us for dead. If I had got treatment sooner, maybe I wouldn't have ended up with a permanent limp. I vowed one day that I would get even with him."

"And did you?"

"I tracked his movements for many years waiting for my chance. I had seen quite a lot of atrocities that he had committed to attain the wealth he has got. He never gets his hands dirty though and hides under that mantle of diplomatic immunity. I have witnessed grown men cry with the punishments Delacot has inflicted on them. So in the end I thought enough, was enough. I had read the story about the miner and the Emerald Bear so I decided to find out more about it. As it turns out there is a secret organisation, that auctions off teddy bears, but these teddy bears are no ordinary teddy bears; once the numbers have been matched to the bears, the successful bidder can claim the prize within. I realised that Delacot wanted the Emerald Bear, more than anything else in the world, so I set about making it incredibly hard for Delacot to acquire it. You see I wanted my revenge and that was the best way I could think of, denying him the thing he wanted most in the world. Having the satisfaction that I had the bear, not him."

"And how did you go about achieving this goal?"

"Well first I read up about these teddy bears and how this auction worked. I had money from my mother and I started to purchase the bears. You are not invited to an auction straight away, you have to build up your collection, it's a bit like building up points; until you have the required amount you cannot progress to the next tier."

"When did you come up with the idea to travel to America with the villagers' Christmas Club money?"

"I had been working on purchasing the bears, but you know, Inspector, it isn't cheap. In fact it is very expensive, we are talking huge amounts, but the bears are worth it and they go up in value and steps. I knew that if I carried on purchasing the bears anonymously, because that was how it was done, I would eventually hopefully get an invite to an auction."

"When the bears were purchased where was the money sent to?"

"To Sunderlands, an offshore account."

"I see."

"Well I had been purchasing the bears for about two years, you see it was like a game that Sunderlands had set up, the ultimate prize being the Emerald Bear."

"Tell me more about the Emerald Bear," Bora said.

"The Emerald Bear is the highest award a person can get. The person who has the Emerald Bear also holds the key to the vast emerald that is worth millions of pounds. It is said that the owner of the Emerald Bear never needs to part with it, because it is not only one's pension, but a safeguard against anything happening to the owner of it. Well I knew Delacot wanted it just as much as many other people around the world, but he wasn't as clever as I am. After giving his daughter some freedom for a few years, he decided he wanted her to do something for him. She lived in London and he sent two of his men to take her back to South Africa. Well he must have persuaded her to carry the bears back to England, in the hope of trading them up to the final tier. He gave her two bears, one was to act as a decoy for the other one, and a sheet with the numbers on. She was supposed to deposit one of the bears, the most valuable one, in a safe deposit box in London, until such time that Delacot could come over and retrieve it."

"And then what happened?"

"Well I realised the girl was in the country and I decided to pay her a visit and take the bear and the numbers from her. I tracked her to this old farmhouse and then I slipped in. I tried to reason with her, but she started to struggle, and I knew that wasn't good. I just knew at that point that it was going to be pointless asking her for the bear even though I could tell her what her father had dealings in. There was a struggle and she started shouting, I didn't want her to raise the attention of any neighbours, so I stabbed her and ripped a bear and the sheet with the numbers on from her hands, before leaving."

"And what about the car?"

"I torched the car some way down the road; it was quite difficult to do as it was a very wet night and I couldn't get the petrol to ignite. Anyway, eventually I managed to light it and drove away in a hired car."

"What happened next?"

"Well now I had the bear and the numbers, I went to the safe deposit box put in the numbers and the box opened. Then I was on the penultimate tier for the bears. That was when I went to America and I was invited to an auction, but in the meantime, I had to purchase one more bear, then I could go for the ultimate prize. I knew Delacot had been to quite a few of these auctions and had so far been unable to get his hands on the Emerald Bear and the numbers. I on the other hand had the money, the bear and the numbers that I needed to bid on for the Emerald Bear. On the second day of the auction I had the bear, I just needed the numbers. I went back to my apartment and waited for the email. I felt a smug satisfaction knowing Francis Delacot would never own the Emerald Bear and would never be able to access its riches. I needed to make one last phone call to Delacot and my revenge would be complete.

"You see, Inspector, the emerald was never inside the bear, it was a bear that was called the Emerald Bear, so you had to have the right combination of bear and numbers in order to open the safe deposit box."

"Jake Barnes, I am arresting you for the murder of Shirley Delacot. Sergeant, read him his rights."

*

The murder investigation had finally been brought to a successful close.

"Well Bora, you still have it."

Christine had gone to the hospital and she had returned minus the boot and the walking stick. She and Nathan had set the date for their wedding.

"Sir, will you walk me down the aisle at my wedding?"

"I would be delighted to, Christine!"

ABOUT THE AUTHOR

Elizabeth worked for many years in the Adult Education Sector, before retiring to concentrate on her writing.

Her hobbies are listening to music, attending the theatre and playing the ukulele.

She lives with her husband and son in Cheshire.

Printed in Great Britain
by Amazon